Wayfarer

Wayfarer

A Tale of Beauty and Madness

LILI ST. CROW

razOr
bill

An Imprint of Penguin Group (USA)

razOr bill

A division of Penguin Young Readers Group
Published by the Penguin Group
Penguin Group (USA) LLC
345 Hudson Street
New York, New York 10014

USA / Canada / UK / Ireland / Australia / New Zealand / India / South Africa / China
Penguin.com
A Penguin Random House Company

ISBN: 978-1-59514-620-5

Printed in the United States of America

1 3 5 7 9 10 8 6 4 2

PART 1

THE GIRL IN THE WATER.

If she isn't dead, she soon will be. Limp and boneless, she makes herself as heavy as possible. Blue ice and green slime closing overhead, crackling and creaking as it shudders and grinds. Fickle and loyal at once, the ice numbs her while it obeys her enemy's raging shrieks.

She always knew she'd drown. The dream comes back several nights in a row, then hides for a while. Just when she starts to relax, it jumps her again. The ice stinging every inch of flesh, her shoes too heavy, sodden clothes dragging her away from hurtful air and into grateful numbness.

A splash, a scream, and frozen water shatters above her. She is sinking fast; the oddest part is how it doesn't hurt. Her lungs burn, but it is a faraway sensation, disconnected. All she has to do is choke, and it will be over. The water will rush in, suffocation will start. Already blackness is creeping around the corners of her vision. This far down the water is darker, full night instead of dusk, and there is a shadow over her.

Fingers wrap in her hair, and now is the time to struggle. Because if the monster pulls her out of the water she'll have to go on living in hell, and that she will not endure. There's a single route of escape. All she has to do is blow the air out, watch the silver bubbles cascade up. Icy water will flood past the stone in her throat, fill lungs and heart and every empty part of her, and there will be darkness.

In that darkness, peace.

The hand in her hair gives a terrific yank, a spike of scalped pain spearing her skull, dragging her toward the surface of hell once more . . .

. . . then, she wakes up.

ONE

ELLEN SINDER SLID DOWN FURTHER IN HER SEAT, MOTHER Superior Heloise Endless Grace's office suddenly, painfully bright. Her eyelids wanted to fall down to protect the vulnerable bits behind them. Her arms crossed tight over her midsection, holding everything in. Her bare knees were bruised and scabbed, and the tinkling silver luckcharms tied to the straps of her battered but polished maryjanes—Cami said she had extra, as usual, and so onto the straps they went—hushed themselves. They wouldn't work inside the school, but they were still nice to have. Sort of comforting.

Mithrus knew she could use all the comfort she could get. This was going to end badly, she could just feel it. *Anytime* her stepmother showed up, inside or outside the house, it ended badly for Ellie nowadays.

"I am afraid the decision isn't yours to make." Golden electric light made the Strepmother's frosted blonde mane a sterile sunburst, and today she was wearing the van Clifs, their spike heels laced with surestep and glittercharms. She'd chosen the eggplant-colored Auberme suit with its forgiving cut since her middle had started to thicken, charmfiber woven into the fabric twinkling a little as she moved. The Strep continued, pitilessly, in that honeyed voice she used to get her way with other adults. "I am her legal guardian, and as such—"

"Ah, yes." Mother Heloise's broad pale moonface, framed by her black and white habit, was, as usual, slightly damp. She really looked like a peeled, oiled, hard-boiled egg. Pale and shiny. "Guardianship. It appears Mr. Sinder—Mithrus bless and watch over him—was *very* clear." A bovine nod, her jaw working slightly. "The conditions of your guardianship are stringent, madam. And one of them is little Ellen's continuation at and graduation from both this school and Ebermerle Charmcollege." A beatific, moronic grin spread the Mithrus nun's ruddy lips, and if you were an idiot you might miss the sharp intelligence in her small, dark eyes. "We have a copy of the will on file, and Mr. Sinder's wishes are quite, quite plain. Yes. Quite plain."

I didn't know about that. It was just like Dad to have things set up, but he'd always underestimated his second wife. Once Laurissa Choquefort-Sinder got her head together with another lawyer, the trust Ellie's father had left would either be drained or so tangled up in the legal system it wouldn't help Ell at all.

Still, it was nice to know he'd thought about it. Ebermerle was *the* college for charmers; if you didn't apprentice with a clan or a powerful charmer you *had* to have a degree to get licensed.

Good luck getting apprenticed with the Strep feuding with half the charmers in town. Charmers were a picky, jealous bunch anyway, and the Strep was an outsider in more ways than one. She'd been tolerated because she was powerful enough to produce a trademark Sigil, that fiery symbol of two high-heeled shoes Ellie sometimes saw in her nightmares.

Well, and also because Dad had been an inter-province lawyer, and you didn't want one of *those* mad at you. He'd loved Laurissa, at least at first.

If Ell's stepmother took her out of St. Juno's Academy, it would be time to put the Plan into action. Hanging around the stone house on Perrault Street all day with the Strep screaming at the slightest thing was not, as Ruby would say, even *close* to copacetic. Neither was charming bolts and bolts of cloth into high-priced couture, or pairs and pairs of footwear that would bear Laurissa's trademark, added after Ell did the charming—which she never saw a penny of, really, but at least right now she could escape to Juno.

Both Rube and Cami would be wondering what was going on. She'd been called out of High Charm Calculus, which was normally a blessing, but as soon as she'd entered the office of Juno's Mother Superior and smelled the Strep's burnt-cedar anger, her stomach had rolled over and given that same sick thump.

"There are much *better*—and more *appropriate*—schools." The Strep was trying, Ellie had to give her that. She didn't give up easy, especially when it came to something that would likely give Ell a lot of pain.

It didn't use to be like that. For a while after Dad had brought Laurissa home, she'd been the picture of patience and girl talk. Ellie still squirmed inside, thinking of how pathetically grateful she'd been for all that attention.

"Oh, certainly. No doubt." The Mother nodded. If she was insulted, she gave no indication; St. Juno's was *the* high-finish school for New Haven's ruling or charm-blessed families. At least the mere-human ones. "But we must obey Mr. Sinder's final wishes, Mithrus bless and keep him."

The Strepmother tried gamely once more. "The question of payment—"

"—was addressed by the estate." Mother Heloise nodded again, a slow, ruminating nod. "The will is *quite* clear." Now her head came up, and her small, close-set eyes too. There was a gleam in her gaze, but her plump hands had not moved from their quiescence, folded under where her breasts would be—if she had any under the black and white habit. You could tell *everything* about Magdala nuns, but not Mithraic Sisters. Sexless and billowy was the ticket for them.

Maybe that was why they were teachers.

"Quite, quite clear." Mother Heloise smiled broadly, blandly, and the exotic sight of the Strep struck speechless would have warmed Ellie all the way through if she didn't know who would end up catching hell for this embarrassment.

And how much it was likely to hurt.

Her stepmother rose, the spike heels grinding into tired linoleum and their sparkcharms crackling. "Ellen. We are *leaving*."

Mother Heloise had different ideas. "Little Ellen needs to run along back to class." She beamed at said little Ellen, beatifically. "Such a lovely child she is, and *so* talented. But she is accident-prone, isn't she? All those bruises and scrapes."

Mithrus Christ. Ellie's mouth was dry as baked charmglass. Her arms cramped, she was holding herself so tightly.

The Strep's Potential flashed, and for a moment Ell was sure she was going to have one of her raging fits. A Sigiled charmer was nobody to mess with, and Mrs. Laurissa V. Choquefort-Sinder was at the top of her field even if she was an outsider in New Haven, a high-priced *haute couturière amulette* with taloned fingernails and enough Potential to burn down a house.

Even if she did have Ellie doing most of the work that made her famous, now.

If Laurissa did snap a curse at Mother Heloise, maybe the school's defenses—built to keep nasty nonhuman or barely human things away from vulnerable Potential-carrying adolescent girls, as well as to keep said girls from relentlessly pranking teachers and each other—would wake, and turn even a Sigiled charmer into a pile of ash.

Wouldn't that be a sight. Ellen's breath came high and short. *Oh, please. Please.*

The office, its dark scarred wainscoting and tired chipped paint comfortable instead of shabby, grew still and oppressively close. The lightbulb overhead fizzled a little, despite the damper on it. Potential was funny around electricity; even the Great Tesla hadn't figured out why the two things, seemingly so similar, had such weird effects on each other.

When Laurissa finally spoke, each word was chipped from a block of ice. "What. Are you. Saying?" Dangerously calm.

Ellie waited for the ancient file cabinets to start shivering and Mother Heloise's heavy desk to shift itself a fraction or two. Her throat was full of scorching-hot liquid, even though she hadn't had anything but an apple for lunch.

The overhead fixture swung slightly, the air turned hard as glass, and the Strep dropped back into her chair, one beribboned, high-heeled van Clif shoe slipping almost off her bony foot despite a carefully applied stickcharm. She frankly *stared* at Mother Heloise, who appeared not to notice her sudden movement.

"Bruises and scrapes, yes." The Mithrus nun nodded, mumbling a little. Then her sharp little eyes focused on Ellie again. "We must watch our Juno girls carefully in this dangerous world. Miss Sinder, you run along to High Charm Calculus now. Wouldn't do to miss the rest of class."

Her joints creaking, Ellie stood up. Slowly, she shuffled for the door, her skirt moving just above her knees, wool scratching. Her blazer was threadbare, but at least she had the luck-charms and the super-thin hairbands that were *in* this year. Her maryjanes were gloss-shining, too, because Ellie charmed them herself.

"She's normally so shy," Mother Heloise continued, piti-lessly. "Doesn't say a word about home, dear little girl that she is. But teachers, especially we Sisters, bless us in Mithrus's name, notice things. Little things, Mrs. Sinder."

Ellie twisted the chunk of crystal glass laden with suppres-sive charms that served as a doorknob and ducked her head as she went through. Sister Amalia Peace-of-Ages, spare and bone-thin in her habit, was nodding over an ancient typewriter, a Babbage screen glowing at eye level on her scarred, ancient wooden desk. More frowning wooden file cabinets and an ancient milkglass window separated her from the hallway, and Ellie almost managed to get past before Sister Amalia croaked, "Hall pass, Miss Sinder."

"Y-yes." She wiped at her cheeks, hitching her bag's knotted strap higher on her shoulder. "High Charm Calc. Lower sixth—"

"—form, yes." The typewriter clacked, and the deathly silence from behind the Mother's heavy door wasn't helping anything at all. What else was Mother Hel saying? What would Laurissa do? Smooth it over, she was good at that. *Really* good, at least with adults.

She's going to kill me. Ellie wiped at her cheeks again. *Probably as soon as I get home today.*

"Fifteen minutes," Sister Amalia said, finally, tearing the pink slip viciously from the typewriter and tapping it with one bony finger. The crackle of a small anti-alteration charm popped off her nail and settled into the thin rosy paper. "Class ends in twenty, dearie. Use the water closet in Third Hall." She turned back to the Babbage's glowing screen, and Ellie's throat closed. She wiped at her cheeks again, and the urge to kick the Sister's desk rattled around inside her like the buckle of the Strep's special oiled belt tapping against the workroom door.

The Sisters meant well, sure. But Mithrus *Christ*, was there going to be a single day in Ellen Sinder's life when she wasn't someone's fucking charity case?

It didn't help that Sister Amalia was right, and Ellie needed ten minutes in the bathroom in Third Hall before she could march, head high and cheeks dry, back into the droning of High Charm Calculus with the tide of whispers following her.

"Seriously?" Ruby's glory of coppery curls caught the sun and threw it back with a vengeance. She leaned against the black Semprena, her blazer already shucked and the sleeves of

her white button-down rolled up to show a clutch of twisted hemp bracelets and smoothly muscled forearms, dusted with gold in the fluid shadow-sunshine. The parking lot around them resounded with chaos as those girls lucky enough to drive home jammed the lanes and honked at each other.

St. Juno's was paranoid about safety. No riding public transport or walking allowed. You drove or took the small, luxurious buses to your gate—provided you were one of the charm or financial aristocracy attending Juno or the other private schools. Ruby was on file as Cami and Ellie's driver, and for such a flighty girl she was remarkably consistent when it came to ferrying them to and fro. She even habitually parked underneath the huge willow in the southeast corner of the parking lot, far away from the school but in the shade, so that Cami wouldn't have to sit in the sun while they waited for the traffic to clear.

Not that it mattered, but it made Cami more comfortable. She had drawn her legs up and sat tailor-fashion on the Semprena's glossy black hood, her folded hands weighing her skirt decorously down. Her long black hair cloaked her shoulders, and her wide blue eyes were dark and troubled as she studied Ellie for a long moment.

Ruby let out a long, aggrieved sigh, but it was Cami's turn to talk now, and she liked to have things straight in her head before she let them out into the world. She used to stutter, but ever since winter the words had come more smoothly.

Ellie suppressed a shudder, as if that just-finished winter had returned. Seeing Cami get increasingly nervous and distant, being able to do *nothing* about it, and, finally, finding out about Cami's birth family—the *Biel'y*, an ancient evil with a cracked-up inhuman queen who survived by eating hearts—reaching out to try and steal her away had been pretty goddamn awful. Snow everywhere, the Strep's increasing violence, the sense of impending doom, and the tunnels under the city, alive with nasty misshapen Potential and hanging with pale lichen—and Cami, lying so still and pale in her hospital bed after they had rescued her.

In the middle of all that, the knock on the door and the news that Dad's train, bringing him back from another inter-province negotiating session, had derailed out in the Waste. At first, Ellie hadn't really understood. She'd stupidly, wrongly thought him being gone on business trips every few months was the worst it could get.

It was barely Marus, Marchmonth, but it felt like a lifetime had passed since then. Cami was due for summer school, too, just to catch up. *That* would be fun for her.

"Mother Hel means well," Cami finally murmured. "But it's going to make it h-hell f-for you."

Exactly. Ellie ran her fingers back through her hair, the slippery blonde strands clinging. The scab at the back of her scalp twinged a little—she was careful not to break its crust. Hitting the door that hard had been a bad piece of luck, and the Strep had kicked her in the stomach as well. "Yeah." Trust Cami to put her finger on exactly what Ellie was most worried about.

Camille doesn't talk much, Ruby said every once in a while, *but when she does, even Gran listens.*

Ruby's strong white teeth flashed. It wasn't quite a smile, just a silent-roar of a grimace. "I could sic the bridge club on that psycho bitch. Gran already doesn't like her."

Cami sighed softly. Her knees, bare and smooth now without the scars she used to have, glowed pearly pale; she shifted slightly and tucked her skirt in more securely. "There's plenty of room at our house," she said, quietly. "Nico will help."

The kind of help I'd get from Nico Vultusino is not the kind of help I need. But if anyone could get him to take an interest in Ellie's problems, it was Cami. And if there was one thing even a Sigiled charmer like the Strep might fear, it was the Family.

Cami just didn't understand that Ellie had her sights set on permanent escape, not a temporary fix. A permanent fix would mean that she wasn't anyone's charity case anymore. Not to mention meaning she could sleep without nightmares and have whole days without bruises and the perpetual feeling of the world slipping away under her feet.

"It's my dad's house." Ellie swung her bag, the knotted strap slippery in her sweating palm. "I should just leave her there? And if I don't live there, will the trust pay for school?"

"The Family—" Cami began, and the open earnestness on her face was almost enough to make Ellie forget what a bunch of cold ruthless bastards said Family was. There would be help there, sure—but every bit of help you got from Nico Vultusino was likely to be accounted for, with high interest, sooner or later. Cami wasn't like that, but then, she'd been adopted in.

Ruby had heard enough. "Just let me at her," she fumed. "Two minutes in a locked room, Ell. *Two minutes.* You can give me an alibi."

"Yeah. Right." *You're tough, Rube. But she's something else.* The thought of her friend facing down the Strep was enough to send a chill down Ellie's spine, even if Ruby had been the terror of Havenvale Middle School when Ellie had arrived. Anyone who messed with Cami got the short end of Ruby's considerable temper—and Cami had from the start somehow made that protection extend to Ellie as well. "The court case would be sensational. *Woodsdowne Girl Eats Charmer, Gets Belly-ache, Film at Eleven.*"

Cami's winged eyebrows had drawn together. "Tuition isn't a p-problem," she said, softly. "We can p-protect you, Ellie. You kn-know that."

You can't protect me from her. Nothing can. I don't want to spend the rest of my life owing favors to Family, either. Ellie shrugged. "It's not that bad." Her stomach cramped slightly, and she knew she was lying. "It's just a few years until I'm of age, maybe I'll even

Sigil or apprentice with someone before then." *Then I'll be hell and gone. Maybe I could even do an exchange—getting out of the city would get me away from Laurissa. That would be nice.*

Even charity cases had dreams.

"Years with the Strep?" Ruby's snort could have won a sarcasm prize. "You should collect hazard pay."

"She knows how to play the legal game." Ellie didn't have to work to sound bitter. "She could sue the Family, even. Make things difficult for them. Even your Gran, Rube. She does all her double-dealing with syrup on top, and stupid grown-ups are fooled. There's nothing I can do." *Except put the Plan into action. Which I could.*

"Good luck suing the Vultusinos." Ruby snorted again. "And seriously, Gran would eat her for *lunch*."

"And get ptomaine poisoning. We'd better get going." Ellie glanced over her shoulder. "It's clearing up. If I'm late . . ." She didn't have to finish.

Cami still looked troubled, but she said nothing as she slid off the Semprena's hood. She just looked at Ellie, that line still between her eyebrows, and it wasn't fair. She was beautiful, and so was Ruby.

Ellie was just . . . a mouse. A creeping little mouse. She hitched her bag onto her shoulder and twisted the silver-and-sapphire ring—the only thing left from Mom, the Strep had seen to that—around her finger. The charming in the stone sparked a little, and its voice was a seashell murmur at the very bottom of her consciousness.

Be brave. Be strong.

The problem wasn't being brave, Ellie thought as Ruby kept muttering *just two minutes, alone in a locked room.* Cami folded herself up in what passed for the Semprena's backseat, Ellie took her place in the passenger seat just like always, and when Rube twisted the key and the engine roused with a purr, deep hollow rock blared from the speakers, shaking anything anyone else had wanted to say into jelly. It was the South Bay Sigils singing about somebody's baby getting a Twist, and Ellie shuddered.

No, brave was easy. You just put your head down and *did* it.

The problem, she realized as she slammed the door and grabbed for the seat belt—Ruby had already dropped the car into gear, and it was time to brace for the ride home—was surviving.

That's what's going to be hard.

TWO

THE DINING ROOM WAS DARKER NOW, BECAUSE THE
Strep didn't like the tinkling crystals of the chandeliers here or
in the foyer. They gave her a headache, she said, and complained
that the high-ceilinged rooms were drafty and dreary. Still, she
always wanted to eat in here when the skeleton staff of household help had the evening off, and it was Ellie's job to serve.

That particular chore had been instituted after Dad's death,
just like a whole raft of other things. It was like the changes in
government during the Reeve and through the Deprescence,
when the world struggled to deal with the eruption of Potential
and the creatures that had lived only in stories suddenly showed
up real and whole. The Age of Iron, when mere-humans thought
they were the masters of the planet, had ended while everyone
was busy with the Great War.

Usually Ell found a little solace in thinking about history
as a pattern, playing itself out in the tiny wheels of human lives

echoing with the bigger wheels of cities, countries, eras, centuries. It was a way to tell yourself that sooner or later even the worst things would end.

Then there were days like today. The quiet snick of the servants' backdoor closing behind Antonia the cook's slow, majestic bulk was a prison cell locking. Ellie braced herself, slipped through the short hall, stepped softly through the arch into the dining room. The gloss of the long table could have been a mirror, and the Strep's reflection was distorted as the charmpolish reacted to a sudden drift of Potential. It always moved oddly around Laurissa; maybe it was her Sigil that did it.

Ellie set the plate down carefully, remembering to turn it so the fan of asparagus spears was pointed away from the Strep. That had been worth a stinging slap once, though Laurissa was usually pretty careful not to hit the face hard enough to bruise.

Don't think about that. "Here, ma'am." Soft and respectful.

"Oh, don't cringe." Laurissa was in one of her irritable moods, but she hadn't exploded when Ellie came home. Her dark eyes weren't hot with anger. If anything, she looked distracted, her blood-lacquered nails tapping the glossy tabletop. "*Despite* what your precious headmistress thinks, I'm not a monster."

"No ma'am." *Mithrus Christ.* Sweat collected in the curve of Ellie's lower back. She hadn't changed out of her uniform yet—since she'd missed most of High Charm Calc, crouching over the keyboard for Babbage study-chat with Ruby and Cami had taken forever; she had to catch up and there was French to struggle with, too.

There was an odd light in Laurissa's gaze, like a sheen of oil on a dark puddle. "It's just us now. Such a tragedy. Just us girls, together."

Yeah, with Dad gone it's just us, and your boyfriends when you want them over. And that baby on the way. Which may or may not be Dad's. Mithrus. "Yes." The sweat was in the hollows of her armpits now too. *Oh, God, where is this going?*

"That's a good girl. Go get your plate. There's a train due tonight."

What? "A train." Ellie repeated it as soft and noncommittal as she could, taking a step back. So she was obeying, but she wasn't *questioning*.

The Strep hated to be questioned.

Her stepmother's other hand rested on the slight curve of her belly. Her talons, glossy Chinin Red, scraped against the fabric of her shirt as she caressed the small mound, probably unconsciously. She'd only begun to show after the train crash, after the news of Dad's . . . death. That was thought-provoking too, wasn't it.

"My sister is coming. Another little girl in the house for you to play with." The Strep examined her plate critically. "I do hope you won't let it affect your studies. Or your chores."

Sister? What the hell? "No ma'am." She escaped through the archway. Her own plate was charmed to keep it warm—Antonia always did that, though she left the Strep's alone. Ellie had given up wondering if it was Miz Toni's comment on the woman, or just that the Strep was afraid of poison charm.

Maybe it was just that Toni felt sorry for Ellie. That was possible too. Laurissa had cut the staff several times, and the first to go were the ones who dared to give Ellie any pitying looks. Laurissa couldn't get rid of Toni, even though she'd been Ellie's nanny a long time ago. At least, she couldn't get rid of a cook of Antonia's caliber *easily*, not if she wanted to keep a certain status.

The Strep was all about that certain status. It was, Ellie had decided, why she'd gone for Dad. Inter-province lawyers weren't celebrities, but they were worth a *lot* of money. Not a lot of people could handle delicate negotiations one day and trips through the Waste on a sealed train the next.

Ellie stood for a minute in the kitchen's safe dimness. Every surface quietly gleaming, the two stoves and the stainless-steel fridges clean and shut like tight-pursed mouths, the squares of pristine cream linoleum flooring charm-scrubbed. Before the Strep, she and her parents had come into the kitchen to eat more often than not, laughing with Toni and playing games, Ellie lisping childhood charms and her father's smile a warm bath of approval.

Of course, the Strep wasn't even the worst thing that had gone wrong. It had all started with Ellie's *real* mother, dead in a matter of days. Six years ago, but she remembered it like yesterday, each of those days crystal clear and painful-sharp. The anonymous wasting illness that had consumed her mother was like a Twist, settling in and destroying everything, leaving Ellie's life unrecognizable. And her father, half dead with grief, easy prey for a charming woman he met over Waste, a blonde bombshell who fluttered around and catered to him before the wedding. She'd even fussed over Ellie, teaching her about makeup and tiny little charms.

Afterward, the siege had begun. Poor Dad hadn't even realized he was in the middle of a war, probably because the enemy only came out of her foxholes when he was gone on one of his inter-province trips. Like the first time, a sudden stinging slap and Laurissa's hissing venom. *Little rich girl, thinking you're so special. Well, you're not.*

When Dad came back, Laurissa was suddenly all sugar and cream again, and Ellie's silent confusion had sealed the deal, so to speak. She had sensed, clearly and sharply, that it would be her word against Laurissa's, and Dad was busy and absent. Even if Ell spoke up, well, she'd still be left alone with the Strep.

A *lot*.

She'd gone over and over it since then, trying to find the way she could have done things differently. There was just all *sorts* of food for thought now that things had changed so much.

Too bad she never had any time to chew it.

She picked up her plate and trudged back for the dining room. She only got a few minutes to herself during the day, enough to take a deep breath and remember what it *used* to be like. Sometimes the stolen time helped.

Sometimes, like today, those few filched seconds just made it worse when she stepped into the dining room again and smelled that burning-cedar anger.

Laurissa looked up from the head of the table. Its gloss distorted her reflection again, and the edge of the Strep's Potential was a smoky ripple, not vibrant like Ruby's or colorless heat-haze like Cami's or shimmersoft like Ellie's own. Lately, the Strep's charm-mantle had been even odder. Almost fraying at the edges, but only when she was at home. Out in public she was the same as she'd ever been—a painted screen nobody but Ellie saw the danger behind.

"Do sit, dear." Laurissa picked up her wineglass, took a mannerly sip, and set the crystal down with a click. "We must discuss a few things."

Great. Each mouthful would turn to sand while she tried to figure out what the Strep wanted next, but God forbid she didn't eat. Ellie settled gingerly in her chair, laid her napkin precisely in her lap, and braced herself for whatever was next.

• • •

The sleek black-gleaming train heaved and snored, pushing its shovelnose chased with dull-red glowing countercharms along with a breathless sigh. Billowing steam and cinders laden with Potential-sparks gushed, as if it rode a cushion of smoke instead of true-iron rails.

Passing through the Waste was dangerous. Out beyond the cities or the electric razorwire and sinkstone borders of the kolkhozes, Twists ran wild, the fey moved through in their own meandering ways, and stray-sloshing Potential messed *everything* up. Even the foliage and wildlife in the Waste got Twisted in places, without charmers to drain off the excess Potential and make it manageable.

So to go through, you had to pay for passage on a sealed train—*and* an indemnity in case you were contaminated en route. Diplomats and inter-province lawyers, not to mention some corporate bigwigs, had travel insurance, but it didn't cover accidental Twists—and sometimes, even true-iron didn't hold back the shifting, and a train derailed.

If it did, your best hope was to die in the accident, because whatever lived out in the Waste would finish the job. Or you'd Twist, and that would be the end of it. Or, one of the hunters from the cities would find you, and you'd be killed on sight.

The risk of bringing contamination into the cities was just too high. Only fey could move between Waste and city, or Waste and kolkhoz. The huge communal farms were where criminals were sent, true, but they were better than the alternative.

Anything was better than the Waste. So everyone said.

Sometimes, Ellie wondered.

She breathed out, then in with shallow little sips. Her stomach still hurt. The after-dinner calm had been punctured only by the Strep's angry scream when Ellie slip-charmed yet another pair of high-heeled boots; the application of Potential had been complex but performed perfectly. It was a charm Laurissa had been working on for days—and not having any luck with. They were waiting for Laurissa to add her Sigil . . . and to sell. They'd fetch a high price.

I shouldn't have done it right. She's just going to sell them. If she didn't bend too much, it wouldn't hurt. The Strep's scream had punched her, Potential like a mailed fist right in the solar plexus, and she'd spilled to the stone floor of the workshop, unable to breathe. The thought that maybe she'd suffocate and save Laurissa the trouble had made a shallow choked sound come out—one her stepmother had to have thought was a whimper instead of a traitorous laugh, because she didn't hit Ellie again.

At least the Strep was going to be more careful about hitting her where it would show, now. Mother Hel had accomplished *that* much.

Hooray.

Her pale hair lifted on a breath of cinder-laden wind, and

Ellie hunched her shoulders. If she held herself *just* right, she could breathe well enough.

"*Seeeeeeal intaaaaaact!*" the platform master yelled, grabbing and spinning the spoked breakwheel with callused hands. Ellie watched the shifting, cascading Potential wed to true-iron, and the train settled with a massive mechanical sagging sound. "*Breaaaaaaak now!*"

She could sense, almost-See, the breakwheel's heavy-duty charming interacting with the train's seal, folding it away in layers and feeding it back into the wheels and rails crackling with pressure and live Potential. Those who worked in the railyards had to have Affinity for true-iron—at least it was *some* insurance against Twisting.

Sometimes Ellie wondered when her own Affinity would begin to show. It would be a sign that her Potential was settling, and that would be a happy day. One step closer to freedom, or at least a better cage.

"Come on," the Strep muttered. Her scarf fluttered, cinders catching in her long frosted mane. She didn't bother with a crackcharm to shed them, and they didn't stick to Ellie's school uniform.

Juno wool repelled a lot of things.

The hatches opened, compressed air blowing and the train taking in fresh instead of mostly recycled.

"The Ten-Fourteen, New Aaaaaavalon to New Haaaaaaven,

now docked!" the platform master, his greased hair with its crust of cinder-crown bobbing, yelled in a singsong. "Liiiiiine up, ladies and gen'lmen! Continuing service to Pocario, Old Astardeane, and Loden Province!" The words reverberated, a simple charm to make them ring over the train's grumble and the noise of those gathered on the platform turning them oddly flat and soulless.

Going through the Waste was only barely scarier than staying *here*. She added it up inside her head again, and came up with the same answer. Two hundred and eighty credits. Not even a quarter of what she needed to pay for passage *and* indemnity. Good luck finishing school or getting apprenticed in another city, too, where she didn't know anyone and had no money for rent or food. She'd be better off getting an apartment in one of the nasty parts of New Haven, except the trust wouldn't pay for her to attend Juno if she wasn't living in the family home. The Strep had mentioned as much this evening, casually, her candy-sweet tone dripping with venom other adults couldn't hear.

The Strep had been awfully forthcoming about some things, but less forthcoming about the terms of her guardianship. If Mother Heloise hadn't looked at the will—or was the Mother bluffing?

I don't care. At least Juno's a good education. All she had to do was get through the next couple years. Year and a half. Year and eight months. Whatever. Ebermerle had dormitories, and the prospect of getting out and away from Perrault Street was enough to give her a small warm feeling of optimism.

Just a tiny one, but you took what you could get.

The Strep glanced sidelong at her, and Ellie's face ached with the effort to keep itself neutral. The woman had a god-damn genius for finding any trace of rebellion in a teenage girl's expression.

Maybe I could be a diplomat. Dad always said they could keep a straight face under torture.

Oh but the thought of her father hurt. Seeing him cave in around the hole of Mom's death, and then Laurissa suddenly there like a fey's bittercake present, sweet candy frosting hiding nasty underneath . . . God.

If there was a God, Mithrus Christ would strike the Strep down. For a moment she was lost in the fantasy—Mithrus descending from iron-colored clouds, book and whip in hand, pointing at the Strep. *For the crime of being evil, you are condemned to . . .*

That was a problem. Ellie couldn't think of any afterworld dire enough. Better to plan her next cred-grab. If she did it subtly enough, the Strep didn't notice a few credits missing from her purse here and there.

There was always Southking Street, too. Even an unlicensed charmer could always make some cash on the sly there, but with her Potential still unsettled, she had to take half price for anything, because of the higher risk of Twist or side effect. Then there was the danger of being caught, though the jack gangs that extorted protection money from anyone vulnerable enough were a bigger headache.

If she could just stay afloat a little longer, work a little harder, she could survive the Strep. Maybe even escape early.

"*Marguerite!*" the Strep cooed, and Ellie returned to herself with a jolt. "*Little sister*, how *are* you?"

Oh, hell. She sized up the girl in a swift glance.

Chubby, her hair a lank mass and her dark gaze half-dead, the Strep's sister clutched a battered cardboard suitcase and flinched as the train let out another sonorous whistle. She looked as disheveled as anyone who had just come off a sealed train would, though there were damp traces on her round cheeks as if she'd washed—or had been crying. Her eyes were red too; cinder-laden recycled air wasn't good for anyone's tender tissues. She didn't even have a hat and veil, just a plaid skirt and dingy kneesocks, a sloppy peach-colored boatneck sweater that could have done a lot for her if it wasn't so baggy and dingy, and sensible, scuffed, unpolished shoes.

She looked like a refugee, or a poor country cousin. A kolkhoz girl, with no shimmer of Potential at all. How could she have absolutely none when the Strep was so high-powered? It wasn't fair.

Ruby would call her a fashion *disaster*, and Cami would

simply shake her head slightly, the compassion in her blue eyes somehow painful because it was so acute.

"Is that *all* you have?" Laurissa was clucking as if someone was grading her on a Motherly Façade of the Year performance. "Poor dear. Was it *bad*?"

The girl flinched. "Not bad." Even her voice was colorless. She didn't seem to notice Ellie, watching the Strep the way a mouse will helplessly watch an uninterested—but still very close—snake.

Maybe she knows?

But the girl actually dropped her suitcase and threw her arms around Laurissa, who, amazingly, didn't smack her for creasing the Auberme suit and the freshly ironed, very stylish Tak Kerak canvas trench coat. Ellie's gorge rose, and she hastily looked away.

"BOOYEAH!" someone yelled, and a blur of motion burst from one of the train's further hatches. "NEW HAAAAAAAAVEN!"

What the hell?

It was a boy, Ellie's age or a little older. He was in an unfamiliar prep school uniform, his striped tie askew and toffee-golden hair sticking up anyhow. Three running strides and he was met by a pair of adults—a beaming mother with dark eyes and a father in a suit, both charmers with a haze-cloud of Potential around them, reacting uneasily as the train settled again.

She recognized him, of course. How could she not?

Avery Fletcher. Mother and father both born into charm-clans, and Dad had knocked back beers with Mr. Fletcher once or twice at the Charmer's Ball or during other get-togethers. Since the Strep had a Sigil and Ellie had Potential, they attended those sorts of things.

At least, while Dad was in town they did. When he wasn't, the Strep had gone alone.

Mrs. Fletcher had her arms around the boy. The surprise for Ellie was seeing how he'd grown. When she'd moved to New Haven he'd been a weedy little jerk, and she'd known him peripherally for years.

Ruby would like him now. Cute enough. But arrogant. Ellie sighed. She still remembered the sandpit, Avery throwing handfuls of it at her, and her own despair as she tried to avoid them. He'd been, what, twelve? Thirteen?

A gnarl-skinned redcap, its cheeks flushed and its too-long arms corded with muscle, brought luggage along the platform on a wheeled cart. It hopped a little, as if the platform burned— of course, redcaps were changelings, and the fey on them would make them uncomfortable around cold true-iron. Still, they didn't Twist, and this was a good job to have.

Fletcher's luggage was part of what the redcap was hauling. The boy surfaced from the hug, his father ruffled his hair, and Avery glanced across the platform like he could feel her gaze.

Heat rose up Ellie's neck, staining her cheeks, and she looked away.

The Strep still had her arms around Marguerite, who had gone pale but nodded eagerly. The naked hope on her round face was almost too much, and Ellie hastily looked away again. Her gaze settled on the train, and she counted the charm-symbols crackling against the black pitted metal, trying to unravel what each one did.

"Hey! Sinder!" Yelling again, across the platform. "*Ellen! Hey!*"

Oh God. She pretended not to hear, staring at the blurring charm-symbols, keeping the Strep in her peripheral vision. Her stomach ached, and the Strep's head came up. She beckoned, and Ellie trudged obediently across the platform, ignoring Avery's last cry.

Talking to him would only cause trouble. How had he remembered her name?

"A friend of yours?" Laurissa inquired, sweetly. Her eyes had narrowed, and her mouth was tight. She studied the boy and his parents speculatively.

"Huh?" Ellie played dumb, hunching her shoulders. "Oh, Fletcher? I saw him at a couple charming events. Hi. I'm Ellie."

The wan, moonfaced sister offered one moist paw. "Rita," she whispered. "Marguerite."

Ellie dredged up a smile. "How do you do, Rita." *Did she*

grow up with the Strep around? That would explain a lot. But she's so young.

Whatever the girl would have said next was lost in the train's blasting whistle, and Laurissa hurried them away with sharp heel-clipping steps, glancing back occasionally at the Fletchers with that same odd expression. For a moment Ellie lost herself in another fantasy—true-iron suddenly smoking and scorching the Strep as she screamed, her spite and rage exposed for all to see.

Ellie's back ran with gooseflesh and she slowed, glancing sidelong. Avery Fletcher stood near his luggage, his father picking up two suitcases, the duffel bag slung over Avery's shoulder. His mother tipped the redcap with a flutter of paper credits. Avery was smiling, his dark eyes merry and warm.

Looking directly at her, for some reason. Or maybe at Laurissa.

She put her head down against the cinder-laden breeze and hurried after the Strep.

THREE

FROZEN WATER'S COBALT WEIGHT, THE COLD BITING
fingers and toes, its claws trickling up arms and legs, a trail of pain
before numbness sets in. She floats, somehow a part of the ice, undu-
lating along its deep glow. Not sunshine, the light comes from inside
somehow, and the freeze is a harsh friend.

It traces up her veins, and soon it will reach her torso. When it has
risen past her belly, up her arms and past her shoulders, it will spread
inward through the arches of her ribs. When it touches her lungs she
will not breathe, and afterward, it will close, almost gently, around her
beating heart.

Everything . . . will stop.

These are the most dangerous dreams, because it is so tempting to
just let go, let the ice creep, until it is too far along to be halted. Then it
will be out of her hands.

No.

As always, there is a shimmer above her. The same smell, of rotting *green and cold metal; the warmth in her nose was blood. Floor wax and the back-and-forth motions as she worked, the squares of pale sunlight on the orphanage floor. Someday she would be rescued. Maybe her mother would even come back, golden hair shining, and—*

Well, even a slave had dreams.

Wake up. Not severe, but warning. There was a stinging all over her, vicious little nips of pain, and a trembling glimmer in the darkness as she sank. Fingers in her hair now, and a scalp-spike of pain as she was pulled.

She didn't want to wake up. The ice was up to her shoulders now, and her legs were inanimate. So easy to just slip under. So tempting. The wax swirled in a circle, her knees aching and her hands chapped and stinging, loose as seaweed in the cold flow.

The ice was everywhere. She should be numb. Why did it hurt?

The sting became a howl of fury, and she finally began to struggle. Not for the surface and for air, but for the ice, chasing the numbness as it retreated, a false friend after all.

Ellie lunged upright, sweat tingling in her scrapes, her hair stuck to her forehead and the faint aqueous light from her mother's ring picking out the grain of rough wood.

This tiny roundish room had a low ceiling; a beam was right over the place Ellie had chosen for her sleeping bag. She had to be careful or she'd bonk her head right on it and add another contusion to her collection. If she had a credit for each one she could escape tomorrow, and a thin rancid giggle at the thought caught in her throat.

Her breathing slowed. She clutched at the blanket she'd filched from the upstairs linen closet and let her racing pulse slowly wind down. Let the brain tune itself to a formless hum, let the body sort itself out. Disconnecting was easy, once you had the hang of it.

When Mom was alive, she'd rock Ellie to sleep after black drowning dreams; night terrors were common for charmer-children. Now Ellie found herself swaying slightly, and the quite natural thought that she could maybe disconnect long enough and deep enough to stop breathing was actually comforting.

Another sharp crackle, and the ring stung her. She inhaled. It was like a Sister's popcharm against the knuckles—not hard enough to really hurt, but it got your attention for sure.

The girl—Rita—now had the bedroom that used to be Ellie's. *Oh no, she doesn't mind, she's happy to be taught how to share*, the Strep had said, calmly gleeful. It didn't matter—Ellie'd taken one look at the stifling, beribboned, pink-laced tomb across from the master bedroom, where Laurissa wanted her to sleep, and privately decided *fuck that noise*. It wasn't any great trick to sneak up here to her refuge, the most forgotten space in the whole four-towered pile of stone that was one of the larger houses on Perrault Street. Especially since the few staff they had weren't enough to keep the whole pile gleaming the way it used to.

Just after the news about Dad came, Ellie had thrashed out of a nightmare in the middle of the night to find a ghost of the Strep's choking *Noixame* cologne hanging in the darkness with the smoky burning cedar breath of anger, smoldering instead of raging flame. Maybe Laurissa had been in her room, or maybe it was just a warning.

Either way, she'd locked her bedroom door and brought up things to this little space by dribs and drabs. A hideaway, a safe spot. Preparation was a girl's best friend, and all that.

Now she blinked, taking stock, her arms around her knees.

A funny little misshapen trapdoor with a bar securely snugged in its brackets, yes. A sloping floor, covered with dust and the marks of her footsteps and dragged things, yes. The chair she'd filched from the smaller dining room, a sleeping bag, a faint gleam from the high, narrow, crooked window. Yes, yes, by God and Mithrus, yes.

There was even a small pile of things that didn't go bad—crackers, wax-sealed cheese, apples that would be mealy but fine enough to eat as long as they were left under a sealcharm, and another charm laid to discourage mice from finding her little trove.

It was bad enough being up here without *rodents*, for chrissake.

There was even a neat pile of paper credits inside an open-work silver box that used to stand on Dad's desk in the library.

A stack of old heavy-sleeved records, too, all she'd been able to save. The two prized Hellward vinyl discs were given pride of place, and Screamin' Jack's familiar face glared at her from the cover of *The Devil Don't Need None*.

Dad had sometimes played those, scratchy and warm, while Ellie did homework and her mother worked thread-fine charm-fiber into her tapestries. Mom had been a charmweaver, and her eye for color had come down to Ellie, or so Dad always told her.

Maybe the ring was responsible for the sudden ease with which Ellie was charming everything nowadays. It wasn't un-heard of, Mom used to say it was an heirloom. From where, though, Ellie had never thought to ask.

Now it was too late.

Her fingers and toes were all pins and needles, and her teeth threatened to chatter. The warming-charm had worn off the sleeping bag. She was looking at waking up every few hours to refresh it against the damp chill from the stone walls burrowing past the bag's thin screen. Or maybe she had to run the risk of stealing a blanket or two.

The room that used to be hers was blue. A sea room, a sky room; Dad had let her pick every shade and tone.

Mom's favorite color. Just like the pool in the back used to be, beyond the rose garden. It was dead-dark and still now, and traceries of algae had begun at its edges. The landscapers who came out were only supposed to bother with the front of the house, what people would see when they peered through the scrollwork of the iron gate. The rose garden was shaggy and ill-kempt now; it was amazing how things could start to look ragged in so short a time.

Ellie put her head down on her scabbed knees. The ring was dark and dead again, and it was awful dark in here despite the reflected cityshine through the high crooked window. She would have to figure out some other light source unless she wanted to charm something to hold a glow, and anything that produced light would be a snap for the Strep to find.

There was a silver lining. The velvet darkness meant nothing and nobody could see her, and the ring's stone was dark. Danger past. And finally, resting her aching head, her arms locked around her knees so tight the bruises—old yellowgreen, blue and deep, or blackreddish new—wept in tiny little groan-voices of their own, she could cry.

FOUR

FRENCH CLASS WILL BE THE DEATH OF ME. AND NOT from a braincramp either. Just from sheer fucking boredom.

Even the dust hung motionless in the air, shafts of liquid gold sunshine braving Juno's charm-latticed windows to fall in orderly diamonds on the mellow-glowing wooden floor scuffed by who knew how many feet. Sister Mary Brefoil droned on about participles and turned the mellifluousness of French into murdered poetry, robbed of all its breath and fire by her flat delivery.

Ruby was openly nodding, keeping conscious in fits and starts. Cami kept giving Ellie little sideways looks, maybe because Ell had been quieter than usual.

Quiet as Cami herself used to be before the stutter broke. At least Ellie had been *useful* during that little escapade, using a High Adelton location-charm to track Cami into the darkness under New Haven.

Afterward, Nico Vultusino had put the fear of Mithrus into

the Strep for a little while. It faded, of course, and then there was double hell to pay. Still, that little bit of breathing room had been just fine by Ell.

She'd *earned* it, too. The High Adelton was almost a fey charm, and it was *also* one you weren't supposed to attempt until years after your Potential settled. The risk of Twisting was there, of course, but the bigger risk was your ability to charm getting eaten by uncontrolled loops in the charm's structure, especially if the thing or person you wanted to find was hedged around with safeguards.

It was powerful, though, and it was one of the few that worked through stone, water, *and* air. The risk, to Ellie, had been ultimately acceptable.

Nobody knew what charm she'd used, but Nico had given her one of his long considering looks, moss-green eyes narrowed. Not much got past him, even if he was brain-soft when Cami was around. It was a good thing he had one little weak point, actually, because otherwise he'd be scarier than even Family had any right to be.

The memory sent an internal shiver through her. *You sure you can find her, Sinder?* As if she was one of his Family boys, fanged and bright-eyed, with their uncanny stillness and their taste for blood.

I can, she'd said, firmly enough that nobody had argued. It hadn't even been difficult.

That was scary in its own way, wasn't it? How easy some things were. Just like slipping underwater.

Now Cami scrawled on a piece of notebook paper, slid it over to her with a practiced motion when Sister Mary turned to the board. Chalk squeaked, and Ellie looked down.

You haven't been sleeping.

Ellie tried not to wince. Trust Cami to notice. Ruby would keep going on blithely assuming everything was grand until disaster loomed, but Cami actually *thought* about things. That was good, because otherwise Ruby would have been even more of a holy terror. Cami probably didn't know how much she moderated their shared redhead.

Ellie waited until Sister Mary took a breath and launched into another droning spiel, then drew a smiley face with two decided slashes for eyes and a shaky arc for a mouth. *Copacetic,* she scrawled, and next to Cami's careful almost-calligraphic letters her own looked shabby.

Run-down. Second-hand. Rubbed through. Just like everything else about her these days. Except the ring, but at Juno its stone was merely blue, pretty and quiescent. If it had charm on it, the school's defenses would have reacted, right? She shouldn't be worrying about whether or not it was helping her keep up with Laurissa's demands.

Of course, every well-done charm was met with a scream and a *Stupid little whore!* As well as a slap or a vicious pinch. It never ended. *Stand up, don't slouch. Look at you, can't you even clean a floor right? You're so useless. Never worked a day in your miserable little life . . .*

Thinking about the constant venom made her dizzy, and she gripped the edge of their shared desk. Cami's fingers drummed once, silently, on the scarred wooden surface. *Fine,* that little movement said, *but I'm still worried.*

There were things Ellie could have written, but none of them could possibly be construed as helpful. Instead, she took a deep breath and settled inside her skin, the subconscious *thump* as centering clicked into place familiar and comforting.

You couldn't charm unbalanced. Well, you *could,* but it wouldn't take as well.

Sister Mary's desk was a towering achievement of organization. She had a cubby or a clip for everything, and the stacked papers were rigidly arranged according to a rule almost as iron as the Mithraic Order's hedge of restrictions around its members.

Like every regimentation, it had its weak spots.

Ellie's fingertips tingled, and the world went away. A thread of Potential slid ribbonlike through the maze of suppressive charms meant to keep Juno schoolgirls from pranking, and sweat prickled on Ellie's upper lip, at the curve of her lower back, under her arms.

Don't get caught.

The glass ink bottle in its scrolled silver stand had been

recently refilled. Red-black liquid inside trembled. Grading ink, charmed so it wouldn't come out and couldn't be altered. That *particular* charm was so specific it was pretty impossible to subvert—but that specificity made it volatile when you knew your *Sigmundson's Charms and Tables of Correspondence* backward, forward, and sideways.

Like Ellie did. At least she was sure the ring didn't have much to do with that; she honestly couldn't tell why some charmers had trouble memorizing them. They were so *simple*, a language of Potential and description that, unlike French, was instantly recognizable.

Cami shifted next to her, but Ellie's concentration had narrowed to a white-hot point. She had long ago perfected the schoolroom art of sitting still and apparently paying attention while doing something else, and a fierce spiked rose of joy bloomed deep in her chest as her charm, subtle and completely opposed to the one shivering in the ink's uneasy fluid embrace, slid home with another satisfying *click*. The two reacted with equally satisfying violence.

CRACK.

Broken glass whickered through the air. Two ghoulgirls—Amy McKenna and Capriana Clare, both with black-varnished nails and jet-bead rosaries, playing at being black charmers—let out a shriek. Steam rose from a spray of boiling ink, and Sister Mary Brefoil, spattered and shocked, let loose a torrent of words in French *and* English that she would no doubt have to say a great many Magdalas on her own polished wooden rosary for.

Ellie exhaled softly, a shocked and amazed expression sliding over her face like the mask it was. Cami's fingers had clenched, and her pencil was in splinters. Ruby was totally awake now, dark eyes wide and her wide grin of delight a beauty to behold.

There. My work for the day, done.

Finally, for the first time since yesterday afternoon, she'd done something right. She finally felt . . . well, *human* again.

At least, she would until she got home.

FIVE

A FEW HOURS LATER, THE BLACK SEMPRENA SKIDDED. Ellie sank her fingers into the dashboard and cursed; Ruby's disbelieving laugh pierced Tommy Triton's wailing. There was no sound from the tiny shelf of a backseat—Cami pretty much always had her eyes shut and her lips moving in silent prayer while Ruby drove.

It was, Ellie often thought, the only way to handle Ruby *at all*.

"What the *hell*?" Rube yelled, and the brakes grabbed *hard*. Smoke rose, the smell of burning rubber thick and cloying as Tommy Triton wailed about being *born bad-charmed, baby, and wasn't that always the way?*

Ellie tried to shriek, but her mouth wouldn't work. Instead, her jaw hung loosely, her heart triphammering inside her ribs as if Tommy Triton's drummer was thocking around in there, high on charmweed and feeling invincible.

The long straight shot of Kelleston Avenue wasn't the most efficient way to get to Perrault Street, but traffic had been terrible and Ruby had decided to swing out and take it. Now they'd found out *why* traffic was so snarled.

The Semprena rocked to a stop. Stood shivering like a nervous horse, its engine uneasy as its cargo's thump-knocking hearts. Inside the thin screen of metal and glass and moving machinery, Ellie's skin came alive, scraped ever so lightly by a charmsilver wire-brush.

"Holy *Mithrus*, do you *see* that?" Rube stared, her dark eyes huge and her knuckles white on the steering wheel.

Ellie sucked in a deep, endless breath.

This ribbon of two-lane pavement snaked down toward the industrial district, and the small shops on either side were closed up tight. Which they shouldn't have been, since right after school's-out was prime shopping time.

Kelleston also ran up the slope of one of the smaller hills New Haven was built on, and the shadow hulking in the middle of the road was proof positive that it wasn't exactly a *safe* street.

If there was such a thing as a safe street. Lately Ellie had been suspecting that a whole lot less of the world was "safe" in any sense. If Dad could die and there could be tunnels under the city that would swallow your friends whole, what *else* could happen?

Her hand flashed out; she almost broke the volume knob on

the stereo with a savage twist, and the sudden silence was almost as stunning as the thing in the road.

"Oh, God," Cami moaned in the backseat, very loud in the stillness. "I'm afraid to l-l-look. Did she h-h-hit someone?"

Oh, God. Don't look at this. "No," Ellie whispered. "Cami, don't you dare open your eyes. Ruby, turn the car around."

Kelleston ran parallel to zigzagging Southking Street for a while. And both of them passed dangerously near the core— the diseased heart of the city, where the Potential tangled and curdled, where anyone too poor or desperate to live anywhere else was trapped. Twist and jack gangs fought for territory inside the blight of the urban core—almost like a piece of the Waste except this was the Potential of too many people living all knotted together. Most cities had a kernel of disfigurement at their centers, left over from the gigantic convulsion of the Reeve after the Great War and just driven in deeper by the crowding of the poor.

Any place old enough to remember the Reeve still held the scars. That was why most cities had *New* somewhere in their names.

The thing lay slumped in the middle of the road, and no wonder the shops were bolted and barred. Thin Marus sunshine ran down the street like liquid, the inside of the car warming dangerously. Little prickles ran over Ellie, Potential flooding her nerve-rivers.

"Is it dead?" Ruby whispered.

"Oh M-M-M-Mithr-r-r-rus *what* . . ." Cami's teeth were chattering.

"It's not dead." Ellie's throat had closed to a pinhole, she had to struggle to produce a croak. The inside of her mouth was dry and slick as dusty glass. "They don't die." *Not until every bit of wild magic has run itself off. And if they get out to the Waste they may not ever die; who knows?*

There was a sharp sound from the back. Cami had looked.

Ellie made a shapeless noise, too, and her mother's ring crackled out a single blue-white spark. The old, shared urge to protect Cami must have spurred Ruby into action. The Semprena's engine revved.

The minotaur raised its heavy, graceless head, a blurring storm of Twisting charm-Potential swirling around it in a perpetual tornado of dust and waving fronds of wild magic. It must have been running for a while, because its flanks heaved as it poured up from its crouch, and you could barely tell it had once been human. A charmer, most likely, wandered too close to the urban core or full of hate or rage.

Strong, bad emotions could Twist a charmer up. But it took the febrile petri-dish of the core or the Waste to birth a minotaur. The head dropped and bone sprouted, ivory-glowing horns spreading wide and wicked, dripping with a dark red ectoplasmic fluid that came from nowhere, the body contorted and swelled until the arms thickened and the shoulders bunched with muscle. It *grew* as long as there was ambient Potential to feed it.

If you got too close, it could kill you. Or worse, *Twist* you too.

The swirling intensified. Electric chill prickled along Ellie's skin. The higher your Potential, the more you had to fear from Twisting. Your bones could sprout through your skin, charm unraveling, each erg of your Potential scraping the inside of your flesh like jeweled bees, limbs corkscrewing and the rest of your short violent life spent creeping in the shadows, contaminating others if their Potential was high enough or they got too close, or even if you were both just unlucky.

Ruby's hands were shaking, gripping the steering wheel with preternatural strength. The twisted hemp bracelets on her wrists were alive with uneasy charmlight.

So there is something she's afraid of. Who knew? The minotaur's bulk bunched up on itself, gleaming with a horrible, dusty, wet iridescence, like oily grit on a puddle's filthy surface. The two mad gleams that were its low-burning eyes, nearly lost in massive folds and rivers of Twisting, bone-calcifying flesh, fastened on the little black car.

Do they smell Potential? Ellie's heart thundered in her chest, tripping along so fast she could feel the vibration all through her. "Ruby." *I sound calm.* "If you do not get us out of here, I will *haunt* you."

Rube's reply was unrepeatable. She spun the wheel and smashed the gas. The car slewed wildly, Ellie's body loose with terror inside the cage of seat and seat belt, and Cami let out another strangled noise.

"*It's f-f-f-following*—" Cami choked back another scream and Ellie felt a queer loose draining sensation, as if the strings of Potential married to her nerves had all twitched at once. The gravitational pull of wild, Twisting magic, maybe, and darkness crawled around the corners of Ellie's vision. The car bucked, its tires squealing in protest, and Ellie heard herself praying in a soft wondrous tone. *Holy Queen Magdala, spouse of Mithrus Christ, watch over us—*

The world righted itself with a jolt, Ruby cursing cheerfully as she held the wheel steady and feathered the brake, then jammed the accelerator to the floor. "Can't catch me!" she yelled, the words muffled under the cotton-fuzz of shock filling Ellie's ears. "*I'm the goddamn gingerbread wolf!*"

That's not the way the rhyme goes. The world came in bright shutterclicks, because her eyelids were fluttering. Every inch of charm and nerve inside her body lit up like a Mithrusmas tree, but by the time she drew in another long endless whooping breath the danger was past.

Of course Ruby didn't slow down. The Semprena wove through traffic like thread through several needle-eyes, metal and rubber both making high stressed sounds as Ruby crowed again and again, wild long trilling whistles and snaptooth obscenities.

Afterward, Ellie was never quite sure of the route, because the city's geography whirled and spun inside her head, refusing to make any sense. All she knew was that the car jolted to a stop near the Sandeckers' place on Perrault, safely far enough away that the Strep wouldn't see them, and it took Ruby a while to quit her snarl-cursing. Spring sunshine beat down, heat collecting under the windshield and sweat raised in great pearly drops all over Ellie's body. Her hands jittered like windblown leaves.

"Mithrus," Cami whispered. "Oh, M-Mithrus. It was one of *them*."

"'Twas." Ruby let out a long shaky sigh. "Wow. We've seen one up close now. Everyone check for Twisting."

"*Ruby!*" The muffled, hysterical giggle from the backseat said that Cami was covering her mouth with one pale, narrow hand. She was safe, Ruby was safe, it should have all been okay.

Ellie's lips were so dry they cracked when she could finally make her mouth work. "You could have killed us."

"No way." Rube shook her long fingers, flashing a dazzling, unsettled grin through the windshield. She patted the dash, a proprietary little smoothing of the charm-shaped fiberglass curve over the speedometer and charmflux meter. "The old girl has some moves. Don't you, baby?"

"That. Was. A *minotaur*." Ellie's hands moved of their own

accord, hitting the seat belt's catch. A spark popped—bright blue, the ring's stone speaking its opinion loud and clear. "You. Irresponsible. *Bitch*." The lock button popped up, and Ellie had the dubious satisfaction of seeing Ruby's jaw drop before she was out of the car, taking a deep breath of fresh sun-washed air and hitching up her bag onto her shoulder. The Semprena's horn blatted, but Ellie ducked aside into the walk-through running between the Sandeckers' and the old Claridge estate's wall, laurel hedges growing wild up against the stone on the Sandecker side and brick, veined with red ivy, on the Claridge's. She walked quickly, her head down, and heard the engine rev. The dusty little path, worn by who knew what since not a lot of people around here walked, was dark even under the sunshine, but the boundary and defensive charms laid into the walls on either side were comforting watchful pressures.

Her breath came in little hitching gasps. She held her hands out as she walked quickly, laurel branches fingering and scraping her hair, examining for signs of Twisting. If it happened to her, she'd lose *every* chance of ever escaping the Strep.

Her legs seemed fine, and she felt at her forehead. No tender spots except the ones from Laurissa's bouncing her around, no thickening bone.

Maybe I'm safe.

She still didn't believe it, not even when she ducked out of the walk-through, rounded the corner, and saw her own gate.

SIX

IT HAD ALL BEEN USELESS, ANYWAY. THE STREP HADN'T even noticed that Ruby hadn't dropped her off. Dad would have been furious. *What I pay them had better keep my baby girl safe,* he would say. Mom would have gotten That Look, the one that promised she would politely but firmly take someone to task. The Strep would have just given some saccharine platitude, and then moved on to making it about *her* in some way.

Still, as soon as Ellie stepped through the heavy ironbound door, she knew something was afoot. She leaned against the door's cold solidity, heart racing and legs limp as overcooked cabbage. Her skirt, its blue and green plaid wearing through near the hem, shivered along with her.

For a moment she closed her eyes and tried to pretend she was just coming home from a normal day, that she would hear Antonia's cheerful *hello there, stranger!* when she walked into the kitchen and the phone would ring—Dad, checking to see she was inside safe. And there would be her mother's footsteps, light and quick, almost dancing, or the thump-whir of a loom as she wove.

Instead, she smelled charmscorch. Disturbed dust. Laurissa was working again today, and exhaustion threatened to drag Ellie right down into a puddle on the black and white squares of the foyer.

God. Not today. Please, not today.

The entire house was buzzing, too. A crackling in the air with the charmscorch and the smoky scent of Laurissa's anger, the scraping and scurrying of motion behind all the silent walls.

There was a slight susurrus, and Ellie opened her eyes to find the new girl, in that same sloppy peach sweater, perched on the staircase like a plump little bird. Rita crouched, and peered through the lace-iron balustrade. Little gleams of eyes, and that lank hair. Scabs on her knees to match Ellie's, and her skirt rucked up almost indecently.

"She's in a mood," Rita whispered, a breath of sound. "Be careful."

Great. "I can tell," Ellie whispered back. *Poor kid, stuck with her all day. Is she gonna send you to school? Where, public? Mithrus.* Public schools in New Haven were *not* fun. At least nobody got knifed in the hallways at Juno.

No, we just get driven home by Ruby and almost get eaten by minotaurs.

Rube was going to want some groveling before she forgave Ellie for losing *her* temper. Another wave of weariness swamped her. Why was she the one always apologizing?

Because you're a useless charity case. It's your role in life, Ellen. Get used to it.

Rita vanished up the stairs, a swift shadowy scuttle. "Thanks," Ellie whispered in her wake. The girl might even have heard.

Maybe Rita could be . . . an ally, sort of. Couldn't she? If she was smart, she'd see that banding together might afford both of them some cover. Laurissa was impatient with the new girl, but not *angry*. Not like she was with Ellie, who for the life of her could not figure out what the hell she'd ever done to make the woman so furious. At first she'd tried harder to maybe make Laurissa like her, but that never seemed to work with any predictability.

Did Rita have some trick to it, one Ellie could learn?

What would it be like to grow up with the Strep? At least Ellie could remember something different. Something better, no matter how far away.

A short, high cry came from the depths of the house. She flinched.

It was the sound of a charmer's rage, and even more dust blew itself through the halls in swirls and eddies. The hurrying sounds became cleaning staff, probably hired for the day, and an involuntary half-laugh escaped Ellie as she realized two things.

One, the Strep was charming in her workroom, and as usual lately, things weren't going well. Which meant Ellie would be called in to help.

Two, it looked like Laurissa was throwing another party. A real one, not just a charmweed bender for one of her boyfriends. Instead of getting some room to breathe while Laurissa and her toy of the moment smoked and laughed and made animal noises behind closed doors, there would be a whole houseful of people the hostess had to impress.

It would be the first party since Dad's . . . accident. Derailing. Death.

Laurissa would be sugar with the guests, but if anything went wrong—and Mithrus knew *something* would—guess who would feel it most?

Great.

A stone rectangle cut into the heart of the house, nothing to soften the bare walls, full of the smell of dampness, heated dust, and the faint odor of live charming changing from day to day, a Twist of its own. Today it was the sharp yellow of vinegar desperation. Yesterday it had been strawberries, sweet just before rotting. They weren't precisely smells, sometimes, but that was how the brain translated them. At least, that was the theory nowadays.

Laurissa stood in front of a stone plinth, her spray-stiff,

mussed hair all but crackling with frustration. Her hands were fists, and Ellie saw with some small traitorous satisfaction that a vein at her temple was pulsing. The back of her suit jacket held a large, visible crease, and her pink stiletto-heeled Pak Chin shoes had been kicked into a corner. Barefoot on cold stone, the Sigiled charmer snarled silently and watched thin threads of steam-Potential unravel themselves from a pair of narrow, knee-high leather boots propped on the plinth. A pricey custom job, it looked like, probably already late to the client since Laurissa had overbooked again. Ellie's gaze swiftly unraveled the failing charm, tracing it back to its source.

Wow. She's really slipping if that's not working right. The repair would be easy, just a tweak of a few threads of throbbing Potential to get them to settle into the leather right.

There was no reason the charm should have been misbehaving at all. It was a ridiculously simple set: surefoot, lookgrabbing, rain proofing. A Sigiled charmer should have been able to do that in her sleep, especially if she produced a symbol when her Potential settled, *and* could reliably produce that same symbol in all her work. A pair of spike-heeled shoes, Laurissa's personal trademark, along with florid overdone curlicues, worked their way into every piece she charmed.

Also, they could be added to every piece Ellie charmed *for* her, since Ell's own Potential hadn't settled yet.

Not all high-powered charmers could Sigil. It took an Affinity for physical objects, a specialization inside the elemental Affinities—water, air, earth, fire, metal, wood, stone—and a healthy dose of luck. Clan sigils were different; as living symbols for a group of charmers tied together by blood, Affinity, or loyalty, they evolved and could die out.

Sometimes a charmer only Sigiled once, when their Potential settled. Charmers who could reliably do it could charge a bundle, since Sigiled pieces didn't unravel, ever. The charm was wedded permanently to the physical base, and the only way to undo it was to destroy the item itself. If anyone could figure out how to Sigil cars, they'd make a *bundle*.

Maybe it was the pregnancy hormones affecting the Strep's concentration. She hadn't been charming right for months now. Usually getting knocked up made a settled charmer's work more powerful in certain ways, but it varied according to age and Affinity.

Too much to think about. Ellie just concentrated on watching.

Laurissa let out another sharp sound of frustration. Shelves of dark wood bolted to the walls jittered a little—bottles and trays of dried or distilled herbs; pieces of feather, bone and fur; canisters of charmahol and colorless volatile sylph-ether spirit; metal or wooden discs in various sizes for temporarily attaching Potential to before it spooled off into complex patterns; all the various supplies a working charmer needed.

You could work with just pure Potential, sure. But it was

easier to anchor it to a physical base, and *way* easier to use sensitized materials that had been sitting in a workroom for a while. You did have to periodically clean things out, because otherwise they'd get . . . well, things would soak up a lot of Potential.

They would start to act almost *alive*.

Ellie had cleaned the workroom herself not three months ago, as winter crouched over New Haven. She'd even waxed the ancient shelves, but the white-glove treatment Laurissa subjected every corner to had found the faintest smudge of dust. The punishment for that had been awful.

A shudder went down Ellie's back. She ignored it, flattening herself against the wall by the locked door; the special oiled belt moved slightly from its hook, its buckle tapping once. It was supple and broad, that belt, and if you didn't move fast enough, it would catch you where it didn't show.

Most of the time the Strep didn't use the buckle. There was that to be grateful for, at least.

On the other side of the door, colorless Rita was doing the same wallflower act, shivering at the stony chill. It was looking like she didn't feel safe from the Strep, either.

That would have been really interesting, but Ellie didn't have any attention to spare.

"Son of a *bitch*," Laurissa breathed. "It's going wrong. Why is it going *wrong*?"

Ellie kept her breathing to short soft sips. The important thing right now was not to be noticed. Rita looked like she had it down to an art form, and Ellie's chest hurt for a moment, a swift lancing pain.

Screw it. I've got all I can handle over here. Her heart pounded, paying no attention to the fact that she was going to pass out if it kept this up. Spilling to the carefully swept floor in a heap was only a temporary measure, though. It would set the Strep off like nothing else, and today that might even mean the buckle. She was just angry enough not to worry if it made a mark somewhere Ellie couldn't hide.

At least she'd been able to change out of her school uniform. Sprawling on the floor with a skirt was *indecorous*, as Ruby would say, rolling her eyes and twisting her glossed lips in imitation of her redoubtable Gran.

She is going to be sooo pissed at me for calling her a bitch.

Laurissa's shoulders sagged. For a few moments she seemed to shrink inside her clothes, and Ellie's throat was desert-dry again. The posture reminded her of the minotaur's slumping shamble and its fuming blur as drops of angry maroon ectoplasmic fluid rose in shuddering scarves.

The jolt of copper terror kept her upright, and she blinked as Laurissa snapped her fingers, a vicious dry click. "Ellen, sweetheart? Come and take a look at this." Dulcet false honey, one of the worst tones she could use. The *soon I'm going to hurt someone* voice that other adults would always mistake for kindness. "It's a little thing, but difficult. Good practice for you."

I'll just bet. Ellie edged forward. Her old trainers were a little too small, pinching her toes, but there was no way of getting new ones. Her jeans were also a little too short, but she'd stolen them a bit oversized and could just undo the hem with a threadcharm. "Yes ma'am. What should I do?" *As if I don't know. At least if I was charm-whoring down on Southking I'd get a credit or two for this.*

"Oh, maybe you can see what needs to be done." She waved her long fingers, the Chinin Red lacquer flashing dangerously under ceiling-moored, insulated electric bulbs. The light in here wasn't the usual gold of incandescents; it was a pale drench passing through buffers wedded to glass so a stray bit of Potential wouldn't explode things and rain danger on anyone below.

For a second Ellie had a mad thought of shattering the bulbs while the Strep was working. It might even be worth it, if she could find a chink in the buffers.

"I don't know." Hedging was probably safest. "It looks pretty complex to me. . . ."

"Oh, come now." Impatient, a toe tapping. "Top of your class, aren't you? My little Margie could learn *plenty* from you. Couldn't you, darling? Don't slouch. Come here and let Ellie show you how to *charm*." The vengeful glee under the words was vicious even for Laurissa, but she probably had all sorts of ways to make her sister feel insignificant.

It was one of her talents.

Margie. What a hideous nickname. It was old and dowdy, and it probably stung Rita like hell. So much for her knowing some way to defuse the Strep.

The girl crept up, mouselike, hanging back almost as much as Ellie did.

Ell let herself take another long look at the boots, even though the charmset Laurissa was attempting was stupid-simple. There was, as Mom always said, no reason not to do even the smallest things *right*.

It was a pinch in a numb place she couldn't afford, thinking of Mom.

The leather was already sensitized by Laurissa's attempts. The charm *wanted* to go on right, there was already a space for it behind Ellie's eyes, in that funny place where she could almost-not-quite physically *see* the pattern Potential wanted to take. It was pretty absurd—Potential ached to obey, longed to be used. Why other people didn't just let it coalesce was beyond her. She would have thought the ring made it easier, except she'd always been able to sort-of-see that unspace. Maybe it was what they called charmsight, though it couldn't be so straight-forward.

Could it?

Her fingers tingled, bitten-down nails fluorescing with golden threads. The threads flowed together in complex knots that were also symbols, leaping off her flesh as Ellie smoothed down the air a half-inch away from the leather—quick graceful movements. She had to stand on her toes to go around the plinth, moving lightly as if she was back at the Vole Academy. Cami had attended in the evenings, but Ellie and Ruby had been in class together during long, syrup-slow afterschool afternoons.

For such an athletic girl, Ruby was astonishingly klutzy at the ballet barre. Just one of those things.

Charming really was like dancing. You found the rhythm, the place where the music wanted you to go, and you went with it. One-two-three, one-two-three, this one was just like a waltz.

What the boots *wanted* was surefoot charm with water resistance and refraction built in. The lookgrabbing charm was an afterthought, but it wouldn't mind tagging along.

Nice and easy, Ell.

Carefully scattered pebbles of colorless glass under the boots twitched. Gold-glowing symbols, hair-fine and delicate, crawled through the leather, inside and out—Ellie dipped a finger inside the well of each boot to make sure it would take. They spread out, a puddle on the plinth's surface, and the broken glass became tiny jewels.

There was a flash, a soundless thunder, and the music halted.

Ellie took her hands away, flicking her fingers as stray golden sparks crackled. The ring was dark, only a shimmer in its depths as the stone hummed a low note of satisfaction.

The boots were taller now, an elegant sweet curve that would mold to the calf, cut away sharply behind the knee. The toes were squarer, and even the heels were subtly altered, lower and also curved, balancing them beautifully. The broken glass, glinting, had smoothed itself up the charm lines as if heated and spun out in delicate fibers. The threads formed symbols and tiny scenes—a spiderweb spinning itself, a filigree horse leaping, a Mithraic sunburst, flowing and melding as the charm caught the interest of its viewers.

Her heart was a rabbit, frantic inside a cage of ribs. *Oh, no.*

It was a beautiful piece of work. Her shoulders came up defensively, waiting for a scream of rage and a stunning blow— probably to the back of her head, but maybe a kick, who knew? The Strep was good at striking where you least expected. A goddamn genius.

There was a tinkling crash.

Marguerite, whey-faced, stood next to a wooden rack full of sylph-ether bottles. One lay broken on the floor, curls of silvery vapor rising, seeking eddy and flow in the sea of Potential around them. Tiny silver flames winked into being, whispering their chiming little cries.

"*Idiot!*" Laurissa flared, and Rita shrank back, her big dark eyes filling with tears. The tiny flames cast an odd white directionless light, and they strengthened, scenting anger.

No. Not anger. Pure rage.

The moment stretched out, and Ellie was suddenly dead certain the sylphire would latch onto Laurissa and start working in, feeding on the sudden shock of finding your own flesh alive with crunching, nipping flame. Smoke rising as if Laurissa was a faust, a dæmon's inhabitation filling her with burning.

How did she die? Well, Officer, there was sylph-ether, and she got careless, and—

The Sigiled charmer snapped a spike-edged catchword and the flames winked out, crying like tiny crystalline children. She spent the next fifteen minutes ranting—*stupid little bitch, clumsy brat, I should have left you on the street to starve*—at poor Rita, who huddled colorless and shaking, her round cheeks wet and her chubby fingers rubbing at her arm where Laurissa's talons had dug in. The Strep forgot all about Ellie, who crept back to the wall near the door and forced herself to watch every moment, silently willing Rita to look at her instead of at the Strep's crimson, contorted face.

The new girl never did, but not taking her gaze away was the least Ellie could do. Because there was no way that bottle, charmed into the rack, could have fallen out by itself.

Maybe, just maybe, Rita might turn out to be okay.

SEVEN

I<small>T USED TO BE THAT</small> E<small>LLIE COULD CREEP AROUND AT</small>
night far more regularly, especially when Dad wasn't home. The
Strep's boyfriends used to keep her occupied, and sometimes
she was even relatively calm after one of them had spent the
night. Judging by the sounds filtering out of whatever bedroom
she used—never the master suite, Dad was absent and love-blind,
but not *stupid*—no wonder she was worn out on those occasions.

Now, though, the boyfriends didn't come by nearly as
often. Good for them. But it also made it harder to slip out and
around.

Ellie slid through the house in an old pair of threadbare
ballet flats, her hair scraped back into a small ponytail—it used
to be a lot longer, but the Strep hated looking at it. So hacked
short was how it was, getting in her face and being stupidly
unmanageable.

Just like the rest of her. Ugly, clumsy, shabby, cringing.

She flattened herself against the wall—here the servants' hallway made a T, the walls probably about as old as New Haven itself and made of cold stone, not dressed with wainscoting past the angle that someone coming out of the bedrooms would see. This place was a heap, and honestly, if she survived the Strep and ever owned the house free and clear, Ellie had a plan for dynamiting it into hell.

Like all plans, the first step was the most difficult.

Stop. Listen.

Little creaks as the whole pile settled, timbers breathing as a chill spring night dropped fine misty rain over the city. The invisible sound of the draft down the bedroom hallway, as familiar as her own breath. Her pulse, a steady metronome inside her ears and wrists. The scrape of her jeans against the wall as her body kept itself upright, making the hundreds of tiny little adjustments necessary to stay stuck to a whirling earth.

The first time she'd fully understood that the planet was round and hurtling through space, she'd been terrified. Now she was just unsurprised. Of course nothing could be steady. Of course it all had to spin. It just made sense.

A soft scrape. A padding. Not the Strep—when Laurissa was ghosting around at night, you could smell the *Noixame* on her, trailing scarves of sicksweet perfume waving like kelp beds, just looking to wrap around and pull an unwary swimmer down.

No, this was a heavier tread, a sloppy shuffling.

Ellie peeked around the corner. The same peach sweater—did she ever take it *off*, even to wash it? The same frayed brown plaid skirt, as well. Ruby would be rolling her eyes so hard right now.

I didn't even Babchat. Homework is going to be dire.

Floating ghostly down the hall, the blur of peach and lank dishwater hair hesitated at the door to the room where Ellie was *supposed* to sleep. One soft round hand lifted as if to knock, Ellie slid around the corner silent as a suppressive charm, and by the time Rita had decided *not* to knock and slid the door open with a noiselessness that implied some practice with such a maneuver Ellie had already halved the distance between them.

She slid through the door just before it closed and put her finger to her lips as Rita stumbled toward the bed, a squeak of surprise loud in the hush.

Both girls froze, staring at each other. Rita's mouth was a loose wet O of surprise. Ellie popped the silencer charm off her fingers, and the immediate deadening of the air around them—not that it needed much help, nobody breathed in this frosty pink room with ribbons on the untouched comforter—was a little gratifying.

"We can talk," Ellie whispered. "But not too loud."

"You're a *charmer*," Rita whispered back, kind of like she would whisper *you're a cannibal* or *you're a minotaur.*

"Born that way." She couldn't help herself. It was a Ruby

sort of crack, the sort of thing she'd just flip into the air and it would sound great. But immediately, she felt a sharp bite of guilt. "Look, I'm sorry. You didn't have to distract her. Thanks."

"You . . ." Rita's soft hands fluttered. Now that Ellie was closer, she could see the shapes under the skin, the high cheekbones and pointed jaw. She could have been pretty, if she wasn't so blurred. Her hair wasn't greasy, it was just really fine, and the cut did nothing for her. It wasn't even really a cut at all, just hacked off at a weird angle, as if she'd done it herself a while ago.

Her eyes were really extraordinary too. Big, and dark, and pretty, thickly lashed. She would really be something when she lost the baby fat.

That's not baby fat, a deep voice whispered, and gooseflesh broke out over her entire body. Rita looked so . . . the only word Ellie could come up with was *insubstantial*. Like all that pudge wasn't really weight that could hold her down.

She shoved the thought away, and it went quietly. No need to borrow trouble, right? They stared at each other for a long time. Finally, Ellie held out her hand, tentatively. "Look," she whispered. "I'm your friend. If you want."

Rita shrank back. She said nothing, her mouth working like a fish's for a loose, wet moment. Those gorgeous dark eyes rolled, and Ellie's hand dropped back to her side.

You should know better, Ell. There's no such thing as friends in this house.

Still, she tried again. The girl had dumped the bottle out of the rack, and got bit pretty hard for it. "Look . . . you didn't have to do that. I'm grateful. If we're together . . . look, she can't hurt us. . . ."

It was the wrong thing to say. Of course the Strep could hurt them, she could hurt them *plenty*, and thinking Rita didn't know it was stupid. She could *see* the walls going up just by the change in the other girl's expression, and there was nothing to say to fix her stupid mistake because Rita was already moving.

She brushed past Ellie like a burning wind, and Ell had time to think *that's weird, she doesn't even smell right* before the door opened—

—and Rita slammed it, *hard*, a sharp biting sound that broke the silencer and was sure to wake Laurissa up. Which meant Ellie had to move, and *now*. She did, just barely making it into the servants' hall before the Strep's bedroom door cracked, a dangerous golden slice of light falling out, cutting off the rest of the house. Ellie peeked around the corner, unable to look away, unable to breathe until the slice narrowed and the master suite's door closed with a soft deadly snick.

Her entire body trembled. She was wet with sweat, and good luck sleeping tonight, even though exhaustion weighed on her like lead.

So much for allies, or friends, or anything else.

Bitch.

EIGHT

Z<small>IGZAGGING</small> S<small>OUTHKING</small> S<small>TREET</small> <small>WAS AT ITS LIVELIEST</small> on weekends. You couldn't park anywhere near, even on Highclere, which meant Ruby did her bargain hunting elsewhere when school wasn't in. That was just fine, anyway, since Ellie didn't want either of her friends seeing what she did when she could escape the four-spired house on Perrault Street on a Saturday. There was a list of chores as long as her arm to come back to, no doubt . . . but she could steal a little time.

Girls of a certain social strata didn't ride the bus in New Haven. Which was why she was always careful. For one thing, she never wore her school blazer, even if it was old and ratty enough to be secondhand. And never, ever a white button-down with a rounded turndown collar, since that was a dead giveaway. No maryjanes, no jangles of silver on her feet, no ultra-thin headbands holding her hair back.

Instead, it was a sloppy gray-washed T-shirt under a jacket

she'd traded a spinning gemcharm to a lizard-skinned jack for, a rough denim thing splattered with paint and with a faint odor of burning clinging to its creases. Jeans frayed at the knees, and a pair of battered trainers she'd done outside chores in for years, pinching her toes but still reasonably held together with dull gray tougher-than-titon-skin charmbind tape. She couldn't do anything about the ring. Leaving it anywhere inside the house wasn't a good idea.

Laurissa sometimes stared hungrily at the star sapphire, though it kept itself dull and dead in her presence. It always had. It was far more active nowadays, though, and sooner or later something was bound to happen.

Anyway, Ellie turned the stone toward her palm before she caught the bus at Perrault and 42nd, so that only the silver band showed. It could have been any metal, really, and she was safe enough.

The bus lurched and swayed all the way up 42nd to Grimmskel, and then lumbered toward Deerskin Station. It was stuffed with cabbage-reeking jacks—feathered and furred, those born twisted by Potential into odd shapes, full of anger and confined to the lowest-paying jobs—and a shapeless mass of non-charmers, some smelling of alcohol and some of nicotine, all of desperation.

Often Ellie wondered if she gave off the same invisible aroma.

She hopped off the lumbering silver beetle of a bus at Deer-skin and set off for Southking without incident, which was a blessing. The first few times, she'd been terrified one of the jacks was going to eat her. There'd been a scuffle at the back of the bus, and a baby screaming, too.

Before they'd moved to New Haven, Ellie had foggy memories of things discussed in hushed tones, adults dropping their voices when they noticed a child was present. It took her a short while to figure out that if you shut up and didn't ask questions, they would drop other hints. Especially because of Dad's work—he knew, often enough, the stories that hadn't made it into the papers and tabloids.

Stories about jacks with a taste for charmer flesh, or charismatic Twists who gathered more than one gang of the dispossessed and allowed criminal hungers free rein inside the blight of the core. There were other dangers, especially for young Potential-carrying girls. Lots and *lots* of them.

Money and connections bought safety, and that safety came with a hedge of restrictions. Only an idiot wouldn't draw the conclusion that the restrictions wouldn't be there if there wasn't a high chance of something going awfully, terribly wrong.

Her usual spot on Southking, right next to what used to be a small bodega and was now a red-curtained shop called Alter-ative Boutique, as if that wasn't a name that would give anyone the shivers, was taken by another scruffy charmer in a long blue denim coat hawking popcharms and eyegrabbers, so she headed against the flow of traffic, uphill.

The hawkers and buskers were out in full force today, a press of tattered velvet, denim, and cheap glinting metal, singing their sell-songs.

"*Pret*-ty silver, *buy* some *sweet*silver, *Miss*?" Shaking a fistful of chiming, thread-thin charmsilver bangles.

Waving a blood-red flower as big as a fist. "*Pe*-onies for a *pen*ny, three days *guar*anteed!"

A jack with a high gray bone crest on the back of his head snapped his long spidery fingers, his nails clicking in time to his cry of "*Buy* some fresh *goff*charms, two for a *cr*edit!"

On the corner of Southking and Bastir, where the latter curved north toward the market part of town, there was a young man playing a violin, his shock of russet hair under the bright spring sunshine matching the red in his coat, clashing with his yellow jeans. The bow trembled as he drew it across the strings, a small charm to make the music audible further away resonating within varnished wood and catgut. A delightful little shiver went through her as she passed, the charm's simplicity and power perfectly married to its function. Nice work. Except there was a brittle undertone to the music that made her think of sharp teeth and beady eyes, a nasty smell like wet fur, so she hurried past.

Further up, there was a space—a bodega's brick wall, covered with an intaglio of graffiti. Nothing that looked likely to give her any trouble, but Ellie still spent a few moments leaning against the wall, her felt hat pulled down low to hide her hair and shade her eyes. When nobody moved to shove her along, she shook her fingers out. The sapphire was a comforting warmth against her palm, and she began searching the faces passing by.

Non-charmers with net shopping bags, jacks with feathers or fur or other odd mutations, carrying backpacks or canvas slings. All with sneaking sidelong glances, credits changing hands in corners, kept down low out of the sightline. You couldn't quite get *everything* on Southking, not the way you could in Shake's Alley or nearer the core where the Twists and black charmers, half-Twisted themselves, sold nasty, expensive, brutal charms for poison, death, curse.

But you could get a lot.

No formal or informal apprenticeship or she'd be producing in a workroom and selling in an atelier. No membership in a charm-clan, producing work under a clan's sigil even if she wasn't powerful enough to have a personal one. She obviously didn't have any sort of license either, or she'd be in a tent over on Rampion or in the Market District proper. It was clear she was too young to have her Potential settled, so any charm she gave might have an unpredictable side-effect, but it was likely to be cheap as well as powerful. There were some valuable things unsettled Potential could do, even if some of the High Charm

Calculus equations went into a tangle of weird inconstant values as soon as someone whose Potential wasn't settled enough worked at them. The intersection of math and magic was never static; it kept responding to every breath of chance and Potential.

Still, you had to at least have been exposed to Calc before your Potential settled. It inoculated you a little bit against Twisting.

A lean, short jack, bone spurs on his cheeks slicing out through the suppurating, too-thin skin on his stretched face, grinned and slunk a little closer. His laboriously multicolored jacket marked him as one of the Simmerside Tops; that particular jack gang was pushing into Southking on weekends to take a cut from those too weak to resist—or those who didn't want trouble.

The edge of Ellie's Potential sparked, a hard sharp dart of light describing the arc of her personal space. *Back off, bottom-feeder.* "Cryboy."

"Bluegirl." The weeping fluid on his cheeks, where the bone rubbed through, glistened. He'd called her a number of things, trying to make her twitch, before finally settling. Now on Southking, she was slightly known. "You been gone a while."

"Busy." *And you're not getting any protection money from me. Mithrus, you're a sucking hole.*

"This is a nice spot. Really nice." Another smirk. What would it be like to have your cheekbones cut that way, to feel the proof of mutation on your face? Every time you looked in the mirror, to be reminded of a difference you couldn't hide?

Not like the Strep. Nobody saw through *her*, at least nobody over eighteen.

Ellie's fingers tensed. The rest of her stayed loose, her heart skipping along a little too quickly, but that was okay. It wouldn't show. Not to *him*, anyway. She'd popped a dartcharm at him the first time he tried to squeeze her for a credit or two, and proved she had enough Potential to give him serious trouble if he pushed harder. Since then he'd just hung around, like a jackal.

As long as Ellie kept him where she could see him, in the middle of a daylight crowd, there wasn't much he would do. If he caught her near dark, or alone in a lonely place, well, that would be different. "Thanks for the compliment. Now run along, jack. You're blocking my sunshine."

"Sure thing, *charmer girl*." He spat it like the jack insult it was, all hot air and halfway to Twist. Ellie restrained the urge to roll her eyes. Instead, she just watched him drift away along the tideline of the crowd.

Business picked up after that. A steady stream of memory-charms to kids her age, two credits a pop. System flushes inscribed on cheap brass discs to get feyhemp or milqueweed out of their bodies before the public schools did another round of quick-release blister testing, five credits. One skinny, rumple-haired, middle-aged woman who handed over a fistful of crumpled paper credits and walked away with a small colorless glass vial of charged sylph-ether Ellie had taken the risk of stealing. The woman's hurrying became an almost-drunken stagger as she vanished, probably running back to her doss where a lamp and a few lumps of tarry poppy extract waited.

Charged sylph-ether gave an extra kick to the poppy tar's high; the woman wasn't far enough along the curve of addiction to start burning it with whatever taper was to hand.

Ellie almost left after that one. Ice and vagrant's tears were hardcore addictions, but they left Potential alone. Feyhemp could burn you for a little while, and milqueleaf made you stupid. Charmweed could addict you if you didn't have Potential; if you did it would just give you a lethargic hangover. But poppy tar fucked you *right up*, and burned any Potential you might have out of you.

As much as she hated High Charm Calc, there was no way Ellie would do anything to irrevocably damage her ability to work with Potential. It was, after all, her only ticket out of Perrault Street. She ran it over and over in her head and came up with the same thing each time. Good luck getting an apprenticeship if a Sigiled charmer dropped a hint that you were unstable or lazy, and good luck getting into a charm-clan when your stepmother was a stranger in town who had made no friends with her avid social climbing.

Most high-powered charmers liked a bit of friendly rivalry, but there were those that took it too far. Funny how nobody seemed to think that maybe Laurissa wasn't a nice person at home, considering how she jostled and elbowed for clients so hard.

That was adults for you. They didn't think about you until you turned old enough, unless they wanted something. Even Dad hadn't thought very hard about Laurissa, or maybe she charmed him right into forgetting everything but her. Who knew?

Even Mother Hel seemed to think everything was just peachy now. Or she was too busy to keep an eye out for Strep-related bruises.

In any case, the only escape possible was saving up, getting into Ebermerle College, and keeping her head attached in the process.

An afternoon's steady work got her a ringing-empty head and a pocket full of crumpled credits, as well as a gnawing belly. It took physical energy to control and contain Potential, especially when you had to be extra careful of it slopping over the sides of the charm and sparking into chaos.

Still, nobody'd had any complaints about her work so far. Stealing the sylph-ether had been an inspired choice, and she was already planning how to grab more. Today had been a good day; being careful until she learned enough to plan for everything had paid off. She'd almost doubled her stash, and all it had taken was a little forethought.

Her gaze flicked through the crowds, and she calculated her exit stroll. She'd learned, after having been chased by Cryboy and his gang of low-level jacks one afternoon, not to shout that she was going anywhere in particular. And *especially* not to relax.

It was just like being at home, really.

She was halfway to Highclere and the beginning of her circuitous route toward the bus station that would let her catch the 151 to Perrault when someone shouted behind her.

"Hey!"

Every inch of Ellie's skin tingled. She didn't stop to wonder if the shout was for her—when your Potential sparked like that, it was best to move first and ask questions later. She didn't know if it was Cryboy pounding the pavement after her, except it wasn't like him to yell unless he was pushing his prey toward his fellow bottom-feeders.

So she took off in the last direction a pursuer would expect—a three-quarter turn to her left, darting across Southking's four lanes. Brakes screeched, someone laid on the horn, but on a Saturday afternoon everything was crowded enough around here to mean she wouldn't get squashed under someone's imported hunk of gas-burning junk *or* a straining pedicab.

"Wait!" whoever it was yelled, but Ellie had no intention of making it any easier on him. She jagged down an alley she'd

scoped out a long time ago, scrambling for a fire escape hanging on rust-eaten screws. It shuddered and yawed alarmingly, but it held her all the way to the top, and she streaked across the roof of the warehouse that was now Beaman's Emporium—shampoo only half a credit per bottle, if you didn't mind the risk of your hair turning into seaweed, and smokes two per packet if you didn't mind them being cut with whatever some jack in some Eastron factory had to hand that day—and clattered down the stairs on the opposite side.

A stitch grabbed her side with sharpclaw fingers, and her entire midriff seized up. She found herself on hands and knees in the Emporium parking lot, staring at pointed glitters of broken glass and a few foil-bright candy wrappers. To her right loomed a huge junker, a rust-colored Porsline truck that had to be almost as ancient as the Reeve itself. To her left was a plain of weed-cracked, open pavement, but there wasn't a single thing moving on its broad, bumpy back.

The Emporium closed at four on Saturdays. Why, nobody knew. Some said it was run by fey, but then everyone who had ever known a flighty-ass Child of Danu laughed themselves sick. Fey weren't supposed to be good at business. They had weird ideas about profit and loss, too.

Still, it would explain a hell of a lot. Ow. Oh, God, ouch.

When she could breathe again, she blinked back tears and carefully heaved herself up into a crouch. Nothing was stirring in front of the Emporium, and she hadn't scraped her hands *too* badly. Her jeans would need more patching, and bright drops of blood welled on her knees and palms.

At least she still had her credits.

It was there, her back to a ginormous ugly-stupid orange truck, that Ellie was startled into laughter again. Ruby wouldn't have run with her—she would have turned around to fight whatever was chasing them. Cami would have tried her best to drag Ruby along, being more of the live to fight another day persuasion. While they were arguing, it would be up to Ellie to make a plan and *solve* the damn problem.

It was ridiculous to think of her friends here, but Cami at least would have understood the sudden burst of dark hilarity.

After all, Ellie had lost her stupid hat. It had flown away during the scramble, and good luck finding it now.

NINE

Getting back to Perrault was anticlimactic.

"She's been gone all day." Rita was as colorless as ever, hunched on a wooden stool at the breakfast bar. Her scabbed knees peeped out from under the brown plaid skirt, and she'd laced her hands protectively over her middle.

The kitchen for once wasn't a trap. Instead, it was warm and bright, full of Antonia's humming, the cook lowering her hefty self down to peer into a cupboard.

"Saturday. Spa day." Ellie dropped onto her usual slightly unsteady three-legged stool. Rocked back and forth a little, just to feel the familiar movement. "She goes to Bianca's downtown." *Gets her claws painted and her skin oiled. Just like a machine.*

"*There* you are." Antonia cast a dark-eyed glance over one broad shoulder. Today her big shapeless dress was pale much-washed blue, with huge splotches of yellow flowers like cancerous growths. She still wore a black band around her left arm in mourning for Mom, part of her wardrobe for years now. She probably didn't dare to wear one for Dad. "Shame on you, Miss Sinder, running around in that getup. Little hoyden."

"I didn't know anyone used that word anymore." Ellie grinned, running her fingers back through her hair. *I never liked that hat anyway, but I'm going to have to find something to cover this up.* The pale blonde was too distinctive. "What's up, Miz Toni?"

Antonia had been Ellie's last au pair, hired before they moved to New Haven. Mom and Dad had arranged for her to get a cook's certification afterward, sending her to Candide Culinary on a full scholarship with references. Keeping her was keeping status among Laurissa's fellow charmers, especially if the Strep wanted to throw parties during the social season—or, God forbid, put in the winning bid to host the Charmer's or Midsummer's Ball.

It was almost a relief to think Ellie wouldn't have to go to a ball this year. Dad would have gotten the invitations for Ruby and Cami as well, because Ell would wheedle him into going and using both of their guest slots. If Ellie hadn't had Potential, Mom's death could have closed the charm community to them both.

It was never difficult for him to get extra tickets for her friends, but Family and Woodsdowne weren't *strictly* allowed in. They could charm, sure . . . but they weren't quite, well, they weren't jacks or Twists, but they were *different.*

Like fey. You didn't invite *them* home.

"Pickles," Antonia grumbled. "Pickled this, pickled that. Well, a pregnant woman, Mithrus bless her. *You* get beef and barley soup, just the thing for growing girls. Perk you up, pale and peaked as you are."

"Certified Twist-free meat." Ellie's face didn't feel as stretched and grim now. "And *organic* barley?" Mom had used to go on organic kicks every once in a while. For just a brief second missing her parents didn't stab her through the heart . . . then the stab arrived, right on schedule.

"Only the best, and a-marketed for cheap." Antonia's grin was wide and white. Her broad dark face was always sheened with a film that was neither sweat nor oil, just a faint moist glow like dew on a healthy orange. "Madam says she plans on changing staff, and during my vacation too. While there's to be big to-doing at the house, and me not here to make all go smooth."

For a second Ell was confused, then her brain kicked in again. *That party Laurissa's planning.* It must have been some bit of social climbing that couldn't wait, since the cook wouldn't be here.

Maybe Toni's vacation was covered in Dad's will too, unless the Strep was planning on firing her. Laurissa sometimes complained about how *dear* Mrs. Cafjil was—it had puzzled Ellie until she'd realized the woman meant Antonia—but how the cook was *simply* the best, and worth it.

Toni was the only piece of Ellie's old life left. Laurissa had hired a few new, gray-faced shuffling domestics. Probably at half the usual rate, too, and it looked like she was getting a fresh crop.

So Laurissa was planning a party with cheap day-temp labor. It was a little too early to really be social season, but she obviously intended to get a piece of whatever action there was. Maybe she wanted to launch this sister of hers into New Haven society, even though Rita was obviously no kind of charmer. It didn't mean she couldn't marry or contract into a clan, seeing as how Laurissa was Sigiled. Potential moved around in families, sometimes, and the chance that Rita might throw a baby with Potential enough to Sigil might be what Laurissa was banking on to buy an alliance with a clan somehow.

"The party . . . It's me." Rita hunched even further. "Tomorrow she's taking *me* there. Bianca's. It's expensive."

"Huh." *Well, if anyone could use a makeover, honey, it's you.* "That'll be nice for you," she offered, tentatively. Did Rita think she was still mad over the other night?

Being mad at Rita was a bad investment. She was just trying to survive, like Ellie was. If she found out more about the girl, maybe she could make a plan about her. What *kind* of plan, Ell didn't know yet.

Still, having a plan was better than just waiting to be surprised. Even pre-plans, or thinking about contingencies, were better than just letting things go their own way. Without plans,

Ellie would have been in even *worse* trouble with the Strep, and far more often too.

Antonia sighed, hefting herself around. Bright silver-scrubbed pots bubbled on the stove, she placed a large stoneware crock on the counter and set about measuring fine-ground salt into it.

More words burst out as Rita stiffened, half-spitting them. "She says I have to not be such a lump. That he won't look at me."

"Who won't?" There was a basket of apples on the steel-shining breakfast bar; Ellie grabbed one even though Antonia would scold her for ruining her dinner.

"The boy." Slumped now, tired as if she'd used up all her energy for the two words. "The one the party's for. She's making a charm."

What? Ellie went cold all over. Antonia's gaze came up; was there a warning in the cook's wide dark eyes? Hard to tell.

"Um." Ellie bit, hardly tasting the sweet juice, the satisfying crunch, tart white flesh under a thin bloom of red and green.

Cami didn't like apples. Oh, she never complained, but she got a funny look on her face whenever you ate one around her.

When Ellie finished chewing, she had her wits back. *She can't mean what I think she might mean.* "Well, lots of charming goes into parties. Everyone tries to waste it as conspicuously as possible; it's part of charm society one-upping. Who's catering the next one?"

"Don't know." Rita couldn't look more miserable if she

tried. Which was amazing. It was, Ellie reflected, an achievement in and of itself to look that hangdog. Even her hair drooped, almost touching the counter. She flushed, too, as if the idea of going to a spa sickened her.

"Oh." That seemed to finish up conversation.

Antonia's mouth was a thin line. She dumped water from a glass carafe into the crock and stirred it, viciously, with a wooden spoon. Sometimes it seemed like she, out of all the other adults, saw what the Strep was doing.

Other times, Ell wasn't so sure.

The corkboard next to the door was bare and empty, no fluttering papers with a long list of chores attached. Maybe the Strep had forgotten. Ellie chewed her way through the apple, slowly. Rita's cheeks were scarlet. She was blinking furiously, and Ellie's chest was tight. Her throat worked dryly at the last bit of apple, and when she bit the core in half Antonia made a spitting noise.

"Avert!" She grabbed a glass bowl full of long thin green scraps of cucumber peel and thrust it over the counter. Ellie obediently deposited the broken core in its tangled nest. "Bad girl. A charmer should know better."

"That's no charm. It's just superstition. No science to it at *all.*" Ellie grinned again as Antonia hissed balefully. "Hey, Rita. Do you want . . . you know, we could take a walk. In the garden. Or something." *After I hide all these credits burning a hole in my pocket.*

"N-no. Can't go outside." Rita shivered. The peach sweater really wasn't that bad. If only it wasn't so stretched and faded, it would have been a great color on her. "*She'll* know."

Not that there was any place to walk to, either, unless they forced a way through the overgrown rose garden. "Okay. We could do something ins—"

"No." Rita slid off the stool, landing with a thump. "You think I don't know what you're doing? Acting *friendly*. Trying to get me into trouble. Just like a *charmer*." And with that, she stamped away, through the swinging door and down the hall with hard thumping footsteps.

No such things as allies, here on Perrault Street.

Antonia splashed more salt into the crock. She said nothing.

Ellie sighed. "When does your vacation start?"

"Monday. I could take a couple days less, but . . ."

"No." A hard little bullet of a word. "You don't have to." She tried to make it sound casual.

Antonia eyed her for a long moment. Ellie sighed, the weight of the credits in her pocket and the tension of having to hold herself so hurtfully *aware* making her heavy and blinking.

"Miss Ellen." Softly. "Are you all right?"

Do I look all right? Does anything here look all right to you? For a moment Ellie gaped at her. Then she shut her mouth with a snap and shook her head. "Fine."

What else *could* she say? Like Rita said, Laurissa would know.

It was only a matter of time before she got rid of Antonia, status or no, and if Ellie said anything, Mithrus Christ, *then* what would Laurissa do?

Of course, Miz Toni had her certification. She could get a job anywhere; she could even indenture for six months to pay passage on a sealed train to some other city or province if she was blacklisted in New Haven. Her escape was guaranteed. She was an *adult*.

"Very well." A wave of the wet wooden spoon, a spatter of saltwater as if she was driving back a smoking faust. "I am not frightened of *Madam*, you know."

Then you don't know her. She could run you out of town, even if she can't blacklist you completely. "I'm okay, Miz Toni." The lie was bitter on her tongue, and Ellie slid off her own chair before she was tempted to say anything stupid. Like, *okay, take me home with you, get me out of here.* Or even, *yeah, don't be afraid of her, that's really smart.*

She made it out through the swinging door and up to her hidey-hole without any incident; the house was utterly silent, not even creaking. Once, she thought she heard something behind her . . . but it was nothing, and within minutes she was curled up on her sleeping bag, dead asleep. No chores meant that for once, all she had to do was wake up in time for dinner. If she was lucky, she just might find out what the Strep was planning with this party of hers.

TEN

IT WAS STILL DAMP FROM MORNING DEW UNDERNEATH the giant willow tree, but they sat there in the mellifluous almost-shade anyway. The concrete picnic tables were sometimes used for Parents' Day and field days, and you weren't quite *supposed* to be out here during lunch . . . but they did it anyway. It was a gloriously sunny day, even if the wind still held a damp chill leftover from winter's bony clutching grasp.

Cami balanced a pencil on her slim finger, trying to find its equilibrium point. "But aren't you guys still in mourning?"

"Mourning?" Ellie rubbed at her arm—the Strep's talons had dug in a good one this morning right before Ruby blatted the Semprena's horn to call Ellie out. *You useless little bitch. Just wait until you come home.*

At least Ruby wasn't mad. She'd just given Ellie a queer look, almost apologetic, and didn't say anything about Friday's episode of vehicular shenanigans. Right now she was lying on her back on the picnic table despite the chill, legs dangling off the edge and her arm over her eyes, magnanimously letting the two of them carry most of the conversation.

"When someone in the House dies, that part of the Family's in mourning." Cami's profile was thoughtful, serene. She finally tucked the pencil behind her ear and handed Ellie half of her sandwich. It was provolone and tomato today, on crusty home-made bread. "There's a l-lot of etiquette. You d-don't throw p-parties for a while."

Mourning. It was a pinch in a numb place. News of the de-railing had arrived in the morning, and the Strep's immediate tears had evaporated when Mr. Engel—Dad's lawyer buddy—had left the house, obviously relieved to be free of the nasty duty of breaking bad news. Laurissa had rounded on Ellie, who was still staring numbly at the front door . . . and slapped her, hard, across the face. *Stop your whining,* she'd hissed, even though Ellie hadn't said a word.

She shook the memory away. It wouldn't do any good. Staying numb was the best policy. "Oh. Charm clans aren't like that. Besides, I don't think anyone could stop *her* from throwing a couple shindigs." Ellie paused, running through everything she'd managed to glean over the weekend one more time, then let out her conclusion. "I think she's got plans for the Fletchers. She was asking about their clan colors and everything." *Because I know the alliances and clans better than she ever will.*

The look of outright horror that passed over Cami's face was pretty priceless. "What kind of plans?"

"This sister of hers—"

"Rita," Ruby supplied, helpfully. "Who isn't going to school."

Stuck in the house with the Strep all day. No wonder she's a bitch. "Yeah. Well, last weekend, Laurissa was all about how she was going to take Rita in and give her a makeover. That she needed something to wear. And Avery Fletcher's back."

"Which one's he, now?" Ruby's foot twitched, the charms on her maryjane making a soft chiming.

Well, if you dated a new boy every week, no wonder they'd start to blur together. "Brown hair, some blond. Arrogant little jerk. Used to throw sand at me, remember Havenvale had the sandpit near the track? There."

Cami eyed her curiously. Eyebrows lifted, her sandwich half-lifted, almost forgotten. "You're still m-mad. That was m-middle school."

"I don't like him, but he doesn't deserve whatever *she's* planning." Ellie's throat burned; she picked up Cami's extra bottle of limon and cracked the charmseal with a savage twist. It took two swallows to wet everything down right. "So she's getting Rita a makeover, and looking at participating in pre-social-season shindig throwing, involving Fletcher clan colors. Want to bet she doesn't have *something* up her sleeve?"

A lock of glossy blue-black hair fell in Cami's face. She brushed it away, an impatient, graceful movement that almost made Ellie's chest burn. Why they let Ellie hang out with them was beyond her. Maybe they needed a third point to make the whole thing work, like certain gemcutter charms. Tricycle, stool, third wheel.

The other word for it was *pity*. There was another term, too. *Charity case*.

She closed her eyes for a second. Now that the first sharp edge of hunger was blunted she could concentrate on really tasting the food instead of just choking it down. Marya—the Vultusino's house fey—always made the *best* bread. Even better than Antonia's chewy delightful rye.

Toni was officially on vacation now.

Laurissa was still making noises about how *expensive* it was to run a household, even though she was raking in credits hand over fist from Ellie's charming. She probably just longed for the Age of Iron days of serfdom or something. Maybe Ellie should be glad she hadn't been demoted to scrubbing toilets instead of cleaning out the workroom. The day maids were mostly invisible, gone before Ellie got home, and the landscaping company responsible for the front and the hedges on either side of the driveway was staffed mostly by jacks who did their work mid-day, when nobody in the neighborhood was likely to be home to see them.

Nobody who mattered, anyway. Perrault Street might as well be a tomb while everyone was at work. Some charmers lived there, true, but they would be down in their workrooms, busy earning the keep that made them able to live behind their walls, with faceless servants doing cleanup.

"She wants to set that Fletcher kid up with her *sister*? Wow." Ruby found this hilarious, and her bright rill of laughter startled something in the willow tree. It rustled, and Cami's head tilted inquiringly. "How old's Rita, again?"

Almost my age. "Fifteen. Kind of weird. Can you imagine the Strep having a *mother*?"

Ruby snorted, still with one arm over her eyes. "Boggles the mind. You'd think the womb that spawned her would have curdled like fey-milk."

Cami's shocked giggle set both of them off, and the willow overhead rustled a little more. The leaf shadows were a spray of coolness, adding to the drenched wind full of waking earth and the breath of exhaust from the city surrounding them. There was a hint of iron-tasting mineral water from the bay, trailing a cold finger down Ellie's back. Her knees, bare under the hem of her tartan skirt, cracked with scabs as she swung her feet, making a companionable jingle to match Ruby's.

For a few minutes, everything was okay again. Cami always had too much food packed into her black lacquer bento box nowadays, and she had a way of just handing it to Ellie that made it so they were sharing instead of Ellie begging for a crumb or two. It had pretty much always been like that, since the first moment Ruby, fists and feet flying, had taken on all comers looking to tease the new girl from overWaste—and Cami had been there, quiet and shy, to hug Ellie while she tried not to cry like a little kid.

Night and day, the two of them, and where did that leave *her*?

The laughter ended on a series of hiccups for Cami, and that made Ruby curl up to sit, bending over and shaking her redgold mane as she struggled for air. Ellie's stomach hurt, but in a good way.

All too soon, the warning tones of the charmbell tinkled over the lacrosse field and interrupted their hitching gasps of leftover merriment.

Cami, of course, had the last word. "If Fletcher's smart, maybe he'll see what the Strep really is," she said softly, handing Ellie the last carefully cut carrot stick from the tiny charmsealed plastic pouch. "Who knows? It's Rita I feel s-sad for."

Not me. But Ellie kept her mouth shut. There was no use in pointing out that they all had to swim on their own.

ELEVEN

THE DAY WORE ON—SISTER MARY BREFOIL HAD BEEN In a Mood ever since the inkbottle incident. She loaded them with double homework, ignoring the suppressed groans. Ellie tried to feel bad about that, but the closest she could get was glad nobody had found out exactly *who* had done the pranking.

Although Ruby had given her more than one long, considering look lately.

High Charm Calc was boring and thankless as usual, and by the time the day ended all Ellie wanted to do was go home and curl up in her hidey-hole. There was no way she was *ever* going to catch up.

She made noncommittal noises while Ruby chattered on, Cami between them actively participating in the conversation for once. They were going on and on about Tommy Triton's upcoming concert downtown at the Palisades. None of them would be allowed to go, of course—after dark, downtown was outright *dangerous*, even if—or especially because—Triton was the anthem writer for the jack population. Ruby's grandmother wouldn't even consider letting her go, and Cami just laughed at the thought of going herself. Nico wouldn't go to a Triton concert, it was kid stuff for him. And of course, the Strep would never let Ell go do anything fun—

"*Sinder! Hey, Sinder!*" A familiar call, except it was a male voice.

Juno's stairs were wide and sharp-edged, faintly gritty stone polished by countless feet. She found herself at the bottom of them, in a press of plaid-skirted schoolgirls released for the day, her arm caught in Cami's and her jaw hanging open.

It was Avery Fletcher, the sunshine picking out gold streaks in his hair. He was in faded jeans and a Charm Dolls T-shirt, and his dark eyebrows were lifted. Nice eyes, dark but with golden threads in the iris, and his nose would have been too much of a proud beak if not for his cheekbones, which had really come into their own. He'd been a gawky, bony, sharp-faced kid, but now his shoulders had filled out and he was actually *taller* than her.

Now he looked downright solid.

"A boy on school grounds," Ruby said, archly. "Who the hell's this, Ell?"

"Fletcher." Her lips were numb. She was suddenly incredibly conscious of the frayed hem of her skirt, the shiny patches worn onto her blazer, the fact that she hadn't washed her hair for a couple days, the way she must look. Her cheeks were hot, for some reason. "Saw you were back."

"Fletcher?" Ruby's expression was a study in pantomimed disbelief. She sized him up, from top to toe. A ripple ran through the crowd of schoolgirls heading for buses and cars, some of them straining to see who the interloper was. "Nose-boy? Ave the Rave? Thought you'd end up on a kolkhoz."

It didn't faze him in the least. "Go steal a chicken, de Varre. I graduated early once I quit skipping, you should try it. Hi, Sinder." He shifted his weight, slightly awkward. "I thought I'd come and see if you wanted to hang out. Saw you at the train station the other day."

"I couldn't stop," Ellie mumbled. Cami was utterly still, probably with amazement. "Sorry."

"Yeah, well, your mom looked in a hurry."

"She's *not* my mom." It burst out, and she stared at him, chin raised, her free hand curling into a fist.

Again, unfazed. "Does that mean you don't want to hang out?"

"N-no." Cami's arm loosened. "She does."

For a second everything paused. Even Ruby was speechless, for once. She stared as Cami slid her arm free, grabbed Ellen's shoulder, and gave her a little push. "Y-you bring her home safe, too." The Vultusino girl fixed Avery Fletcher with a piercing, blue-eyed glare, spacing each word deliberately. "Or I'll *g-get* you."

What the hell? "Cami—"

"Go." Now Cami scowled at her, with a softening around her pretty mouth to take the sting out of the look. "Go on. You n-need a break."

"I have homework." Ellie couldn't manage more than a hoarse plea for Cami to take pity. "I don't think—"

Ruby had caught on. "Please," she snorted, tossing her coppery mane. "As if we won't catch you up. I can do your handwriting standing on my *head*. Ta-ta, lovebirds. Don't do anything I wouldn't!" She proceeded to drag Cami away, her laughter a bright fluttering ribbon over the surf-noise.

Leaving Ellie, cheeks afire and mouth hanging open wide enough to catch flies, gawping at Avery Fletcher.

He stuffed his hands in his pockets. The bubble of silence around them drowned out the staring, the giggles, the engines of the small luxurious buses grumbling.

"Hi." One corner of his mouth hitched up, tentatively, and Ellie realized she was actually dizzy.

She got a breath in, closed her mouth, and shrugged. "Hey."

"I parked in the visitor's lot. You, I mean, do you need to call, or check in, or . . ." A little puzzled now, like he couldn't quite figure out what he was doing here. Of course, neither could she.

He's asking if I have to call home. "No." If Dad had been alive . . .

It was as if he'd read her mind. "I heard. About your dad."

"Everyone did." As soon as it was out of her mouth, she regretted it.

Now he didn't look uncomfortable at all. The sun painted streaks in his hair and lit up his eyes. "I guess so. Look . . . I'll drive you straight home, if you want."

"No." *What am I doing?* "Somewhere else. I mean, I could go somewhere else."

The smile took over his whole face, then, and she saw the ghost of the kid he'd been, throwing sand at her and taunting. There was something else, too, some shadow she couldn't quite place. It would take time and thought to suss it out.

He didn't give her a chance to change her mind. Instead, he offered her his hand, as if they were at a ball, about to waltz among streamers and glittercharms. "Sure. Anywhere you want. Come on."

TWELVE

THE CAR WAS AN OLD PRIMER-PAINTED DEL TORO THAT nevertheless purred when he twisted the key. The Fletchers could of course afford better, but Ellie decided not to ask him why he was driving such a heap. He grabbed the steering wheel and shot her a look as the engine settled into its silken rumble, but Ellie stared straight ahead, at St. Juno's rising gray and colonnaded above the sweeping bank of its front stairs. You could see the Mithraic temple it had once been, and the giant *tau* cross worked into the masonry above the arched front doors was a frowning algebraic symbol.

He didn't drive like Ruby, which was a relief. In fact, his driving was damn near *sedate*. Ellie sat, ankles crossed demurely, and stared out the milky-edged windshield, charmglass growing a cataract just like outside Mother Hel's office. After they turned left on Holyrood Street, massive oaks stretching their green arms overhead, he finally cleared his throat, and she almost flinched.

"So where do you want to go?"

I'm alone with a boy in a car. Dad would have a fit. Her heart was beating a little too quickly. She kept her face a mask. "I don't care. Just not home."

"Huh." Then, very carefully, "How bad is it? At home."

I should have known. "Pull over."

"What?"

"Pull *over*."

He hit the signal, slowed, and turned right. The network of residential streets around here was old and thickly grown with oaks, elms, and huge beeches, the houses small but expensive. It was far away from the castles of Perrault; it was more like Woodsdowne, where Ruby's clan lived, under the slim iron fist of her formidable grandmother. Edalie de Varre took a slice of every import and export through the Waste, and the Seven Families did too. Everyone took a cut in New Haven, it was how business was done . . . and sometimes, Ellie had desperate thoughts of mortgaging whatever she had to, just to get sent *away*.

It wouldn't be a solution. Nobody would help her for love, which just left credits. Of which she had a small—but growing—pile.

She counted them up mentally, again. Even with the new charming on Southking, they still added up to *Not enough*. And here he was, asking her about *home*. About how bad it was. Like he could have any idea. Like she was a charity case to *him*, too.

Everyone coming off their pedestals and casting bread upon the stagnant puddle that was Ellen Sinder.

He braked to a stop in front of a small white-painted cottage, a violently lush bramble hedge greening early along its leaning picket fence, under the sunshine and leafshade. Ellie reached for her seat belt buckle, and was out of it in a hot second, reaching for the door handle.

"Don't." He didn't yell, but the quiet force of the word halted her hand.

The engine sang to itself, softly running inside its carapace of metal and charmfiber. He hadn't turned the ancient radio on, either. She could hear him breathing.

"You ask me about home, and I walk." Her throat was dry. The bruise on her arm gave a twinge, every muscle in her body tightening, ready for action.

"Okay." Did he actually sound frightened? Maybe. "Relax, Sinder. I don't want you to walk."

Why not? "Just don't ask." Well, didn't she sound ridiculous now. "Okay?"

"I already said so. You think I drove all the way out here so you'd get out in a hurry?"

"I don't know *why* you drove all the way out here, *Fletcher*."

"Put your seat belt on."

She did, wishing the burning in her cheeks would go away.

He pulled away from the curb, cautiously, and proceeded to

drive through the neighborhood with mind-numbing slowness, punctiliously obeying every traffic law. She could actually sit and watch the world slide by outside the open window, a flood of fresh air teasing at her hair. It was a nice change from screaming while Ruby tried to kill them all, but she was already thinking about the hell she was going to catch if the Strep saw her getting out of someone else's car. Or if she got home too late.

If it wasn't that, though, it would be something else. Laurissa was *always* finding something wrong. It didn't matter what Ellie did one way or the other. So what if she was in a car with a boy?

I should warn him about Laurissa. "So, Fletcher . . ."

"Avery. You might as well."

Charming of you. "I didn't even call you that at Havenvale." She snuck a sideways glance, and found out he was smiling as he navigated the tangle of streets to the south of Juno.

"Not my fault. Hunter's Park?"

"What?" Her fingers knotted together. Maybe he drove so slow so his conversation could leave her in the dust.

"Hunter's Park. We can sit under a tree and hang out. Or if you're hungry, we can swing through Dapper's. I haven't had a D-burger in a long time."

Her stomach cramped. Dapper's DriveThru had been one of Dad's all-time favorite outings. He'd take her there on Thursdays sometimes, so they could get berrybeer floats. *I need time with my favorite girl,* he'd say. For that brief span of time he was all hers, listening to her chatter, telling her stories, a warm sun-bath of attention. "They closed."

"Awww, *nooo!*" He actually smacked the steering wheel a good one, and Ellie's heart leapt in her chest. She tasted cop-per. "*Damn* it. I leave for a measly year and a half and see what happens?"

I'm sorry. For a moment the words trembled on her tongue. She shoved them away with an effort. Mithrus, what was *wrong* with her? She leaned against the door, and kept track of his hands with her peripheral vision.

He was silent, checking the traffic both ways on Silverthorn Boulevard. He waited a long time for a clear spot, his fingers relaxed and his face set. The pulse beat in his throat, and the T-shirt stretched over his chest. He was built pretty solid, not at all the weedy kid she remembered.

"You used to have braces, didn't you?" Her own voice caught her by surprise.

"Hated 'em." His grin was like Ruby's, strong white teeth. Muscle moved in his forearm. "You can relax. I'm not about to kick you in the shins and call you . . . what was it?"

Ellie Belly. God, I hated that. "You called me a lot of names."

"Yeah, well. You know about guys."

Are you kidding? Juno's all girls. "Actually, I don't. So if you think that's why I'm in the car—"

"Mithrus Christ, Sinder, I'm just trying to *talk* to you. Been looking forward to it ever since I got home." He reached over, snapped the volume knob on the radio—a *Marconi*, that was how old the car was—and Baltus the Golddigger was singing about the sealed train coming around the bend.

"Baltus," she said.

That earned her a startled dark-and-gold glance. "You're into blues?"

"Dad was. He had a bunch of old vinyl rounds. Two-Tail Harry, the Montags, Screamin' Jack Hellward—"

"Vinyl? *Really?*"

Yeah. The Strep put them all in the dustbin. I saved what I could. "Yeah." Her throat was full. "He loved that stuff. My parents met at a Hellward jam before the band broke up. Mom told me I was a child of the blues." Her mask was cracking, she could feel it. But the smile that was rising didn't seem dangerous, because he was watching traffic. It was really nice, she decided, to be in a car with someone who wasn't driving to impersonate the Wild Hunt.

She had to repress the urge to make an *avert* sign with her left hand. He really had her rattled if she was thinking about kid horror stories. Still, with the fey, it paid to be cautious, didn't it?

He was talking again. "Damn. So you were conceived at a Hellward concert. That's *amazing*."

Oh, eww. Trust a guy to go there. "It was their first meeting. I don't know."

He actually laughed, and her own giggle took her by surprise. She rolled the window further down, and by the time he pulled into the parking lot of the low chrome bullet that was the Briarlight Diner—he was on a nostalgic kick for sure, because the last time she'd been here was *way* back in middle school—she was wiping her cheeks and her stomach ached. It was kind of like being with Ruby or Cami, except . . . her heart kept wanting to pound, and the world looked a little less dreary.

He cut the engine, and BessieDean Browne's throaty voice turned off midway through the howling chorus in *Digging Mah Tatoes*. "Come on, babe. I'll buy you a milkshake."

She struggled for breath. "I don't—I don't have any credits." It was a lie, but she had to save everything she could. Her escape fund was growing way too slowly.

"I said it's my treat. God, you think I'd take a girl out and make her pay for her own lunch? Come on."

Her stomach cramped again. She was hungry, but still. "I don't—"

He popped his door open. "Stay there."

Then he was gone, and the car was full of the sound of the engine ticking as it cooled. The Briarlight was a long low rounded building, shining from far away, but close up you could see the flecks and pits in its galvanized walls. It used to be *the* place to hang out in middle school, and there was probably still a chunk of the vanilla beechgum she'd habitually chewed stuck under a table halfway down and to the right. Navy vinyl seats, the smell of old grease—she could almost *taste* their waffle fries, crispy on the outside and fluffy inside. The waitstaff had been kids attending Haven Community College; some of them probably never left.

Her door creaked as Avery swung it open. He was wearing engineer boots, she saw, and they were charm-brushed. She even caught a breath of cologne. Was he shaving already?

How had he turned into this guy?

"You're gonna have a milkshake at least," he informed her. "And even if you had credits, babe, I wouldn't let you pay. And after that, I'll take you wherever you want to go."

"My name is not *babe*," she returned. *I'm actually sounding huffy.*

"It's Ellen Anna Seraphina Sinder. I know." He rolled his eyes, and another laugh caught Ellie sideways, spilled across the parking lot like gold. "I snuck into the office and read your transcripts. I know all about you."

"You did *what?*"

"Milkshake." He offered his hand. The braided leather bracelet on his wrist wasn't charmed, it was just worn and faded, as if he'd had it a long time. "Please?"

"All right." She slid her legs out of the car. "You snuck into the office? Past the Titon?" *Mrs. Triumph, that was her name. That red lipstick, and her gold necklace, and those liverspotted hands. God.*

"Yeah. Almost got caught." He paused, and a cloud drifted over the sun. A cool wind touched the backs of her scabbed knees, and she brushed at her skirt to make it fall right. "I had to find out about you, though."

"Find out what?" What could possibly be interesting enough for him to brave *that* beast?

His grin widened, if that was possible, and he swung the car door closed. "Anything I could."

Inside, it was just the same, except there were no middle-school kids leaning over the backs of the booths, catcalling, pooling their allowance credits for greasy food and tall milkshakes in frosted glasses. The tough, cheap navy carpet was a little more worn, the corners were a little dirtier, and the faces of the waitstaff were a little grayer and older. Maybe the community college kids had moved on to a place that had better tips.

Deserted and drowsy, the grill in back hissing and a tired iron-haired waitress in thick-soled shoes shuffling toward them with all the speed of a damned ship limping into harbor. For a second the past doubled over into the present and Ellie half expected to see Ruby in their old usual booth, her head thrown back and her short hair—she'd taken clippers to herself in middle school, and ended up looking waifish and adorable—

glowing, a much younger Cami next to her with that slight pained smile and the scars she used to have, roping up her arms.

Avery laughed, a short surprised sound. "Wow. Nothing ever really changes here."

Do you not see it? You've been away for a while, you should. "Some things do." She essayed a bright smile for the waitress, who had finally hove into port.

"Two," Avery said, and Ellie shuddered inwardly. The woman's left eye was filmed with a webby, milky covering. Was she a jack? They'd never hired jacks here before.

Shuffling away, listing slightly to the side, the woman led them right to Ellie's old booth. Ellie slid in on her old side, sweeping her skirt underneath her with a practiced motion. The vinyl was just the same—faintly sticky—but the table's surface was clean, at least. The salt and pepper shakers were the same mismatched glass pair, but there was a new spray of artificial silk flowers in a small, cheap yellow plastic vase. *New* was only a relative term, since they were dusty and obviously had been battered a few times.

The view out the window was just the same, too—the parking lot, mostly empty because nobody *drove* here, they cadged rides from older siblings or, in Ruby's case, cousins, or were lucky enough, like Cami, to always have someone who could drive her around and most times pick up Ellie too.

"You still have the old milkshake machine," Avery told the

woman, who blinked and nodded, dropping a couple yellowing, fluttering menus between them.

"Oh," she said slowly. "Thing breaks down twice a week an' the cook charms it inta workin' again. But still here, ayuh."

"Can we have two big ones? Chocolate? Unless you want something else." He looked at Ellie anxiously, and she realized he was *nervous*.

Why would he be worried, though? He was the one in charge.

"Chocolate's fine." On impulse, she dropped her hands into her lap and waited for him to look away.

"Two chocos." The waitress turned and shuffled off, her hips thick and stiff, the hairnet over her graying bun tattered, bits of hair sticking out. There was another hiss and a muttered groan from the kitchen, as if something had gone wrong.

"Wow." He looked a little embarrassed, too. "Place has gone downhill a little. Sorry."

Her right-hand fingertips found a familiar bump on the table's underside. It was beechgum, and it maybe still held the marks of Ellie's younger teeth. A scalding wave of feeling— relief? Embarrassment to match his? Both, or something else?— roared through her.

"It never was that uphill to begin with." She searched for something else to say. Dropped her hand back into her lap. "It's nice, though. It's quiet. And you're here." Her cheeks still burned. Maybe he wouldn't be able to tell.

They stared at each other for what seemed like a long time. The milkshake machine began to whirr, and its racket filled up all the empty space just like the breathing of a sealed train.

When it stopped, Avery was smiling. "I used to really torment you, especially at lunch."

That's one word for it. Harassment's *another.* She settled for saying something non-combative. "Yeah."

"I liked you."

"You did *not.*" Hotly, as if he'd called her a name again.

"You really don't know about guys, do you? Of course I liked you. But you wouldn't look at me unless I was teasing you." He picked up a menu, started rolling it into a cone. His fingers were supple, with square nails—charmer's hands. "I didn't know what else to do."

"Figured it out yet?"

"Not really. You're complex." His grin came out, sun peeking from behind a cloud. "But I'm gonna keep trying. If you'll let me."

"Why?"

"Jeez, if I have to explain *that* to you—"

"Maybe I'm stupe-Twisted. Or maybe I just want to hear you say it." Her mouth was working independently of the rest of her, and for a second she was sure he was going to slide out of the booth and leave.

Instead, he just laughed. It was, she decided, a nice sound.

Honest. Kind, sort of like Cami's laughter. As if she was included, instead of being laughed *at*. When had that changed? Away at prep school?

"You're a lot smarter than you want anyone to think, Ell. I like that about you."

"Keep talking." The girl who was in charge of her mouth now sounded almost cocky. She sounded like she could handle anything. "Especially if there's anything else you like."

She sounded like the sort of girl who could hang out with Avery Fletcher, or maybe even scratch up enough credits to escape the Strep for good.

"There's a lot of things I like." He leaned back against the booth, relaxing, and Ellie's shoulders dropped a little. "I'm going to keep some of them to myself for a rainy day, though. Hey, so your stepmom won the bid for my welcome back party. Nice of her."

"Yeah, well." How could she put it? "Just . . . be careful. She's not . . ." Caution warred with the urge to warn him. If Laurissa had a plan, odds were it was something Avery would want no part of.

The Strep had adults fooled. Except maybe Mother Hel, but she seemed content to leave everything alone now. Even Cami and Ruby had no idea how bad it was, how bad it could *get*. They were lucky, even Cami with her mostly vanished stutter and fully vanished scars. The lucky golden ones always made it through.

Where did that leave her? Beaten down, threadbare, busted, and trying to plan an escape. Fletcher was probably safe, he was one of the goldens. He had a whole family, a whole charm-clan, to back him up if he got in serious trouble.

He waited, but when she couldn't find the rest of the words he just nodded. "Okay. I hear you. You want a burger?"

Do you really hear me? She studied his face, wondering if there was something below the surface. Wondering if he was playing some sort of game, or . . . what? Was there anything else he *could* be doing?

Who knows? Be careful.

She looked away, out the window, as if checking the parking lot. Giving herself a chance to collect her thoughts. When she looked back, he hadn't moved. "We can share," she offered, finally. "If you want to."

"Deal." His smile widened, and something inside Ellie's chest loosened a fraction, then a little more. "Next time I'll take you somewhere nicer."

I'm not sure there's going to be a next time. He was her ride home, so she agreed with him anyway. "Okay." Ellie finally relaxed, settling back against tacky navy-blue vinyl. She took a deep breath, opened her mouth without knowing what was going to come out next, and the words shaped themselves on her tongue like an auditory charm. "So tell me about boarding school."

THIRTEEN

SHE WAS LATE, OF COURSE. BUT THE STONE HOUSE WAS empty. Avery dropped her off around the corner, and Ellie thought that maybe he might have tried to kiss her cheek or something. But in the end, he just grabbed her hand and squeezed for a second before letting go, his cheeks turning scarlet. *When do you want to see me again?*

Day after tomorrow, she'd managed to say, and scrambled out of the car before he could change his mind.

Now she leaned against the front door, smelling stone and floor wax and the burnt-cedar residue of Laurissa's constant anger, and tried to breathe.

Think logically. Is she out looking for me?

No, chances were the Strep was out shopping, or sweet-talking a client, or getting her work—*Ellie's* work—shown in a boutique. Ellie's footsteps echoed as she made her way to the kitchen, checking the chalkboard by the garden door.

Sure enough, there was a list of chores. With Antonia gone, Ellie was responsible for dinner, too. Was Rita hanging around somewhere?

It didn't matter. There was enough on the board to keep her busy until the Strep came back. Waxing the kitchen floor, reorganizing the charm indices in the library, entering the month's income into the Strep's ledgers, dusting the Strep's vanity—now *there* was a double entendre of a task, Ellie thought, and her lonely little giggle fell into the kitchen hush with a thud—and arranging a menu. What kind of menu, and for what? The party, the rest of the week without Antonia, *what*? Probably both, but if she guessed wrong . . .

The party.

Nagging doubt just wouldn't go away. Working on a charm for Avery, Rita said. And Antonia's look of warning. Miz Toni had a little Potential, just enough to keep a pot from bubbling over. Or had Toni simply been frowning because of something else?

It could, Ellie supposed, be a perfectly innocent gift. Even a traditional one, from a Sigiled charmer to a clan she wanted warm relations or even alliance with. The Fletchers were a middle-sized charm-clan, but very respectable, and they took in only the best from outside their kin. They had always steered clear of Laurissa, or maybe it was just because their areas of specialty were less fashion and more medical—they had a lot of charmstitchers for humans and veterinary stitchers for pets and livestock; their Arcadia Clinic near the core was a charitable concern tending to the nonhuman, the jacks, and, some whispered, to Twists as well.

On the other hand, the Fletchers were allied with the Graingers, and Hebe Grainger and Laurissa had a not-quite-friendly couturier rivalry going on. Hebe had stolen a couple of Laurissa's clients during last year's Spring Week, and Laurissa had retaliated by spreading a dirty rumor about some of Grainger's fabrics. Ellie could have told her that wasn't a good idea, because the Graingers had married or apprenticed into all the *big* fashion charm-clans, including the two who had connections overWaste. But the Strep wouldn't have listened, so why bother?

Anyway, if the Strep planned to present Rita at the party and launch her into New Haven society even if the girl wasn't a charmer, well, that was a message too. She'd be advertising her intention to start building her own clan, or looking to buy inclusion into one that maybe had a mudge—a kin-member with no Potential—to spare, to make an alliance with. A mother-in-law was technically clan-kin, and could leverage that for closer connections because she'd be invited to plenty of clan occasions.

It could be perfectly innocent.

Yeah, right. The Strep's real good at innocent.

If it wasn't, if Laurissa had some plan aimed at one of the

Fletchers, or at someone else, she'd use the occasion of Avery's return to get to . . .

Ellie found herself going down the stairs, and miserably knew beyond a doubt that she was heading for the workroom. Her maryjanes clicked against the worn wooden treads, the luckcharms—no good against Laurissa, of course—making a sweet muted music. Her skirt made a soft sound as well; it was so *quiet* here. Deserted.

It's probably nothing. Even if it is something, you shouldn't get in the way. If she finds out you even thought of getting in the way, every-thing she's done up until now will seem like cupcakes and candy. Keep your head down, save your credits, this doesn't concern you.

She would just check the workroom, she decided. There was no harm in looking, right? It meant she'd be prepared for whatever came down. Preparation was good for planning, right?

The door was locked, but Ellie had a key—one of her little secrets, just in case. Every old house had forgotten keys, and Ellie had quietly stolen this one ages ago off Dad's ring. He hadn't noticed—he wasn't a charmer—and who knows if the Strep had even known he had one?

Still, before she twisted the key, she stood for a few mo-ments, resting her forehead against the chill of the massive door, still struggling to breathe. Two bony fists were squeezing her lungs, and her heartbeat was a thin high gallop, thudding in her ears and wrists and ankles. Now would be a good time to go take a shower, while she could be reasonably sure the Strep wasn't going to interrupt. Anytime you were in the bathroom, you were vulnerable.

Why was she doing this?

Well, however much Avery used to annoy her, he wasn't being annoying now. He was maybe trying to make amends. Which was a nice thing, and he was decent enough. He didn't deserve whatever Laurissa had planned.

Why am I so sure she's after him?

Arguing with herself wasn't going to do any good. She twisted the key and pushed the door open, alert for any telltales or trapcharms. There were none. She slid into the workroom, every inch of her skin alive for the sound of the Strep's return, or a footstep, or God alone knew what.

She glanced around, then let herself look at the plinth, where any charm in progress would be lurking. Her skin grew cold as she stared, her gray eyes widening, and for a moment she looked much younger than sixteen-and-three-quarters. The color drained from her cheeks, and she actually swayed.

The Strep was aiming for *someone*, that was for sure. Looking under the screen of charmglow, sensing the tangled Potential and its humming ruthlessness, filled her with unsteady nausea.

See, right there, the loop and that line of glyphs? They were in Sigmundson's Charm Indices, but not the paperback they let kids have in middle school. No, these were from the unexpurgated ones in the back stacks of the public libraries, the shelves you had to sneak your way into, or an adult with settled Potential had to sign in and out, plus vouch, swear, and release all legal claim against the library if they caught a Twist from bad charm.

When her eyes stopped watering she found out the physical base was an *incredibly* tacky Rhalfex watch, brand-new and gaudy. A welcome-back gift, with a sting in the tail—Laurissa was planning on hiding the nasty charm under a screen of showy glitter. All it had to do was touch the victim's skin, and that would be that.

Making it harmless was a fool's job. Anything she did, Laurissa could potentially spot. Except Ellie's Potential hadn't settled yet, so she had a chance of remaining anonymous. If she slipped another layer in below the blacklove charm . . . but why would she do that? If she got close enough, it could Twist *her*.

Leave it alone, Ell. She swayed again. *Leave it alone. Go upstairs and leave it. Just walk away.*

Ten minutes later, she backed carefully out of the workroom, holding her breath. The door closed silently and she locked it, then backed across the hall as if the room held a—

—*a minotaur*—

—a monster which wasn't particularly amenable to containment, something strong enough to bust down even a reinforced workroom door. She whooped in a breath, shaking the remains of Potential off her fingers in a cascade of golden sparks. Her knees shook, but she slid along the wall toward the stairs, the chocolate milkshake and hot greasy waffle fries inside her stomach revolving and threatening to escape.

If she threw up *here* there would be hell to pay.

She made it up the stairs in a rush and into the main floor's servant's bathroom, a dingy room with ancient peeling wallpaper and an even more ancient porcelain commode, before losing everything she'd eaten in the past week into the wide, discolored bowl.

There were some things you really shouldn't attempt before your Potential had settled, and she suspected she'd just found a *big* one.

What else could I do? Miserably, kneeling in front of the toilet and shaking as if she had charmweed fever. *If I end up Twisting, well, okay, but what could I do? That would have made him . . . God, I thought only black charmers did that sort of thing!*

What if Laurissa *was* dabbling in the black? That would make *everything* exponentially more dangerous, and Ellie still didn't have enough credits to pay passage, let alone rent, somewhere else. And forget about food.

Ugh. Yeah, I'll forget about food all you like. Eww.

The trembling came in great waves. Each wave was a little less intense than the last, and finally she was able to stand up, flush the mess away without looking at it, and wash her face in the autumn-leaf-colored sink.

She glanced up, and the bruised circles under her eyes were almost as shocking as the dead pallor in her cheeks. Her hair looked odd, too—a little paler than usual, despite the fact that she hadn't washed it.

Her lips moved slightly, aimlessly.

What else could I have done?

There might have been an answer, but just then she heard a faint scuffing sound and whirled. There was nobody out in the dim servant's hallway, and Ellie trudged upstairs to put her bookbag in her hidey-hole and change her clothes, her head down and her steps faltering whenever another wave of shaking came back.

There was a lot of work to get done, and who knew how long the Strep would be gone?

FOURTEEN

From what Ellie could hear, the party was a roaring success. Laughter and murmurs of conversation floated through the walls, the bustle of the servers hadn't given rise to any huge disasters yet, and she could see some of the charm-clan kids playing in the newly trimmed rose garden outside the kitchen window, shrieking as they lobbed balls of colored charm-light at each other and knocked against foliage clipped by jack day laborers Laurissa had hurriedly hired. The pool was behind a fold of temporary chain-link fencing hissing red with a warning-charm, a green-algae eye staring blindly up at chilly blue spring sky. There was an edge to the wind that promised rain later.

She plunged the pot into soapy water and started scrubbing fiercely. There was a lot to get done, and the kitchen was a babble of activity as the catering staff, licensed and charm-bonded, came and went. A chafing dish had almost exploded, the Strep hadn't ordered enough canapés, the chicken was too dry, one of the servers had already broken down in tears after being groped by an old goat of a guest from the Hathaway charm-clan, and the back door kept squeaking as it opened and closed, each time narrowly avoiding colliding with someone hurrying past.

That dry rattling squeak would have been enough to drive her *insane*. If she hadn't been so goddamn busy.

If Dad was still alive, Ellie would be out in the middle of the party, sneaking a honeywine cooler or two and staying out of the Strep's way. Maybe Cami would be here, and the two of them could play tipbobble or charm-tennis.

Her eyes filled, but she scrubbed even more viciously. Even a loosening-charm could only *help* get some of the stuck-on gunk off; this stuff was almost bonded to the bottom. If Dad hadn't left for those inter-province negotiations—

He had to keep working, you idiot, you know a place like this doesn't pay for itself. Hadn't the Strep reminded her over and over again just how much it cost to feed Ellie even scraps? *You should be grateful*, she would sneer. *Look at you. What are you good for?*

What indeed. She was elbow-deep in soapsuds, scrubbing caked-on remnants of whatever sauce the asparagus had been drenched with, her pale hair scraped back into a ponytail and her T-shirt splattered with dishwater. Her school skirt—she'd grabbed it this morning to wear without thinking, and heartily regretted it—was soaked near the waistband where she leaned against the counter. Barefoot, her lips moving as she muttered a loosening-charm to get the worst of the gunk off the bottom of the pan, she supposed she probably looked like one of the catering staff.

Maybe I could work as a dishwasher. A stupid thought. She couldn't get licensed until she turned eighteen, and good luck charm-bonding if the Strep badmouthed her after she left. It was another no-win situation, and as she banged the pot down in the rinse sink and flipped the hot water dial, she cursed under her breath and thought about how the world was a trap just waiting for someone, anyone, to plunge through the ice.

"Ma'am?" The head caterer, a short pluglike man with a smooth, domed, utterly bald head, looked a little nervous. "They're, well, there's a lot of alcohol out there."

She glanced over her shoulder, gauging what he really meant. Charmers and loosened inhibitions were enough to make anyone nervous. "Do you have any more suppressors?"

"We do, but . . ." His eyes, protruding like poached eggs behind his thick spectacles, blinked moistly. "We don't really have the authority . . ."

"The release is on file, and I'm resident at this address." Ellie took a deep breath and a much firmer hold on her temper. "Take out another five suppressors. Turn 'em on. No reason for your staff to have to worry about *that*, too."

"Yes ma'am." Relieved, he scuttled away. Black turtleneck, black jeans, he looked just like a hideously pretentious South-king busker, one that did pre-Reeve spoken-word instead of music. And who didn't understand why the pickings were so meager.

Ellie bit back a laugh and returned to scrubbing. A flick of a drying-charm, water shedding from metal, a kid's trick, she set the copper pot on the counter and it was whisked away immediately to be pressed into service for some other hapless chunk of food to be choked down by Laurissa's guests. She grabbed another one from the pile to her left and plunged it into the sink, sighing the single word that would make the loosening-charm come alive and help peel off whatever was stuck to it. Looked like lemon sauce and little bits of the too-dry chicken, smothered to make it more palatable. If Antonia would've been here everything would have gone like clockwork.

Still, the entire house was throbbing with merriment and Potential. The Strep would be overjoyed. If she wasn't busily looking for tiny little things to give Ellie hell for later.

Rita hadn't been much in evidence the last couple days. When she did show up, she was dead pale, her new haircut—a layered affair that meshed uneasily with her round cheeks—stuck up anyhow, and she reeked of a colorless fume that Ellie knew all too well.

Desperation. Plus a healthy dose of terror.

Better her than me, she told herself. *We've all got to swim on our own.*

It was no use. Her brain just wouldn't leave it alone. And that was only the first thing it wouldn't stop pawing lightly at.

Avery.

She'd come to her senses, she supposed. Ruby complained loudly about heading out the side door instead of the front when the school day was over, but Cami had quietly supported Ellie's desire not to see the guy again. *If she s-says it's what she wants, Ruby, then that's what we'll do.*

She'd told him *day after tomorrow* and hadn't shown up in front of the school. Maybe he'd been there, maybe he hadn't. Ellie didn't see any point in finding out. She'd done all she could for him; it was stupid to keep hanging around when he was part of the Strep's plans. The risk was just too high.

Who knew? Maybe he would even find Rita dateable. Stranger things had happened. At least he wouldn't get a gift with a blacklove charm on it. It was all she could do for him.

It wasn't enough.

She told the funny feeling in her chest to go away, rinsing the now-gleaming pot and snapping the drying-charm like a wet sheet in the hands of an enthusiastic laundress. Her other hand shot out, and someone gave her the next pan, a wide, flat affair with burnt bits of rice fused to the metal. *Great.* "Thanks. I'll have this done in—"

"What are you doing back here?" Avery Fletcher stood next to her, the sleeves of his navy-blue button-down rolled up to expose his forearms, his hair an artistic mess and a vertical line between his eyebrows. Freshly pressed chinos and polished loafers. The edge of his Potential sparked against Ellie's, a brief scintillation. He was *obviously* a guest, and some of the catering staff were giving him nervous looks.

He was older than her, from a charm-clan, and going to take the summer off before he apprenticed or went to charm-college. With his clan connections and Potential, he could do what he wanted. What was he doing sniffing around *her*? He was going to be a star in the charming community, and Ell . . . well, she was a sinking ship.

"Working." She dumped the pan in the sink. "What are *you* doing?"

"Looking for the girl who's been ignoring me."

"What, there's only one?" *It's safest for both of us that way.* "Learn to take a hint, Fletcher."

"It's a charmer's party. Why aren't you out there?"

Why do you think? For a second, she couldn't remember the charm to loosen stuck-on food, and a chill ran down her back. "You get your present?" Because now, she knew it had been for him, and the knowledge turned her cold all over.

"Yeah. It's . . . tacky. My mom took it." His nose wrinkled briefly. "Look, Ellie . . ."

It's better than it was, kid. Waaaay better than it was. That charm would have turned you upside down and she would have had a field day with you. "If I get caught talking to you there's going to be trouble. I don't want you here."

"I'll take care of whatever—"

A real knight in shining, this guy. "You can't. Just go out and enjoy yourself at the goddamn party. It's in your honor. Congratulations."

"Is that really your . . . is that really Laurissa's sister? I never heard she had one."

"So she says. She's from overWaste; both of them are. Not my business." Ellie took a deep breath. The water was getting cloudy again. Her hands were going to be raisin-wrinkled for a good while. Outside in the rose garden, someone started laughing hysterically, a high young voice. "She was on your train. Didn't you see her?"

"She wasn't in my carriage. Ellie—"

I'm not in your carriage either. "You really need to go back out there, guest of honor and all." She rinsed the gleaming circle of the pan. The drying-charm caught itself between her teeth but she forced it out, and the cleaned metal went on the counter with a bang. "You're being rude."

He stood there while she scrubbed two more pots. The pile to her left was finally getting smaller. Maybe she'd be able to catch up.

You won't ever catch up, Ell. Don't even try.

"Fine." A single clipped syllable. Something soft landed on the counter, and she didn't look at it until the sense of his Potential, a fizzing bath of frustration and hurt, faded completely. She could tell he was gone by the way her skin turned back into dead clay instead of sparkling charmlight.

It's not so bad. He's safe, for the moment at least. Laurissa won't be looking for effects for a couple days.

A blacklove charm. He'd be desperate for whoever it was tuned to, probably Rita. The other possibility . . . well, it didn't bear thinking about.

Blinking furiously again, she washed another hunk of cooking-metal before a drop of hot water traced down her cheek. It fell into the thinning soapsuds, and she yanked the plug, turning on the water to rinse everything down. She'd need a fresh sinkful to deal with the last of the main-course pans. After this there was the sorbet, and then the great towering cake, its fondant sky-blue and deep gold in deference to the Fletcher clan's colors, would be wheeled out of the coolroom and down the hall, to the parquet floor and small carved tables that hid under dust-stiffened draperies until a grand event came along. She could almost hear the sigh of wonder that would go up at the cake, and thought grimly that it was a good thing Laurissa had handled the negotiations with the baker herself. If the entire confection decided to melt all over the ballroom's parquet, at least Ellie wouldn't be blamed for it.

Oh, you know you will be anyway. She sighed, popped the sink stopper back in, and dumped more harsh dish soap under the stream of hot water before she let her gaze drift to her left, casually, as if she didn't care.

Her heart leapt into her throat. The world grayed out, came back in a rush of color and sensation.

There, next to the pile of food-crusted plates beginning to come back from the dining room, was a shapeless black felt cloche hat, familiar and strange at the same time.

Her hat. So Avery Fletcher knew she'd been down on Southking? Had he been the one chasing her? He could get her banned, he could maybe even get her banished to a kolk-hoz. You weren't supposed to charm for money if you weren't licensed, and you doubly weren't supposed to do it before your Potential settled.

Was it a warning? Was he going to tell?

Great. She grabbed the edge of the counter, told her knees to stiffen up, buttercup, and swallowed hard, twice. Her throat was so dry she heard a click. *And I was just a jack to him. Smooth move, Ellen. All he has to do is tell someone, anyone.*

Maybe even the Strep.

She set her jaw, rolled up the hat—there was something that crackled inside it—and tucked it under her sodden waistband.

She'd figure it out later, and make a plan. Her back ached, and she splashed a pile of plates into the rapidly filling sink.

I have to get more credits. Enough to escape the city. Soon. As soon as I can.

Blinking still, Ellie scrubbed.

FIFTEEN

EVERYTHING, SHE DISCOVERED, COULD ALWAYS GET worse.

"God *damn* it." Laurissa's fists, white-knuckled at her sides, almost creaked. "*Why* is it not *working*?"

Rita hunched near the workroom door. The new haircut actually did her some good, but her soft helpless terror just made you want to pinch her. Each time Ellie glanced to the side the urge rose, and shoving it away got harder each time.

That'll Twist you, Ell. Just keep still.

"You!" Laurissa rounded on her. "*You*. Make it work!"

So you can hit me again? Already, her head rang, and she was having trouble breathing. It wasn't so much the light, stinging slap she'd just been granted, it was the rage pouring off the Strep in heavy colorless waves. Her Potential moved oddly, too, as if it was unable to grasp the pattern the charm wanted to flow into.

"I can't," Ellie heard herself say, a dull throaty whisper. "It's too hard."

The lie was a pale attempt, but the best she could come up with.

"Not for *you*," Laurissa sneered, forgetting how it creased the corners of her eyes and mouth. "You think you're too good to work a little for your keep? Daddy's little girl. Charm it, or I'll throw you out into the street."

That would be great. At least I'd be rid of you. For a moment Ellie actually contemplated pissing off the Strep enough to have her make good on the threat . . . but then she thought of Southking, Simmerside, the urban core. Desperate faces on lumbering buses, scrambling to charm enough to keep a roof over her head, maybe being kicked out of Juno.

Maybe worse things, like being caught by Cryboy and his jacks. She knew what could happen to an unprotected girl out there.

So she stepped forward, trying not to brush against the Strep's cloak of crackle-angry Potential. Her head felt full and strangely light.

The base matrix—the physical thing Potential would attach to—was a pair of black patent-leather pumps, chunky-heeled and already singed from Laurissa's last attempt. Small copper beads steamed, scattered in odd corkscrew swirls on the plinth's surface. Even the stone was smoking a bit, and the resultant throat-scorch reek was enough to make her eyes water.

Why is everything going wrong for her? I wouldn't mind so much if it wasn't running downhill.

She took her time looking at the wreckage, even though Laurissa's aggrieved sigh made the air dangerously hot and close. These were signature pieces, so they had to incorporate Laurissa's trademark curlicues and florid overtones. Good thing Ellie's Potential hadn't settled, because she could convincingly fake some of those touches. They'd sell, and maybe the Strep would lay off a bit while she was counting her credits.

And maybe Ellie could steal a few of those crumpled paper notes.

Her fingers tingled. She shook them out, delicately, and nodded as if the Strep had spoken. "Yes ma'am." Soft, conciliatory.

She just said to charm it. She didn't say with what.

The thought was so absurd it halted her in mid-movement. Then it seemed natural and right, and she kept her face its usual mask as she stepped forward, finding the music—a harsh dissonant jangle, sort of like the Russian composer right after the Reeve, what was his name?

Figure it out later. She moved with the rhythm, stepping sideways, her battered trainers brushing the workroom floor. Laurissa's anger fell away; all that mattered was the charm. It was a spiky one, its sharp points digging into the tenderness behind Ellie's sore and reddened eyes, but she held it anyway.

Potential leapt to obey, crackling like Tesla's Folly from her fingertips, spidery blue-white crawling veins. They grabbed the shoes and lifted them, tearing at the architecture of the real world, copper glowing red-hot as the beads flung themselves upward popcorn-quick, spattering and spitting with fury.

I know! Stravinsky. The name flashed across her consciousness, a meteor of Potential. A hand striking a rickety table loaded with delicate wineglasses, a crash and a tinkle, the red flare of a charm gone sideways and her own voice raised, shouting syllables she should not, could not know. . . .

Darkness, spangled with lightning like the Waste, crackling and receding. The sense of force bleeding away, and a fierce joy, like running flat-out when you didn't have to, just like a kid. Flinging yourself along, just because the buzzing of happiness *demanded* you go as fast as you could.

Blackness, then, soft and restful. She came back to herself piecemeal. Cold stone against her cheek, faintly gritty.

What just happened?

Rita sobbed in a breath. "Maybe she Sigiled." It was a terrified whisper. "Mommy—"

"Shut up, brat." No trouble identifying this voice. It was Laurissa, heels clicking—she must have put her shoes back on. Why?

Am I hurt? Ellie took stock. *Did she hit me? Maybe? I don't know.* The inside of her skull was scraped clean. Empty. A great ringing silence, as if she was six again and had attempted a charm too big for her age. Her mother would be white with fear if—

My brave girl. This voice came into her head without bothering to pass through her ears. A stinging on her hand. The sapphire—was it lighting up? She couldn't afford to have Laurissa notice it.

Mom? Had she heard Rita say it, or was Ellie just dreaming of her own mother, of cool fingers against a fevered forehead, the warm perfume and soothing touch that was the best safety in the world, the softness and the power of knowing there was nothing that couldn't be fixed, *nothing*, once the voice that moved the world sounded all around her?

"Well." The Strep, sounding thoughtful, but thankfully not burning-furious. "Isn't this surprising. They're very light. A little clumsy in the turnaside charm, but that's to be expected in a first."

"M-m-m—" Rita, stuttering.

"Shut *up.*" Casually cruel. "Get your things out of her room."

The silence turned cold. Almost scaly, a dry quiet full of whispering rasp.

"B-but y-y-you s-s-said—" Rita, gamely struggling. Ellie could have told her the Strep wasn't going to look kindly on *any* questioning. Not in her current mood.

I think I'm all here. She tested—fingers, toes, everything seemed still attached. It felt normal. A cool bath of dread slid down her back, raising gooseflesh and leaching through her like the cold of the stone floor. *Wait. Did I Twist? Oh, please, Mithrus, tell me I haven't Twisted!*

A sharp sound—openhanded slap, cracking against a face. Rita's half-swallowed sob. Ellie curled around herself, her limbs sluggish. If Laurissa was coming down on Rita, well, three guesses who was next, and the first two didn't count, right?

The hinges on the workroom door squealed slightly as it was wrenched open, and the patter of soft fleeing footsteps meant Ellie was alone in here. Alone, on the floor, and with her head still muzzy.

Great. Wake up. Come on, wake up!

A nudge in her ribs. A sharp point, the toe of a shoe digging in. "Well, well, little Ellen. Look at you."

I really wish you wouldn't. She could only produce a groan. What was *wrong* with her? If she'd Twisted, shouldn't Laurissa be screaming and running away?

I'd pay to see that. I really would. And I need all the credits I've got. Only four hundred twelve, because she's been staying home on Saturdays. No more spa days.

Where does all the money go? She takes in tons of it. Where is it?

She tried to hang onto that thought, it seemed important. There wasn't any *time*, though, and she needed to be awake and alert for whatever Laurissa would do next.

"Upsy-daisy." An edged, girlish giggle, and there were hands on her. The Strep's hands, narrow and hard, lacquered talons scraping. "There's a good girl."

Ellie found herself on her feet, swaying, blinking, and staring at a world alive with too much light. The workroom walls crawled with charm-symbols, thin threads of Potential wedded to the very stone—but it wasn't the usual buffers and shielding meant to make sure a charmer didn't blow a house up while dealing with difficult, dangerous Potential-channeling. Not so much the channeling as the idea that it might interact with another bit of Potential and set off a quake through the snarled fabric of reality.

No, this was as if she was seeing the charm-energies inherent in the physical objects themselves. The flux of energy that made matter once it slowed down enough, a dense thicket of light and air and force.

Her head throbbed a little, and Ellie blinked. The plinth was empty but she could see the ripples, a rock thrown into a Potential-pond, spreading out from whatever had happened there. *Did I do that? Wow. What happened?*

Crunch. A sharp pain, as if her entire hand was squeezed, her mother's ring singing a seashell song that was almost, almost audible . . . and Ellie thumped back into her own body so hard she was surprised the entire world didn't rock underneath her. She tore away from Laurissa and stood trembling in the middle of the workroom, the light fading as charmsight receded.

It had to be Sight, but that was *impossible*, her Potential hadn't settled yet! And she'd never read about people seeing charmlight in *walls* before. Oh sure, Potential could be charmed into buffers and defenses, but seeing the structure—it was impossible.

What's going on?

She stared at Laurissa, Laurissa stared back, and a sudden hard, delighted smile transformed the Strep's face. It was the kind of smile that turned the mouth into a V and the eyes into narrowed slits, the enemy peering out from castle embrasures at dawn. The Strep's belly had grown bigger, if that was possible, or were Ellie's eyes just fooling her again?

"This is so nice," the Strep purred, finally. The smile widened, and Ellie had the sudden vivid image of the top of the Strep's head flipping open, cracked by the sheer scary satisfaction the woman radiated. "We're going to make a lot of money, Ellen dear."

SIXTEEN

A COUPLE WEEKS LATER, SHE BLINKED HER DRY BURNING eyes and tried to settle.

"*Blessed Mithrus, watch over us, We are the lambs—*" A swelling chorus of girl-voices, the ancient organ wheezing and thundering along as Sister Alice Angels-Abiding, one of the music teachers, hammered at the yellowed keys with her equally yellowed, knotted fingers. Mother Heloise was at her place in the small pulpit, her broad face a smudge of paleness atop the black sail of her habit. Her hands were folded pacifically, and she beamed across the heads of her students as if her holy spouse was going to come floating down the central aisle at any moment.

Ruby, as usual, sang with great gusto but little skill. Cami's throaty alto—surprisingly deep and sweet—could barely be heard, but she had always enjoyed singing. *Singing d-d-doesn't s-s-stut . . .* There she used to stop and smile a little, pained and shy.

It was enough to break your heart. She didn't really stutter anymore. At least, not badly.

Ellie just mouthed the words. She knew them all by heart, why bother?

Morning Chapel was halfway over. If she propped herself against Cami just right when they all sat down again, she could steal ten minutes of sleep while Mother Heloise read from the Book. In some schools they tested you on the scripture and homily, but at Juno you just had to sit still. Maybe Mother Heloise thought it would drip inside your head anyway, water over stone.

Of course, considering what some of the ghoulgirls and the socials got up to in their spare time, the evidence would tend against that particular theory. But that only raised the question: Would it be worse if the Mother wasn't always going on about Chastity, Charity, Good Works, and Loving Mithrus with All Your Heart and Soul Like a Good Girl Should?

It was like one of those Unspeakable Riddles black charmers were always using to trip up heroes in feytales.

Thinking about black charmers dragged her back to thinking about Laurissa, and that wasn't going to help her get any rest.

The final chord rattled around the rafters, and everyone waited for Mother Heloise's placid "Be seated, children," before dropping down on the aged, varnished wooden pews. Each girl swept her skirt under in her own way; the uniforms only made you look harder for the variances. Even in the middle of the most stultifying conformity there were tiny little individual outcroppings, crocuses sticking up their tiny green heads.

Ruby popped the wad of choco-beechgum back into her mouth and proceeded to chew furiously, her right foot tapping to her own private beat. Cami folded her hands in her lap, straight-backed, and stared wide-eyed at a point over Mother Heloise's head. Ellie settled herself against Cami's side and tried not to think.

It was no use. She couldn't get away from it.

The first pair of shoes—their heels higher and arched, the copper turned to burning russet gold, their toes wickedly pointed and scrolled with a chimecharm to make the wearer's footsteps tinkle like crystal raindrops—had sold immediately. Of course, Ellie never saw the money. But the Strep was calm for *days* afterward. It must have been a considerable amount, and each pair afterward—plus the backlog of commissions from the Strep's charm not working right—had similarly been snapped up, calming Laurissa's temper even more.

She'd stopped having Ellie go through the ledgers, too. Now the Strep did the bookkeeping, and it was a funny thing—the ledgers were locked behind a glass door in Dad's office, where Laurissa had never ventured before. There were the familiar blue ones Ellie had been working in . . . and another set in rich red leather.

Interesting, right? Or it would have been, if she'd had time to think about it.

Rita was demoted to the pink bedroom, and Ellie's blue nest was all her own again. The door locked, sure, but the lock was an ancient crusty thing, and the right charm could tickle it open in a heartbeat.

It wasn't safe.

So Ellie snuck out each night and slept in her little garret. Which was great . . . except when she'd climbed down *this* morning, she'd heard a noise. A soft sliding step.

Rita? Probably. The girl wouldn't even *talk* to her. Antonia was gone for good—the Strep had summarily fired her, claiming the vacation time had really been the cook just not showing up to work. Miz Toni disputed that, but not too loudly—she just took the pittance of severance pay and left with her ample mouth set in a thin worried line.

Because after all, if a Sigiled charmer took it into her head to blacklist a former employee, where in the city would said employee ever find a decent job again? Maybe Miz Toni just didn't want to move to another province. Ellie couldn't blame her.

Afterward, the Strep had smiled at Ellie, that peculiar little smile that didn't reach her eyes. *She was not a good influence, Ellen. Mustn't get too friendly with the help, I've told you that before.*

So it was Ellie's fault, after all. A heavy sigh, flavored with pine-resin incense, escaped before she could stop herself, and Cami glanced over, a flash of blue eyes in the dimness.

Above, the stone was frozen into ribbed arches, carved with grapes and bull heads with wide curving horns in honor of the Sacrificed One, thorny *tau* crosses and the sad eyes of the Magdalen worked over and over with long tapering lashes. The Magdalen had seen a lot, that was for damn sure, and sometimes Ellie thought that maybe things would be better if the bitch had closed her eyes for once.

Like you, maybe? The Strep's been awful nice lately, wouldn't you say?

She told that voice to go away. She needed all the sleep she could get, and this was a golden opportunity.

She wouldn't even think about the scrap of paper folded into her shapeless black felt hat, with Avery's writing on it.

A phone number, and his blocky letters. *Call me. Please.*

Not a chance. Where would she find the time, now? Homework and charming after school, hours and hours draining away on Laurissa's projects.

Plus, the further away Avery was from Laurissa, the better. She was bound to be wondering why the charm she'd attached to his gift didn't bring him back to the house. How many of her other boyfriends had she snared that way? Was it any good to wonder? Avery wouldn't have been the first one just over legal age, and he probably wouldn't be the last one either. She went through them pretty quick, and by the end of it they were usually hollow-eyed and . . .

Nausea flooded her, and she shut the thought away. It was useless. She should just try to get some rest.

Juno's huge Book was open on a stand like a charmer's plinth, and Ellie had never noticed that before. Was there charming in churches? Did anyone care? Mother Heloise touched the pages reverently, intoning something about a wedding and a bridegroom, stupid virgins and smart ones.

Mithrus was looking in the wrong place if he expected to find a ton of virgins *here*. There was Binksy Malone in the pew right in front of her, a certified socialite slut if Ellie'd ever seen one, and right up front was the chief ghoulgirl, Manda Hogan, her dyed-black braids swallowing the glow from massed ranks of candles. She was notorious for never turning down a dare, even from the guys at Berch Prep.

And Ruby, well, Rube was Wild, in red capitals and underlined. No two ways about it.

Well, if Mom and Dad were still alive, you'd be wild too, Ell. Wouldn't you? You can only run like that if you're sure there's someone who can catch you if you trip.

Maybe, maybe not, and that was a bad mental road to go down too. Because the grief was a stone in her chest, and the only time that stone rolled away was when she was charming for Laurissa.

The charms came with frightening ease, and the blank space that flowered inside her head while she was working them was frankly terrifying. Each pair of shoes—she was doing two or three a day, and they sold as quickly as she could make them, which made Laurissa happy—had odd markings, way more restrained than Laurissa's florid curlicues.

Almost . . . well, almost as if they'd been performed by a Sigiled charmer.

Ellie's Potential wasn't settled yet. If it *had*, she'd be switched into a different Basic Charm class, and that would take her away from Rube and Cami. High Charm Calc would have started making sense in different ways, and *that* wasn't happening.

It is, though. Those equations all but solve themselves. You're cheating to get the wrong answers, for once.

She told that little thought to take a hike, too. If she got wrong answers, fine. Getting put in Advanced Charm would mean she would have to charm *more* to keep up with in-class labs, and the idea just filled her with unsteady dread.

"This story," Mother Heloise half-chanted, "tells us some very important things, my children."

Nothing that can help me, thanks. Another sigh heaved itself out of her. Soon the homily would be over, and they would all stand for the closing hymn, and then it was out the door and back into class.

She tried to let her mind drift. Cami's stillness didn't alter.

How she could sit and pay attention through all this was just incredible. She even *thought* about the things Mother Heloise said, and sometimes could be persuaded to comment on them. Living with Family, maybe that sort of thing was dinner-table talk. You could probably think about a lot of religion if you lived a long time, and even the ones that didn't transition into Unbreathing had incredible life spans. Probably fueled by the red stuff they drank. Cami called it *borrowing*.

As euphemisms went, that one was a doozy.

Ellie concentrated on her own breathing, her eyes half closed. Cami smelled of sunshine and a breath of roses from her shampoo, and a faint spice that was all Family. The Vultusino house on Haven Hill was a fortress, and it was a damn good thing too. Cami was too fragile for the world out here.

Ruby was all but wriggling with impatience, a hint of chocolate from her gum striking through the incense and candle scents for a moment. The problem was, Rube's running speed was about fifteen miles faster than the rest of the world's. The world was too big to speed up, and Rube too impatient to slow down.

And here I am in the middle.

Maybe she just provided some dead weight to make the whole trio stable. Who knew?

You're still avoiding thinking about it. She couldn't even get out to Southking at all, she was just too tired and muzzy-headed to charm right, not to mention keep one step ahead of Cryboy and his gang. Or any of the other bottom-feeders who preyed on the buskers and street charmers.

Item one: Rita was in the pink bedroom, and Ellie was back in her own blue nest. Two: the shoes Ellie charmed were selling like oatcakes. Three: the Strep hadn't hit Ellie in a good two–three weeks, and the belt had been moved back into the master bedroom. Laurissa was even downright *pleasant* sometimes, the false dulcet honey she put on when she wanted to impress someone or get her way. Four: the Strep had even bought her new clothes, including a brand-new school blazer.

Which Ellie didn't wear. She remembered the last one, the one Cami had bought her, shredded by Laurissa's screaming rage. Why get attached to anything nice? Sooner or later the weather would turn again, and Laurissa would start screaming.

You filthy, lazy little cunt! No wonder your parents left you to me! I'll make you behave!

"Doing good deeds," Mother Heloise sleepily half-sang, "makes its own reward visible."

Not in New Haven. It was almost funny enough to make her face want to crack up into a smile, but that took too much energy.

It was useless. The homily was almost over, and she hadn't slept a wink.

Great.

• • •

For once, Ruby didn't turn the radio on as soon as she twisted the key. She just waited until Ellie had her seatbelt buckled and gave her a funny little sideways look. "You're awful quiet lately, Ell."

Exhaustion will do that to you. She fished out her ancient pair of shades and jammed them on, blinking behind their comfortable dark screens. "Got a lot on my mind, Rube. Turn on the radio."

Ruby didn't, and Cami was a stillness in the tiny shelf of a backseat.

A *suspicious* stillness.

A sigh fetched its way up out of Ellie's middle. "Is this an intervention or something? I'm not on charmweed *or* milque. Turn on the radio and *drive*, I've got to get home." *If I'm late for charming . . .* It didn't bear thinking about.

Ruby dropped the Semprena into gear, looked over her shoulder, and backed out sedately. "Have you looked at yourself lately?"

I try not to. "Am I fashion impaired? So sorry."

"Ell—"

Shockingly, Cami cut Ruby off. "We're worried about you."

Join the club. "I'm fine. I—"

"You're not fine," Cami continued, softly but with great force, leaning over the back of the front seat. She must have practiced what she wanted to say, but she still spoke slowly, enunciating with care. "You've lost weight, and you look like a g-ghoulgirl with those circles under your eyes. Your hands are shaking, except for in Charm c-class or Calc. What is she *doing* to you?"

She's been my best friend lately. As long as I keep charming shit that sells like oatcakes, I'm golden. "Nothing," Ellie mumbled, shoving her shades up with a fingertip to hide her ghoulgirl eyes.

Trust Cami to notice things. Had she put Ruby up to this? *Honestly, Ell's just fine,* Rube'd probably said. *Who wouldn't look peaky with the Strep beating on her all the time? Let's go shopping!*

It wasn't fair, but then, nothing was. How many of the other girls at Juno knew *that* yet? Probably Cami, because of last winter. Still, everything had worked out fine for the Vultusino princess, hadn't it? Look at her now—no scars, not a lot of stutter, and Nico Vultusino still crazy about her. The darkness and terror had only been a passing thing. Everyone beautiful just floated through things, and Ellie was left holding the bag.

Holding it while it squirmed and fought, keeping it closed tight to keep everyone happy. Or trying to, at least.

"Oh, come on." Ruby twisted the wheel and they nosed into the line of cars heading for the exit. "If you get any thinner we'll be able to see through you on a sunny day. *Hag* is not a good look on you, kiddo."

"Seems to work for Laurissa," Ellie cracked, and Ruby loosened up enough to snort a half-laugh.

Cami didn't. Her worry was like static, a continual buzzing against the back of Ellie's tender skull. "What is she d–doing t–to you, Ellie?"

The hint of stutter, returning like yesterday's curse in the old feytales, rasped against Ellie's nerves. *Fair* didn't mean things were erased, or that the clock would be turned back and the people you needed would be alive again.

No wonder your parents left you for me to raise!

Even *fair* wasn't fair. If either of them got in the Strep's way, or drew her attention with a misjudged gesture—like, God forbid, saying something to Mother Heloise, or who knew—Laurissa would roll right over them.

Now that the Strep was playing with black charm—because the watch *had* been, there was no denying it—she was *incredibly* dangerous.

Too dangerous for her friends. There was another unwelcome thought: Had Laurissa become too dangerous for Dad, too?

Had the derailing out in the Waste saved her father from something *worse*? How long had Laurissa been playing with black charm? Nobody would believe Ellie if she told, and if she *did* go to a magistrate and make an accusation . . .

For once her imagination failed her completely. "Nothing I can't handle. Can we please get off the subject? Mithrus *Christ*."

As soon as she said it, the quiet inside the car changed as if a cloud had drifted over the strengthening spring sunshine. A breeze from nowhere riffled against every surface. Ruby's eyes widened, and she jammed on the brakes; Cami's shocked exhalation arrived a beat later.

"Sorry," Ellie mumbled. Her head rang, and her fingers tingled. It was just a Potential-pop, like a weather front moving through, and she knew she shouldn't have let it slip like that.

If anyone suspected how *easy* charming had become, how the equations were making sense, the whole thing might fall down around her ears. The thought of trying to pick up the wreckage again made her even more tired.

"I don't like this." Ruby eased the car forward again. "You used to tell us things, Ell. Now you're just . . ."

"Quiet." Cami's hand was on her shoulder. "Please. Talk t-to us."

What can I say? "I don't have anything to talk about."

The rest of the ride passed in excruciating silence. Cami's hand didn't move, and she squeezed a couple times, gently but with the iron river of a Vultusino's strength running in her bones. She wasn't born into the Family and she didn't talk about what had happened, but Nico had probably done something to make sure she wouldn't leave him behind again.

Avery Fletcher hadn't said anything to anyone about Ellie selling charm on Southking, because she hadn't been hauled out of class to account for it.

There. She'd done it. She'd thought about him again.

Ellie sagged into the seat and closed her eyes. They let her pretend she was asleep until they reached Perrault Street, and she was through the high iron gates with the Strep's Sigil worked into them before Cami could struggle out of the Semprena's backseat. The door slammed, Ruby gunned it, and she'd switched the radio on, because the thudding of the bass suddenly thumped out from the little car as it arrowed down Perrault to turn on Woodvine and head for the Vultusino castle.

Ellie stood in the sunshine, little tremors like a bird's heart-beat running through her bones, and felt cold all the way through.

SEVENTEEN

Spring Break was traditionally around Fish Day, and the Friday before it started was full of fertility-festival jokes. Women young and old were buying swellfree tea or anti-conceive charms; Ellie could have made a pretty penny down on Southking if she hadn't been trapped in the stone workroom every moment she wasn't at school or allowed to sleep.

The shoes were still selling. Beribboned red pumps with lightfoot charms, cushioned platform wedges with chips of glitter imbedded in the heels and weight-balance charms to keep the wearer upright, boots and more boots, brown and black and red and sky blue, some with heels, some without, all with tinkling music-step charms, a whole series of black patent-leather shoes with supple brass scales holding minor lift and attraction charms . . . It was endless. Homework blurred together inside her head, her tongue jumbled, and if Cami hadn't covered for her in French the results would have been dire indeed.

As it was, there was hour upon hour of charming after said homework, because Laurissa would drift past the door of the blue bedroom every fifteen minutes or so. *How much longer, little Ellen? There's work to be done . . .*

The ledgers were still there behind the glass door. She tried to plan a way to get to them, maybe find out what the Strep was hiding, but every second she wasn't working had to be used for sleeping, and it was never enough. Her brain would just shut down, the plan never quite taking form.

She regularly fell asleep in High Charm Calc now, but the equations had stopped being troublesome. Often she'd wake with a jolt to find her pencil scratching through a test or a pop quiz, writing equations and solutions in a cramped version of her usual slanting narrow handwriting. She got most of them right, too, only fudging the ones she was awake enough to unwork.

It figured.

"No plans for Break?" Ruby kept asking. She also didn't poke the radio into full blare until after dropping Ellie off, probably so Ell could snatch a few minutes of rest. Cami gamely tried to keep up Ellie's part of the conversation as well as her own, and her leftover stutter had largely vanished. Maybe the extra practice was greasing the words free or something.

Today, Ellie sighed, looking down at the linoleum as the flock of girls freed from Juno's restrictions for a whole week spilled for the front door. "Another party," she managed. Her tongue didn't seem to want to work quite right. "I guess." *She has Rita doing the cooking, and the maids were cleaning top to bottom again.*

"Is the Strep still trying to catch that Fletcher kid?" Ruby kept asking about *him*, too.

The sharp jolt behind her breastbone woke her out of her daze, briefly. *Be cautious.* "Don't know. Don't care."

Cami was silent, and Ellie didn't realize trouble was coming until they hit the front door instead of the side doors. Later she thought maybe Cami had been steering them that direction, or maybe it was just habit. In any case, Ellie dug in her heels, but it was too late.

Because down at the bottom of Juno's wide granite steps, oblivious to the girls milling around and whispering and some of them doing everything but pointing at him, was Avery Fletcher, the gold in his hair throwing back sunlight with a vengeance. He stood there like he had all the time in the world, and he was looking right at her.

Oh, Mithrus. Ellie let herself be carried down the stairs. It was too much effort to protest. Maybe he'd just see she was tired and leave her alone?

No such luck, because he brightened visibly the closer she got. Then he looked puzzled, eyebrows coming together. By the time the trio hit the bottom of the steps, his expression had changed. The brightness rubbed away, and his jaw was close to dropping.

Ruby popped her gum, hopping off the last step. "Hey, Fletch. You're persistent, I'll give you that."

"You look *awful*," he returned, and for a lunatic instant she thought he was telling *Ruby* that. It would have been worth a chuckle or two, except he was staring at *her*, and all of a sudden every rubbed-bare, worn-through, shabby or broken spot on her started to throb painfully. "And . . . Christ, have you been on charmweed?"

Ellie found her tongue. "You're an asshole."

"Young love!" Ruby addressed the air over Avery's head, obviously delighted with this turn of events. "It's shameful how you two carry on—"

Cami stepped forward, grabbed Ruby's arm. "Shhh." And wonder of wonders, she actually *shut Ruby up*. "Maybe *you* can t-talk some s-sense into her. It's her stepmother."

"Choquefort?" His nose wrinkled. "Yeah, she's a piece of work; Mom says she's a barracuda. But . . ." He stopped, a curious look spreading over his face. Ellie swayed, wishing Cami was still holding her elbow. It was somehow easier to move with the two of them bracketing her—and when had she become the meat of the sandwich? That was always Cami's job. "Huh."

There, in front of the school and everyone, he stepped forward. Ellie almost flinched, but his fingers were on her cheek, warm and gentle. He stared into her eyes for what seemed an eternity, and she had time to see the threads of gold in the dark forest-green and brown of his irises, and the faint dusting of freckles across his tanned nose. Even his skin held some gold, and she felt a dozy sort of surprise.

"Mithrus," he breathed. "I think I'd better take her to a stitcher."

"Is it that b-bad?" The fear in Cami's tone mixed with a tide of whispers and pointing.

Ellie didn't care. Some strained muscle inside her had been tearing, and when it finally gave way she leaned forward with a sigh, and her forehead hit Avery's shoulder. He was solid and comforting, and for a moment she wondered how the weedy little kid she'd known had turned into this wall.

There was a subtle *click*, as if the world had stopped, some linchpin dropping into place. Ellie exhaled, and maybe Fletcher was stiff with shock. He just stood there for a moment, and she heard Cami speaking. It wasn't important. What was important was that the spinning had stopped, and for a moment she could really, truly rest. The inside of her skull wasn't full of noise now. Instead, it felt like her head was full of brain again. A heaviness, meaty and comforting.

Just a little unwelcome, too, because it meant she had to use the heaviness to think, to plan. Something . . .

Something is very wrong with me.

"You can follow if you want." Avery sounded amused, and very calm. "But I plan on driving pretty fast, de Varre."

What am I doing? Her entire body ached, and the little tingles all over her were a product of his nearness. Why did he do that? Was it just because he was a charmer from a pretty powerful clan, or was it something . . . personal . . . about him?

Did it matter? So far, the Strep hadn't twigged to the fact that Ellie had tampered with the blacklove charm. If she did find out, or if she got any breath of Ellie hanging out with Avery Fletcher . . .

She jerked her head up and tore away. Fletcher made a short swift movement, as if to catch her, but she flinched quickly enough that his hand closed on empty air. "Leave *off.*" Her tongue felt funny, a little too big for her mouth. "What do you think you're doing here, charmer boy? Run on home."

He just regarded her levelly, his hand dropping back to his side. "You need a stitcher, Ell. You're so drained you're almost transparent. Where have you been working freelance?"

"Working?" Ruby cracked her mouthful of chocolate beechgum, a popcharm noise, as she stared at the circle of onlookers. Most of them dropped their gazes and edged away, and her white, white smile widened a trifle. "What?"

Cami was utterly still, her blue gaze locked to Ellie's profile. And of course, she was the one smart enough to figure out what Fletcher was saying.

"At home." There was no point in lying. "She's a Sigiled charmer, Fletcher. I might apprentice." The lie was immediate, and hot against Ellie's teeth. "Drop it."

"So *that's* what's been—"

Ellie had her wits about her again, thank Mithrus. "Look, I *told* you to leave me alone. What does it take, huh?" She pitched it loud enough to be heard by every blessed girl in front of the school, and had the small squirming satisfaction of seeing him flinch and blanch a little. She took in a deep endless breath, and the lightning-flash of intuition inside her head told her what would hurt most.

I can't say that to him. I just can't.

So she settled for the next best thing. She turned on her heel, her mouth stinging with the words she wanted to let loose, and stalked blindly away. Ruby hurried after her, and the smell of burning insulation on the breeze was crisp and nasty.

I'm doing that, she realized as the stairs to her left shimmered, the defenses sensing hurtful, active Potential trembling on the edge of taking spike-edged charmform. *It's me.* A bubble of silence formed around her, and she kept her head up and her movements brisk. *It's anger. Like the Strep. Mithrus, please, Mithrus, God's-son, please, don't let it Twist me. Don't make me a minotaur.*

"Ell?" It was Cami, the luckcharms on her maryjanes jingling and tingling, silvery-sweet. "Ellie *please wait*, he just wants to talk, Ellie!"

"I don't think she's in the mood, honey." Ruby had to actually hurry to keep up for once, and she sounded a bit breathless. "What was he talking about? Do we need to visit a stitcher? Gran can—"

Charity. Always with the fucking charity. "No!" It burst out, high and hard, and Ellie fought back the charm wanting to take shape. Forced herself to think of High Charm Calc equations instead, the difficult knotty ones that returned a different answer each time before your Potential settled. It was work trying to get them to react as if her Potential was unsettled, they kept serving up a single unambiguous answer now. "I can't. She'd *kill* me."

"This might save her the trouble." Cami glided along beside her, not put out by the speed of their passage at all. "What did he mean, huh? Freelance? Ell, come on. C-come on. P-please."

"Leave him *out* of this!" It was almost a scream, and her throat was dry, aching with the effort to keep rage-hot Potential pushed down, put away. "Mithrus *Christ*, just leave me *alone!*"

Ruby's fingers locked around her arm. She yanked Ellie to a stop, and their skirts both swung, flirting with a breeze that was part spring but mostly disturbed Potential, shimmering between them as the barriers of their personal spaces flexed and receded.

"No." For once, Ruby de Varre sounded—and looked— completely serious. "I am *not* leaving you alone. Something's going on, and I'm going to get to the bottom of—"

"Quit being a self-centered bitch, Ruby." The words flew out before she could stop them, that hurtful little intuition telling her what would hurt Rube the most. "I realize it's your default, but just *try*, okay?"

The other girl's fingers bit in, and for once there wasn't a fresh bruise hurting somewhere on Ellie's body. The Strep hadn't touched her for a while now, all that was left were yellow-green ghosts on her skin.

They didn't know anything about how bad it could get, and Ellie had to keep it that way. It wasn't fair, it wasn't *right*, but that was the way it was.

She was trapped.

"I'm gonna overlook that," Ruby said softly, "because I *am* a self-centered bitch. Fine and good. But *you need help*."

"D-d-d-don't fight." Cami was breathless, and the edges of her straight black hair lifted on the uneasy breeze. "Please don't f-f-f—"

"Too late," Ellie informed her curtly. "Shut up."

Cami's hand flew to her mouth, caging broken words. Reddened lips, slim fingers, her skin glowing like an alabaster lamp, the Vultusino girl stared at Ellie with wide, tear-brimming blue eyes.

Ruby's grip lessened. She stared at Ellie like some exotic new type of bug crawled wet and stinking from beneath a rock, waving its misshapen feelers as it clacked its mandibles.

The strained, stretched feeling inside her tightened painfully. Her skin was too taut, as if she was Twisting *inside* where nobody could see. Was that what it felt like when a minotaur began?

Boiling up inside her, black and viscous, the words crowding up behind her teeth tasted like burnt metal. Why stop at just one hurtful thing? She might as well go on.

Was this what Laurissa felt like, right before she started screaming?

The pavement around her rippled, as if she was throwing off sunheat. Ruby's hair blew back, and Cami leaned forward a little, pushing against the resistance.

No. Don't hurt them. You can't hurt them. Even though she just had. And it was so easy, so goddamn easy, to just open her mouth and let the rest of it fly.

So she did the only thing she could.

Ellie whirled, her sleek blonde hair ruffling out, and ran.

EIGHTEEN

IT WAS RIDICULOUSLY EASY. SHE JUST PLUNGED RIGHT through the front gates, where cars and buses were locked to a standstill by the appearance of a fragile fleshly body in their midst. Someone screamed, one of the small cushioned buses laid on the horn, but she was out the gates in a flash, taking a sharp right and pounding along the cracked heaving sidewalk under the whispering elms shading this part of Juno's northern wall.

They had black bark and violently green leaves, those trees, and Juno's defenses resonated through living wood, Potential turning them into towering giants with fringe-fingered arms. Their shadows clutched, but she tore through them, a bright scarf of Potential-sparks tingling in her wake before winking out, one by one.

Ellie ran. And ran, blindly, until there was a *snap*, more felt than heard, and the buckle on her much-abused left maryjane broke. She went down in a heap, spilling onto a grassy verge in front of a small brownstone house, its white window casements secretive raised eyebrows. Its picket fence looked like tiny teeth, painted sticky sugar-white, and stood ruler-straight, barely holding back candybright red roses with queer frilled petals. It was too early for those roses, but the shimmer around them told her they were charmed, and the thought of charming made her sick.

Hands and knees, her entire worn-down body rebelling, she retched pointlessly and shivered, great gripping waves of shudders coursing through her.

A charmstitcher would be able to see what she'd been doing, maybe. Might be able to probe the vast empty space inside her head that opened up and let those wonderful pieces of work through. And they *were* wonderful; they sold as fast as Laurissa could show them. Her own blue bedroom was only hers now because she was making the Strep some money.

How long could she keep *that* up? Laurissa was a wide gaping maw; how much would it take? Where was all of it *going*?

Between her hands, velvety grass sent up a crushed green reek. Thin green blades tickled her wrists, softly, and she could almost hear them singing a piping little chorus of water and light and rest, roots a matted tapestry in damp earth. The roses answered, a high sleepy buzzing that almost—*almost*—made words.

I could just collapse right here. Oh wait, I just did. There were charm-symbols flashing through her brain, awful ones. Those tables in the back of even the paperback copies of Sigmundson's weren't supposed to make sense to anyone whose Potential hadn't settled, but she could see them clear as day. Charms to seize a victim's breathing, shear metal and splinter wood, blight a tree or a small animal. Any charm that black carried the risk of Twisting, but would you care about that if you could, say, work up enough reflected Potential to stop your *own* heart?

Suicide by charm. Just because the books never talked about it didn't mean it wasn't theoretically *possible*, right?

The thought wasn't scary. What was scary was the ease with which her brain began to bubble with calculations.

"What have we here?" Soft as the breeze through the twisting elm branches and fluttering leaves.

Ellie jerked in surprise, and glared up at the white picket fence.

Behind it, among the roses, was a brown face, its lower half splitting in a very white V-shaped smile. The eyes were large and liquid-dark, and for a moment they seemed simply black from lid to lid, like Marya the Vultusino house fey's. Marya's gaze was kind and absent, though, and this was a piercing stare.

Then the split-second seeing was gone, and she found herself looking at a perfectly ordinary old woman with scant white thistledown for hair and a kind tilt to her thin mouth. She was small and round, and her housedress was splashed with violently

blooming orchids on a pretty horrendously bright blue back-
ground. Miz Toni would have loved it.

Immediate hot, reeking guilt filled her mouth. She had to
swallow another retch.

That thistledown hair had bits of leaves stuck in it, as if the
old woman had been gardening and run her dirty hands back
through it, and her weathered skin said she spent a lot of time
outdoors.

Ellie was lying right in front of her fence. "I'm sor—"

"She's storm-eyed, this wanderer," the woman continued,
in a chirrupy leaf-whisper. "Pale-haired too, and burning like a
candle. What brings you to Auntie's house, wayfarer? She looks
hungry, yes she does."

She's a charmer. Ellie felt awake for the first time in days.
Awake . . . but terribly worn, scraped thin like an old-timey hide
window. The ones they used to paint with ochre to keep evil
out, before the Age of Iron. The Potential flowing around the
woman was a little odd, sure, but Ellie had been seeing a lot of
weird things lately.

The old woman's roses leaned around her, drinking her in.
Their frilled petals throbbed, redder than red, and the picket
fence shimmered, too. There was a hazy murmur of bees, and all
of a sudden Ellie smelled flowers and crushed grass and spiced
honey, and a tang of black freshly turned earth. Her nose was
waking up just like the rest of her.

Ellie took stock. Her shoe was never going to be the same. Even a mending on the buckle seemed like too much goddamn charm to scrape out of her weary body. Hunger knotted in her stomach, and everything on her ached.

"Perhaps she doesn't know?" the charmer continued. "Lots of them don't know why they come see Auntie. The lonely and the wanderers, they are all Auntie receives."

She's crazy, too. Most charmers got a little eccentric by middle age. She didn't seem to be Twisted, though. "I'm sorry." Ellie finally managed to make her mouth work. "I just . . . I ran."

"As if the white hounds were after her, yes. Yes yes." The thistledown head nodded, bobbing like one of her flowers. "Come in. Auntie will make tea."

"I really should—" But what was there *to* do? Figure out how to get home, certainly, and deal with the Strep wanting her to charm until her head broke, and there was homework and Babbage chat with Cami and Ruby, who would *not* be happy with her.

Well, tea. Why not? It was just an old charmer woman. A low-level one who wasn't part of a clan or the social climbers who showed up during the season. Maybe she liked her privacy. There were a lot of solitary charmers; even Sigiled ones sometimes retreated from the world.

It sounded like a great goddamn idea.

"Tea. And she is hungry, this little wayfarer. Be nice to

Auntie, lonely old Auntie." The old woman's tone brooked no refusal. "She's hurt." She pointed, and Ellie realized her palms and knees were skinned. Pavement burn, probably, before she'd tumbled onto the grass.

"Yeah, I guess I fell." She levered herself up painfully, and the sapphire ring flashed once in the mellow leaf-shaded light. The old woman didn't notice; she had already turned and was picking her way toward a gate Ellie hadn't seen before. The posts were striped with vivid red paint, sort of like the peppermint sticks hung on traditional trees every Yule. The trellis arch overhead was sticky-white like the fence, though, and the roses were beginning to climb it lazily. By the end of summer they would choke it with greenery and frilled blossoms. "I'm Sinder." Awkwardly, but she had to offer something.

"Sinder, a burning name. It matches her, yes it does. Auntie greets you, Sinder. Come inside."

A burning—oh, yeah. Not the first time someone's said something like that. She examined the white and red wooden gate, and when she was satisfied there wasn't any bad charm on it, she stepped through. It was so thickly painted it felt a little soft under her fingers, and as soon as she stepped onto the crushed-shell path the air felt warmer. Summer, instead of spring, and the shells made little crunching noises underfoot. The spiced-honey smell intensified, her stomach rumbled, and now she could see bees, zipping drunkenly from flower to waxen flower.

The walk led up to the brownstone's fudge-colored door, painted to match the stones. Between them, the masonry oozed creamy white, and the chimney was a darker stick, a thread of white smoke issuing from it. Why have a fire on such a nice day? Charmers didn't usually work around open flame. Hopefully her workroom was insulated; Potential behaved oddly around live fire.

The steps were weird quartzlike stone, almost translucent and freshly washed by the way they gleamed. The fudge door was open, and through it came the most heavenly smell.

Brownies. Not just *any* tiny little chocolate bars of goodness, though. These had a slight bitter undertone and a dot of bright cinnamon, and the smell pulled Ellie irresistibly forward.

Just like Mom's, she thought, and followed Auntie into the house.

That first afternoon remained full of light for a long time, a bright island in a sea of ink.

The foyer was floored in licorice black and whipped-cream linoleum squares, polished until they shone. Stairs went up along the right side, but a parlor opened off to the right as well, comfortable and overstuffed, all in shades of peppermint and cherry. The smoke from the chimney came from the kitchen toward the back, the dining room a tiny nook, with a round wicker table draped with a cinnamon cloth.

It was what Laurissa would sniff at as "*country* chic, you

know," and for a moment the stuffed scarecrow in a blue velvet coat, propped against the dining room's wall, seemed to twitch, its sad painted eyes eerily lifelike as it gazed over the table and the two noodle-colored wicker chairs with eggplant cushions.

Braided strings of garlic and other less-identifiable things hung from racks, and the kitchen's copper pots and cornhusk-green towels and touches were a little shocking by contrast. There was a wide brick hearth with an ember-glowing fire under a large iron cauldron, whose bubbling lid let loose bursts of colorless steam. It was the more prosaic stove and oven Auntie turned to, her housedress now appropriate amid all the other colors, an exotic bird in its soft delicious nest.

The tea was heavy and rich, full of cream and spice. The sandwiches were watercress with thick pale cheese on snow-white bread, peppery and fresh; the cookies round sunwheels full of candied ginger. The brownies Ellie smelled were nowhere in sight, but that didn't matter, because for the first time in a long while Ellie could eat without her stomach cramping.

Auntie kept pouring the tea, and Ellie knew she was maybe shocking the old lady, but all of a sudden, there at the cinnamon table, she found herself pouring the entire story out. The old woman nodded, thoughtfully, asking a question every now and again. She wasn't interested in Avery or Cami or Ruby—though Ruby's name stirred a faint bit of brightness in her dark eyes—but she was *very* curious about the Strep.

The funny thing was, Ell could never afterward remember much of what *exactly* Auntie had said. Just that the questions had been penetrating but soft, incisive but not impolite. That she had a way of drawing Ellie out, and that nobody had listened to her, really *listened* to Ell, in a long time. She was a stranger, not a charity case, so the old woman evinced no surprise or distaste.

One thing she said Ellie remembered a long time after. "A daughter, yes. Old Auntie wants a daughter, but may have none. So she is Auntie." The old woman gave her a considering look. "A wandering, wayfaring daughter, her family must be proud."

Proud? Of me? It was such a novel idea she shook her head immediately. "I guess Mom was . . . but she's gone, and Dad . . ." Yet the soft, quiet idea that maybe they *had* been proud was a balm, and it turned the key in the lock. Her words spilled out, faster and faster.

Ellie babbled on, weariness falling away as secrets dropped onto the tabletop beside the bone-china teapot and the delicate cups, the ravaged plate of dainty sandwiches and the piles of cookie crumbs on platters delicately painted with ripe fruit.

Through it all, Auntie listened and nodded, and patted Ellie's hand with her own soft plump paw.

Long afterward, Ellie would realize that the old woman ate nothing at all.

NINETEEN

FINDING A BUS TO PERRAULT WASN'T EASY, AND IT WAS twilight by the time Ellie made it . . . home. Suppose you had to call it that, or something. Wasn't home where they had to take you in when you showed up? But they didn't *have* to. Surely Laurissa would be a lot happier if Ellie just . . . vanished.

Not just the Strep, either. Ruby and Cami could probably do without her bitchiness, and *definitely* Avery Fletcher could do without her doing whatever it was that kept making him show up like a puppy just begging to be kicked.

The front door was unlocked even at this hour—well, if it hadn't been, she would have gone around and through the kitchen. The servants—the few of them left, that is—were long gone for the day, and there was no way she could paper this over with an excuse.

She's going to be furious. Ellie sighed, dread a lead ball in her stomach, and pressed the thumb-handle down. The door creaked open slowly, announcing her presence with a screech that shouldn't have been there, because the hinges were always kept well-oiled.

The foyer was dark. An unfamiliar feeling began in the center of her bones. She froze as the doors swung closed behind her, latching with a tense *click*, and tried to figure out what the buzzing almost-burning inside her was.

Something's going to happen. But that's not it. She closed her eyes, searching inward.

The answer came just as there was a harsh sobbing noise, and a fluttering.

Ellie didn't move. *I feel . . . strong.* As if pouring everything out to Auntie had done something, changed her. It was really amazing, what just having someone listen could do.

She opened her eyes.

Rita was there, crouched at the bottom of the steps. Her pallid little face was open and avid, and there was a strange click-tap-drag from upstairs, unfamiliar footsteps.

"Rita." Her throat was dry. "Hi. You—"

"She found your money," the other girl whispered, scurrying aside. "All of it. Upstairs in the little hole. Your rat hole."

For a second the words made no sense, an exotic gobbledygook. The click-dragging footsteps upstairs drew nearer, and the smell of burning cedar anger rolled down the risers, a colorless fume twining around the balustrade.

The Strep was coming for the stairs, and she was *pissed*.

There were dark jagged shapes on the floor, and Ell was momentarily confused before realization exploded inside her. They were records. If you dropped them from high enough, they would break. Especially the old, brittle charm-wax ones. The fluttering bits were the album sleeves, shredded and crisped, a charmer's rage smoking up from them.

"You told her." Ellie was suddenly certain. "You *followed* me."

Rita's pallor flushed, and for a moment she was almost pretty. The beauty submerged under a swift grimace, lips skinned back and eyes rolling. "Charmer girl. No more blue bedroom for you." She nipped through the silent swinging door into the servants' back hall just as Laurissa came into sight at the head of the stairs, the chandelier overhead tinkling as Potential drifted and eddied, foxfire specks and sparkles showing the grime and dust on crystal beads and dead lightbulbs.

She hates all sorts of light, doesn't she. Maybe it burns her. Ellie stared.

The click was from Laurissa's red Githrian pumps, but the drag was because something was wrong with her left foot. She hauled it along, scraping the side of the pump along the floor, and her frosted-blonde mane stood straight out, aggressively lacquered. Her belly had swelled—surely it hadn't been that big before? Now it jutted in front of her, and her free hand raked its long nails lightly over the bulge, scraping against the soft fabric of her crimson Lethbridge jacket. Her skirt was slightly askew, a sliver of creamy lace from her slip showing underneath, and her jacket was buttoned awry.

Ellie's jaw was loose. She shut her mouth with a snap, and her hands curled into bloodless fists. Her stepmother's face was shadowed except for the burning coals of her eyes, glimmering under a shelf of winter-blonde fringe.

Mithrus, she looks terrible.

"Little Ellen." The Strep grabbed at the balustrade, peering down at her. Every word was smooth honey; her tone had lost none of its terrible false sweetness. "You'll have to come up, darling." Her knuckles stood out, her hands bonier than ever and horridly graceful.

The foyer trembled around Ellie, miserably trapped like a fly in amber, staring up at the Strep. If she went up the stairs and did what Laurissa said, maybe she wouldn't be hurt too badly?

Yeah, sure. The shredded album covers rustled, rustled. The broken discs twitched, little sliding sounds. The Hellward ones had probably been first off the ledge.

She destroyed *everything*.

The tip of the Strep's nose was a pale dot. The chandelier tinkled, sweet ominous music, and Ellie realized dreamily she was directly underneath it.

"Ellen." A thin crust of false solicitude over a deep screaming well of rage. "Don't make me come down there."

When did I ever make *you do anything?* That was something Ruby might say. Channeling Rube at a time like this would probably be hilarious, but not really guaranteed to calm anything down—

An ominous *creak* overhead. The chandelier jingled, jangled. Like thin icy bracelets on a skeletal wrist.

Laurissa took another step, dragging her foot. The charms on her shoes hissed angrily, raindrops hitting a hot griddle. Her face was still a shadowed hole, and Ellie was dozily glad of that.

"Ungrateful girl." The Strep reached the first stair, twitching her good foot forward and landing heavily, wobbling. "With your nose in the air like you're so *special*, at your little school with your little friends. I teach you everything, and this—*this*—is how you repay me? By *stealing?*" Her free hand flicked forward, and the smoking wad in it was paper credits, fluttering like trapped birds.

The silver scrollwork box hit the foyer floor and crumpled into a ball, shrieking.

Ellie made a shapeless sound. Her escape money, four hundred twelve credits, unleashed itself from Laurissa's bony fist, shredding and sparking into flame. Smoke curled, a tang of heavy charmed credit-paper sharp and nasty under the burnt cedar of the Strep's rage. There was another nose-stinging reek too, one she couldn't quite place. Whatever it was, it made her vision blur, and a hot trickle of water slid down Ellie's cheek.

"I *worked* for that!" Her sudden shout smashed the whispering tinkling of the chandelier. Another sharp groan from overhead, this one full of creaking and popping. "I *earned* those credits, you *leech*!"

A sneer twisted Laurissa's face, rising from the shadow of her hair like a cottage-cheese moon. "Who would pay you?" She hobbled down one more step, and another. "Little slut, who would pay *you*?"

I'm not a slut! I go to chapel! The injustice of it closed Ellie's throat, and the mounting buzzing vibration in the middle of her bones *demanded* words to let it free. "*You're* a whore! That's not my father's baby! You got it off one of your boyfriends, and *I hope it rots in you!*"

The curse flew free, stinging-black and sharp-feathered. It shaped itself from trembling Potential and flashed through space before Ellie could pull it back. Ever afterward, she would sometimes wonder if maybe she *would* have been able to pull it back . . .

. . . but just didn't want to. Which made what happened afterward her own damn fault.

Just like everything else.

Laurissa screamed, the familiar, piercing, Potential-laced noise; she was so used to disorienting and overpowering her prey. Ellie's own cry was higher pitched, a terrified animal struggling in a snare, and the curse hit her stepmother's face with a bonebreaking crunch.

Ellie backpedaled, not realizing she was still screaming until her shoulders hit the front door and she had to stop to whoop in a long, endless breath full of choking smoke.

The Strep tottered, her dead foot pulling itself up in a terrible corkscrew, blood spattering in a bright hideous rain as the curse clawed and shrieked in its own train-whistle voice, not heard with the ears but felt like a drill through the front of the skull. Ellie scrabbled for the door latch, her battered maryjanes striking deep black marks on the marble, the mended buckle—when had *that* happened, maybe Auntie had done it—chiming as luck-charms sparkled and spat. She was too slow, caught in hardened syrup again, nightmare-time making her fingers clumsy and scraping as Laurissa fetched up against the bottom of the stairs, legs indecently splayed, her body twitching nauseatingly.

Oh God I've killed her oh my God I killed her with a curse Mithrus Christ forgive me—

She barely had time to finish breathing in to scream again before the Strep sat up, the curse falling away and shattering into shards of smoking obsidian, and her mad gaze focused on Ellie through strings of frosted, writhing hair.

"You little bitch!" she yelled. "Look what you've done!"

Yep, that one was me, Ellie thought, dark hilarity bubbling under the panicked beating of her heart. *This one was all me. You should see what I did to an ink bottle last week. Or was it last month? How long ago was that?*

The thing about time was that it slipped through your fingers. Like Potential, and charm, and one day you woke up in your own house with your parents dead and a madwoman lurching up from the marble floor, her once-immaculate hair daggers of dyed string and her nasty bruise-making talons twisted into claws. The red suit was more than askew now, and Laurissa's flesh underneath its gaping was dead white.

Fishbelly white and somehow, in some way, *wrong*. Something twitched under the gravid lump of the Strep's middle, reaching out. Bile slapped the back of Ellie's throat. She fumbled for the door afresh, its handle slipping greasily against sweating skin. None of this was very important. There was no use in fighting. The Strep was going to cross the white and black floor, and then everything she'd done up until now would look like picnics and chapel compared to what she was *about* to do.

A crunching squeeze on her right hand, the star sapphire shrieking as it flashed. A splintering, creaking moan, iron staples popping free of roof beams, and the entire pile of Perrault Street stone shuddered on its foundations. The chain holding the chandelier made a horrifying sound as it slithered through rusted hoops, and the entire tinkling, chiming thing descended with ponderous grace, a slight arc bowing it toward Ellie before the ring spoke again, a Tesla's Folly flash of blue lightning, and she found her hand had flung itself up as if it could stop the Strep from lurching into the path of the chandelier.

The funny thing was, it maybe did, because the chandelier was jerked off its course. By a single degree, maybe; Ellie didn't have time to calculate.

But that single degree was enough.

It hit the marble floor to one side, fetching up against the rise of the staircase instead of its foot, and shattering bits pierced the air in all directions. Laurissa screamed again, a cheated howl, and the door finally flung itself open, spilling Ellie backward onto the front steps.

She tumbled down, bruising her shoulder, her head hit the pavers with stunning force; for half a second everything grayed out. That brief starry interval was all the rest she was granted; the ring gave its tongueless shriek again, and she remembered the only time she ever saw her mother truly angry. There had been a car, and a screeching of tires, and Mom hunched protectively over a much younger Ellie, her hand flung out and the sapphire ring sparking just as it did now as metal shredded and her mother's face for a moment turned dark as a storm cloud. The shadow on her mother's face, that was why Avery looked familiar, because sometimes his cheekbones looked—

The sky was purple now, and the wind was chill and damp.

Ellie scrambled to her feet, every muscle rusty-screaming like the chandelier's chain, and backed up, her head tossing nervously as a horse's. The open door spilled a crazycrack flutter of blue-white light, Potential fluorescing as Laurissa snapped a firecharm and eldritch flames splashed against the steps, smoking.

She means business, Ellie thought, and skipped back a few more steps. *She'll roast me alive.*

Only if she catches you, a quiet, determined voice inside her head that sounded like Cami's answered, and under that depthless twilit sky, Ellie ran.

TWENTY

SOUTHKING STREET WAS A DIFFERENT BEAST AT NIGHT. Still crowded, but the regular shops were locked and barred, the daytime tents and stalls darkened. Caged foxfire charmlights hung in the traditional slotted-tin lanterns, showing where the nighttime trades were conducted.

Poisonseller, blackblade knifemartin instead of a dealer in clean honest steel, fortune-makers and charmthieves, the entire street a chamber in the beating heart of New Haven's shadow economy. The Families, like Cami's, took a cut from each transaction after dark too; the raw materials for some of the blackest work had to be imported and thus toll was paid to the de Varres as well—Ruby's Gran, kind as she was to her granddaughter's friends, did not keep her stranglehold on the import and export business with cupcakes and charity.

Charity case. Well, I'm bound for hell now.

Ellie leaned against the counter, taking deep breaths flavored

with the steaming of smoke-hot peanut oil. The jack running
the food stall was broad-shouldered, wearing a flannel shirt despite the heat from the grill, and the pattern of green scales on
her cheeks flushed red every time she glanced at Ellie. Her hair
was aggressively short, and Ell kept a careful eye on the jack's
expression.

She was probably driving away custom, leaning here in her
school uniform and nursing a cold-sweating bottle of limon.

Why, of all places, had she come down *here*? Southking
was dangerous even during the day, and she had her blazer on,
and . . .

Her brain froze. She shivered violently to get it working
again.

Where do I go?

Going to Cami would mean getting mortgaged to the Family, and while Cami was a friend, there wasn't anything good
about the rest of them. Even non-charmers knew *that*. Family
meant *blood*, and they kept what they took.

Ruby . . . well, her grandmother was kind, all right, but also
scary as fuck with those white, white teeth and that unblinking
gaze. You never wanted Edalie de Varre angry at you, that was
for damn sure, and really, after Ellie had been all bitchy, Ruby
might get in a snit and . . .

Well, that wasn't really fair, was it. Ruby would go to the
ends of the earth, for Cami. Last winter, both of them had.

Ruby had even shown up outside the house on Perrault to pick Ellie up. *Cami's in trouble, it's bad.* And out the window of the blue bedroom Ellie had climbed, into the killing cold.

The bigger problem was what would happen if she ran to one of her friends and Laurissa came to fetch her. Laurissa had meant to do something final, something irrevocable, and neither Cami nor Ruby were capable of handling . . .

Her brain froze again. She couldn't make a plan with all the noise in her head and the freezing between her synapses.

"How much longer you gonna stand around, girl?" The jack barely turned her head, addressing the words over her shoulder with edged disdain. "Scarin' off my business."

I doubt anyone finds me a threat. "Soon," Ellie replied dully. "I'll leave when I've finished."

The fan of scales marching up the jack's cheeks swelled a little more, each one rising individually and flushing, turning from gem-green to bright crimson. It was oddly fascinating, but staring wasn't polite. Born Potential-mutated or developing latent feathers or fur when they hit puberty, jacks were always angry. *A jack's a powder keg*, the saying went, and after seeing a few streetfights on Southking during the day between Cryboy's crew and interlopers with other gang colors knotted at wrist or knee or forehead, she believed it.

"Mithrus *Christ*," the jack at the grill hissed. "Stop crying, charmer bitch. You shouldn't even be here. Go home."

I don't have a home, thanks. She took the quarter-bottle of limon and stepped away from the counter, uncertainly.

The night sighed around her, New Haven taking a breath before another squeeze of its hidden hearts propelled Potential through its tissues. Even the trashulks, gray and squat on their squares of charmgrass, were dozing as they digested the day's rubbish. She looked down at the pavement, starred with bits of quartz and lumps of dirty beechgum and other refuse pounded flat, and the vision of each bit of concrete as a ribbon artery feeding into the inner Waste of the core where the sirens howled and minotaurs lurked in a cloud of uneasy chaos-driven Potential threatened to explode her skull and leave her a witless wandering jobber.

She forced herself to think, or at least try to. If she went to Cami or Ruby, the Strep would certainly follow. Mithrus Christ alone knew what would happen then. She couldn't bring the Strep down on them.

Where? Juno? I can't live at school.

That was another thing. She'd miss homework, and there was school in the morning. Mithrus, who cared? There were bigger problems. Like where she was going to sleep tonight. Her stomach cramped a little, but she wasn't hungry.

Not yet.

Her schoolbag bumped against her hip. She should have tucked her credits in *there*, and carried them with her. Stupid, stupid Ellie, and she thought she was so smart. Her hands and knees throbbed, scabbed over and swelling with each beat of her hummingbird pulse. She swung the bottle of limon once, twice, the sweet carbonated liquid fizzing and sloshing.

Why am I doing this? Like it's a weapon.

Then, miserably, she knew. Her chin lifted, her gaze swinging across the street . . . and there, lounging in the shadow near a knifemartin's tent, Cryboy turned his head. Negligently, slowly, and in a moment he was going to see her.

Ellie's breath slammed out so hard soft black flowers bloomed at the edges of her vision. The weeping fluid slicking the jack's cheeks under the bone spurs sliding along his cheeks glistened in the shifting dusklight, and for a moment she saw how it might have been if he hadn't been born a jack. He might have been handsome, in a cruel sort of way, with the soft shelf of dark hair over his eyes and his full lips.

Her fingers tightened on the bottle. If he saw her—

A hand clamped onto her arm. "What the hell are you doing *here?*"

She looked up, blinking away a strand of pale hair, and met Avery Fletcher's green-gold gaze.

Oh, hell. And despite trying not to, Ellie Sinder burst into tears.

"I should have known." A muscle in his cheek twitched. "All of a sudden I get this overpowering urge to wander after dark, it just won't let me be, I go out for a drive and end up here. I should have *known* it was you."

Do you think I charmed you or something? Ellie swiped at her wet cheeks with her free hand. Cryboy was still across the street, but maybe he hadn't recognized her. Mithrus knew she'd never worn a Juno uniform here before. "G-g-g-go—" The words refused to come, as if she was Cami and her tongue kept tripping. Her heart was going to explode if this kept up.

"Stop telling me to fuck off, will you? It gets old." He examined her from top to toe, as if he'd forgotten his hand was clamped around her aching arm. "Mithrus, did you even go home today? You're a wild one."

I went home. Almost got killed, too. The injustice of someone else's assumptions, as usual, stuck in her throat, a dry rock stopping anything she might want to say. Instead, she glared at him through the scrim of tears and, amazingly, Avery Fletcher threw back his head and laughed.

It was a merry sound, and it caroled over the hushed bustle of Southking at night. Cryboy's chin continued its circuit, and for a moment his gaze locked with Ellie's. But he looked away a split second later, as if he didn't recognize her—or didn't care.

It was a goddamn miracle.

Avery didn't quite shake her, but his grip tensed again, and she was suddenly aware of how his fingers met around her biceps, and how they rubbed against the bone through a thin

Wayfarer

screen of flesh. He watched her, the threads of gold in his hair muted now, wearing only a navy T-shirt and jeans against the chill, his trainers new Flotjes imported from overWaste. If he wasn't careful he could get beaten up badly and robbed of them here so close to the core.

Strangely, though, she didn't feel like warning him. His shoulders were way wider than hers, and his calm self-possession made it seem like he could even walk through the core unscathed. Maybe because he was older?

What would it be like, to just wander around unafraid? Calm and knowing you could handle anything that showed up? Was it something someone could teach like algebra or French, or did you have to have an innate capacity, like with charm?

"Here." He subtracted the limon bottle from her unresisting fingers. "This is not where you want to be, Ell."

Her lungs filled. If he kept looking at her like that, her heart *was* going to explode right inside her chest and save Laurissa the trouble of hunting her down. "Sh-shows what *y-you* know."

A single shoulder lifting, dropping, he couldn't quite be bothered enough to really shrug. He was looking at her, with that odd intent gaze that made it so hard to breathe. "I know a lot. Just not what I'd like to."

"Fletcher." She managed to make the words stop jittering and shaking on their way out. "*Avery*. Look. I'm trouble, okay? Bad trouble."

She meant to say *in trouble*, but the preposition just vanished before it could get out. Because she wasn't just in it up to her eyebrows. No, trouble was all through her, and it was seeping out, and any minute it was going to swallow the world whole. *She broke all the records. Or did Rita toss them over the banister?* One at a time, liking the sound they made when they broke? Not that she blamed the other girl; being on the receiving end of all the Strep's rage would make anyone do whatever they had to, just to get a breath. Just to *escape*.

Pointless sadness filled her and swirled away. She was just too tired to keep it.

"I know." Mithrus strike him down, but he actually sounded cheerful. "I knew it the minute you showed up at Havenvale. Fortunately, I *like* trouble."

Not this kind. If Laurissa ever found out . . . Imagining her screaming at Avery threatened to dry Ellie's mouth up completely. Her heart hammered again, hard enough to break through her ribs. "Go home. Leave me alone."

"I thought I told you to quit telling me to fuck off." He glanced over her shoulder. "Let's go. Jacks all around, and it doesn't feel good. What are you doing here, Ell? Or is that another question I'm not supposed to ask? Talking to you is like trying to get through InterProvince Customs with a bag of wasteweed."

"How would *you* know?" She didn't mean to sound sarcastic,

actually. This was shaping up to be the most interesting conversation she'd had in weeks, and it just had to happen during a total disaster.

It has been weeks. A shiver ran through her. *I've been dead on my feet for a while. Mithrus.*

He actually *wiggled his eyebrows* at her, pulling her along the sidewalk. "I have a *lot* of hidden talents, Miss Sinder."

"Hidden deep, no doubt." She scrubbed at her cheek with her free hand again, tears stinging as they dried. Crying always chapped everything, salt water caustic and relentless. Her maryjanes felt awful thin, and every step jolted all through her.

"You keep sweet-talking like that, I'm going to start thinking you like me."

How did he make her feel better? She was in trouble, and feeling better was something she couldn't afford. She had to get somewhere safe, to sit and think and plan . . .

There *was* nowhere safe. Not for her, and not for anyone the Strep might suspect of harboring her. Laurissa was black charming, and she was Sigiled, powerful enough to burn down a house. Imagining Avery in the path of that tornado was just . . . too much.

It wasn't fair. She *did* like him. Anyone else, even Cami, wouldn't have understood anything about this. Maybe he didn't either, but at least he was keeping up. "That's your idea of sweet talk?"

"From you, I guess so." His pace quickened; her skirt swung as she tried to keep up. God, did he have to drag her so *fast*—

"Cute little charmers, out all alone," someone sneered behind them, and a sickening thump of fear echoed inside Ellie's chest. Oddly, it wasn't as crippling as she would have expected. Maybe her fear-maker was busted.

Avery almost skidded to a stop, dropped her arm, and turned on one heel. A prickle of painful stormfront pressure passed through her, like the sun on already-reddened skin. Of course, he was older, and his Potential had settled. He was going to step smoothly into his life, while hers was shattering.

She managed to turn around, her body straining against itself. *God, please. No more tonight. I can't take it.*

"Well, hello there," Avery Fletcher said politely, as if he was at a season event, charmers gathered around and the masked dance of manners, alliance, feud, and one-upmanship in full swing. "One, two, three little pixies. Oh wait, four, slinking in the shadows." A half-delighted laugh. "Run along, boys. I'm the one taking the lady home tonight."

Cryboy slunk forward. "She's a firecracker, charmer boy. I don't think you're up to it."

Her fingers found the crook of Avery's elbow, warm and solid, the pulse leaping from his flesh to hers. A spark popped between them, and he cast her one golden, sideways glance, shaking her off as she pulled, gently.

"Leave it." She tried to sound soothing. "Come on. Just leave it."

"Oh, is the widdle charmer girl *scared?*" Cryboy's cheeks gleamed. It was Ralfie and Hopscotch behind him, Hop with his dreaded-out feathery hair and skinny legs, his three-fingered hands opening and closing at the end of his too-long stick-thin arms. Ralfie was bulkier and moved with scary, oily fluidity, his joints cartilaginous and flexing in ways they shouldn't. "Been waiting to talk to you all alone, Bluegirl."

"Just leave—" Ellie began to repeat herself, but two things happened at once.

Avery stepped forward, right hand coming up, fingers flicking loosely. A brilliant blue-white flash cast sharp-ink shadows; goose bumps popped up on Ellie's skin, tingling and prickling.

She had to blink several times before what she was seeing made sense.

Cryboy, his leather jacket smoking, sprawled on the pavement, rolling back and forth and making a small *heeen* noise. Ralfie crouched, shaking his head with weird boneless broken-neck twitches. A reek of burned hair and gunpowder; Hop lay crumpled and unmoving. There was another slumped shape in the shadows, near the mouth of an alley to their right; she found out she didn't want to look at it.

Mithrus Christ, what did he—

"Warned you," Avery said quietly, and took Ellie's arm again. "Come on, Ell."

She didn't resist. He didn't walk very quickly either, maybe because she was hobbling. Her feet were killing her, and everything else wasn't too happy either. The entire damn day had just caught up with her.

He'd parked on Highclere, but down at the far end where Ruby never did, on the left side of the slender frost-cracked street. The houses here were narrow and frowning. Expensive shotgun shacks, Dad had called them.

The thought of her father was a pinch inside her chest, a hard twisting one. Had she really called Laurissa a whore?

I can't go back. The knowledge jolted, a painful precise slice inside her chest. *She'll kill me. And not just figuratively.*

So, what, then? Sleep on the street? Wait until school tomorrow and . . .

Her brain seized up yet *again.* Hard to think when you were tired and terrified, and she hadn't slept since last night. It felt like a long time, though. It felt like she hadn't slept in months.

His car was the same primer-painted heap, and maybe he kept it that way because it blended in here. There were empty spaces on the street, which never happened during the day. The cars belonging to the neighborhood people were older and heavier, battered and repaired, soft-glowing anti-theft charms visible as the breeze stirred spindly tree branches and mouthed the houses.

"What did you do to them?" It was a stupid question, but that looked like a really useful charm to have, and never pass up the opportunity to learn, right? If she could get something out of this, maybe the day wouldn't be such a total, incredible pile of wasted everything. Broken discs, torn-up paper, what few clothes she had left probably shredded now too. She had nothing but her schoolbag, and her mother's ring, and the uniform she stood up in. How could things get worse?

She had to wince, and her left hand tingled, wanting to make the *avert* sign. It could always, *always* get worse. Laurissa had taught her as much, hadn't she.

"They don't send you to Academy to learn knitting." He unlocked the passenger door, letting go of her arm slowly, reluctantly. "Medic charms can hurt as well as heal. Besides, I wasn't about to let them do anything to you."

So he'd settled into his charm-clan's specialties. Good for him. "Could you teach me?"

He actually looked shocked. "Mithrus, no. It's not a charm you want, babe. Not one you should be throwing, either. You're not even—"

She could finish that sentence in her sleep. *Good enough. One of us. Pretty enough. Worth it.* Whichever one he meant, well, it wasn't like it would hurt her, not after today. "I might need it," she persisted. "I couldn't see what you did."

"Good. Get in the car, please?"

Why? "If I do, will you teach me?"

"No. I'll drive you wherever you want to go, though."

"How about New Avalon?"

An easy shrug. His irises reflected oddly, more gold than dark at the moment. Had he really come out just on intuition, looking for her? "If you want. Getting through customs might take some doing. But your dad was a diplomat, right? You still have a passport?"

Of course not. Laurissa took it. She's probably burning it right now hoping to charm a rebounding sympathy onto me. "No. I don't . . . no."

"I'll figure something out. I'm not kidding."

She searched what she could see of his expression. Oddly enough, she believed him. "Why are you doing this?"

"You don't know? Mithrus, you're so smart, but . . . what's a guy got to do, Sinder? Pretend we're back at Havenvale and tease you again? Throw myself into the bay? Walk through the core singing a Hellward tune?"

Well, you could find me a place to spend the night. Caution warred with desperation. A crazy idea hit her, and she looked up at him, tall and absurdly comforting, his face shadowed as true night folded her soft wings over New Haven. The beech tree behind him rattled its leaves, reminding her of the flicking of his fingers as his charm laid waste to jacks. Medic charms looked awful handy, but her Affinity wouldn't show until . . .

The thought refused to coalesce.

He might have thought she was looking at him for a completely different reason. Because he leaned down, his breath smelling of peppermint beechgum, and his lips touched hers.

TWENTY-ONE

WARM, SOFT, TENTATIVE, AND HER EYES FELL SHUT without any prompting on her part. His tongue probed for entrance, and a flash of *oh my God I don't have enough practice to do this right* went through her weary, aching skull, right before her hands crept up to cup his face and her own mouth opened. Stubble a slight roughness under her fingertips; he had certainly grown up, hadn't he? He had to bend down, and she had wondered sometimes if your neck got tired when you snogged a boy.

It didn't. And practice, she learned, was not incredibly necessary. All it took was attention, his hands carefully on her waist and she liked the feel of that. She liked the warmth of him, the way he blocked out the breeze and the night, the car solid behind her too. Caught between those two solidities was a space just her size.

He made a sound way back in his throat, and all of a sudden

she wondered if Ruby was wild because she liked this feeling
of safety. But that was ridiculous, right? Rube was super-safe.
Her life was a picnic compared to Ellie's. She was a de Varre, for
God's sake, what did she have to be afraid of?

The crazy idea returned, and she had to break away to
breathe. Avery leaned into her, and she found out she liked the
slight hint of cologne on him, too. Something woodsy, almost
like pines, and a tang of silvery coldness. The space between
his neck and shoulder was warm and oddly vulnerable, and
just right for her to rest her face in, nestling up close. There
wasn't enough room to work a slipcharm between them, and
she found out she liked it that way.

If only everything was this *simple*.

His arms were around her now, and he rubbed his jawline
against her hair, a shudder going through him. His soft outward
breath became a word. "Wow."

Her smile caught her by surprise, and she was sort of glad
her face was hidden. Everything inside her turned warm and
soft for a moment, her bones full of heated honey. "Yeah." Her
breath made a warm spot against his collarbone, and he moved
a little, restlessly.

He stilled. Deep breaths, and Ellie matched his. It was nice
to breathe in unison, she decided. If she could just stay here for
a little while longer, things might not be so bad.

"So tell me what I've got to do," he finally said, into her

hair. "Then I'll drive you wherever you want. Okay?"

I really would just like to stay here. That wasn't really an option, though. Neither was asking him . . . what could she ask him? *Hi, take me home and protect me from my crazyass Strep-Monster?* That would go over really well.

Who would believe *her* once Laurissa put on her charming face and reminded everyone she was Sigiled, an adult, a stepmother who'd kept Ellie after her dad derailed in the Waste?

When all was said and done, Ellie was just a kid. A stupid, worthless, brainless little bitch who ruined everything for everyone. Ruby and Cami believed her about the Strep, because they were her friends . . . but adults, even Mother Heloise, believed Laurissa couldn't be *that bad.* There was nothing anyone could do. Until she was eighteen or apprenticed, she *belonged* to her legal guardian.

She was owned.

Besides, she'd heard about Province Homes and orphanages. They were pipelines leading straight to the kolkhoz, if you survived them.

No, she had to start planning and moving, and quick. The crazy idea returned for the third time, and the decision only took her a heartbeat.

What else did she have to lose?

"You can drive me to Juno." Her throat was tight, but she managed to get the words out. "I have to go near there. And maybe soon you can teach me what they taught you at Academy. That's what I want."

"I can't . . ." He sighed, his arms tightening. "Mithrus, you really know how to put the rack to a guy. Damn."

"I'm sor—"

"Nah." He actually kissed her hair, and the warm shivery feeling that went through her almost made her weary knees unlock. It was a good thing there was nowhere to fall; he had her against the car so hard she could barely breathe. It was only for a moment before he loosened up, stepping back and holding her at arm's length as she blinked up at him. "You know, I had dreams about doing that."

"About driving me around?" Her cheeks scorched, and she almost leaned forward. The little betraying tremble in his arms told her that he'd let her, and that he wouldn't be averse to going back to that fascinating new thing called kissing.

"Sticking my tongue in your mouth."

"You have no romance."

"I have *lots* of romance. I'll show you sometime." Was that a grin on his face? She couldn't tell, it was too dark now.

"Keep it under wraps, Fletcher. I'm a nice girl." The wise-cracking felt good. Like she had everything under control. If she could fool him, maybe she could make herself believe it.

"Yeah, you are. When you're not hell on wheels. Get in the car, Sinder."

So she did. He held the door for her, and closed it with finicky, careful softness. He even waited until she locked it before going around to the driver's side, and she took a moment to shut her eyes in the dark, there inside the shelter of his car, and let herself pretend it was going to be all right.

"Here?" Puzzled, he peered up the street. Under the elms the darkness thickened, even the ancient wrought-iron streetlamps struggling to pierce through. "Who lives around here?"

"A friend." Ellie reached for the door handle, hesitated. "Hey."

"What kind of friend?"

A batty old lady. Who nobody, especially Laurissa, would ever connect me to. And it needs to stay that way. "Just a friend. Listen . . ." The words dried up. What did she even want to say?

The engine purred. His fingers didn't restlessly tap the steering wheel. He stared at his knuckles like they were the most interesting thing in the world. In the soft glow from the instrument panel he looked older. Twenty, maybe, or even further along. It was a funny thing, to see what he'd look like in a few years. His cheekbone had a good arc to it, and the shadow along his jawline looked interesting enough to touch.

So she did.

Her hand hung in the air between them, and he was a statue. She traced the bottom of his cheek, marveling at the texture, so different from her own skin. A muscle flicked high up on his cheek, and his knuckles had gone white.

She snatched her fingers back. *Don't, Ellie. This could burn you. This could burn you bad, and you don't have a lot of wick left.*

As casually as she could, she reached for the door. "Thank you." Hoarsely, because her throat had gone dry. "I lost the number you gave me. Your parents still in the phone directory?"

"Yeah." He still stared at his hands. Was he angry? Or maybe some other guy feeling, mysterious as the Seventh Layer of DeVarian's Charms? "They're bidding for Midsummer Ball, too, so the guest rooms are being redone. My dad had a couple extra phone lines put in."

Bidding for Midsummer this early? Someone's eager. Maybe it was Laurissa.

Ellie found, to her weary relief, that she didn't actually care. "So if I call . . ."

He shook his head. "Someone will answer, they'll get me. Just tell me where you want to meet me."

"And you'll show up?" *Well, now I sound clingy. Clingy little Ellie.*

"Yeah." He didn't even hesitate.

She had to ask. "Why?"

"You want me to say it again?"

"Maybe. No," she interrupted when he opened his mouth. "Don't say anything, okay? Let's not ruin it. I'll call."

"Sure you will." He said nothing else as she got out of the car. The engine idled, and he didn't move.

She stepped onto the sidewalk. Up a block or two and to the right was where she thought Auntie's house was. If it wasn't, well, she was going to look really stupid wandering around here at night. Someone might even call the cops. *There's a prowler . . . it's a girl . . .* Then maybe she'd have to find a lie that wouldn't tell them where she belonged, so they wouldn't drag her back to Laurissa.

She was so tired coming up with a lie that good just didn't seem possible. Not to mention the fact that if they didn't drag her back to Perrault Street, she might be taken to someplace like Jorinda Hall or Crantsplace Juvenile.

That was enough to make even Laurissa seem faintly welcoming. So Ellie put her chin up and her shoulders back, walking into the shadows under the elms. The sound of the primer-dipped Del Toro's humming faded behind her, and when she crossed the street it cut off as if with a heavy knife.

She didn't look back.

For a few moments she stood staring, in dull disbelief. At night Auntie's house seemed even narrower, its slightly crooked chimney glowing at the top with a red smokelifter charm, its picket fence grasping fingers. The garden hummed to itself, and when Ellie stepped under the trellis arch she found the gate was open, held back by the twining vines of those queer frill-petaled roses.

She almost wanted to stop and look at the charm used to train them, but her head throbbed at the thought. The crushed-shell walkway ground under her tired maryjanes, and there was an odd slipping sensation—as if the shells were melting, or as if she was being drawn forward without moving, the house looming larger and larger as the path became a river and Ellie a tiny boat rocking on a deep current. She hitched her schoolbag up on her shoulder, the knotted strap digging in, and had her foot on the first slick, quartzlike step when Auntie spoke.

"Come late to Auntie's door, the wanderer has. They come back to Auntie late at night, always."

Ellie whirled, almost losing her balance. There, in the middle of a stand of waist-high green fern set back behind tall blood-colored hollyhocks, black in the darkness, the old woman stood. Fireflies danced around her white head; she'd freed her thistledown hair, a thin but oddly vigorous river down her back. Her brown face was scored with deep lines, but just as night had made Avery look older, it made Auntie look younger.

"I . . ." Ellie floundered. "I'm sorry, Auntie. I have . . . I don't have anywhere else to go, and—"

"Yes, yes, Auntie knows." One plump hand waved, fireflies rising from the fern's depths to follow the gesture. "Inside the lonely daughter goes, and the smallroom upstairs is hers. Tomorrow we begin."

She was too tired to care *how* the woman knew, or to examine the tiny secret thrill that went through her at the word *daughter.* "Begin?"

"Bright light inside Auntie's weary little dove. We train it, we shape it. We teach thee to charm, Columba. Yes, a singed little fiery dove. Go inside."

It's about time something went right for me. "I can't pay—"

"Auntie doesn't want *money*, little Columba. Go, and rest."

Something in her lifted a weary protest, a murmur of danger. If Auntie had been a man . . . well, she never would have come here. She was smart enough for *that*. "Thank yo—"

A spark kindled in those dark eyes. "Do *not*, no *thanking*. Insult to Auntie it is. Inside, or we deny thee shelter."

The implicit promise—that if she hurried, Auntie would at least let her stay the night—propelled her forward. Ellie forced herself up the steps. The fudge door opened, and strangely, once she stepped inside, she felt almost safe. It swung shut behind her with one high-pitched squeak, and she made it up the stairs and down a narrow, dusky hall. Four doors, three of them closed tight and secretive, but one left half open to show a soft gray bedroom with fans of white feathers over its empty fireplace and a small white-painted rocking chair by the tiny window. There was a bathroom the size of a closet, and a closet pretty much only big enough for a broom and two hangers, but it looked damn near like a palace.

The door even locked, but she didn't find that out until later. Ellie dropped onto the deep gray velvet quilt on the narrow single bed, its iron scrollwork glinting in the bright moonlight—strange, that there was moonlight coming in through the window, because it was a cloudy night . . .

She fell asleep.

PART II

TWENTY-TWO

IT WAS PRETTY MUCH HEAVEN.

Each morning began with strengthening sunshine spilling through the glazed windowpanes. There was no tapping of lacquered talons on the door or lunging into terrified wakefulness thinking she would be late for school. The bathroom was small, but she didn't have to worry about the door creaking open or a false-honey voice bouncing off the tiles right before the madness started.

Instead there was the clink of thick glass milk bottles on the front step—Auntie was old-school, and had morning groceries delivered at dawn. She could probably afford it—she could charm rings around just about any teacher Ellie had ever had. Still, she never left the house, so maybe she was retired? She must have saved and invested a pretty penny to be so reclusive, but it was rude to pry. As early as Ellie tried to get up, she never caught the milkman.

Auntie always made a big breakfast, floating around the kitchen with her thistledown hair braided into a coronet. The scarecrow rustled each time Ellie sat down at the table, but when she glanced at it, it stilled. Maybe it was an experiment, maybe it was just sensitized material reacting to the fact that there were *two* active charmers in Auntie's house now.

Because the old woman didn't want her to leave. *Stay, and learn. Auntie offers sanctuary, she does.*

After so much bad, Ellie was finally getting a little luck. It was, as far as she was concerned, about damn time. If only she could stay here until she was eighteen . . . but that was Too Far Ahead. Maybe all that planning really didn't do anything, since every single one she'd had turned into a worthless jumble.

After breakfast, Ellie washed the painted dishes and Auntie dried, moving in companionable silence except for the old woman muttering the name of a charm symbol and Ellie lifting a soapy, drenched hand to sketch it in trembling air.

She hadn't missed one yet.

Auntie didn't charm in a workroom. Or rather, the whole house was her workroom, and the garden too. She didn't seem too concerned about stray Potential breaking things or mutating. "Must flow, yes yes," she would mutter. "Like water, or oil. See, little dove?"

The empty space still opened inside Ellie's head whenever she charmed, but it didn't matter. Auntie taught her how to set her feet in the ground before it flowered, toes sinking in like roots, and it was amazing how such a simple thing made the emptiness friendly instead of scary. There was a fuzzy sense of what was occurring when she did it, a sleepwalker's sensibility of the earth moving around her.

"Watch the rose, Columba," Auntie whispered, and Ellie would sink down in front of a single flower, barely breathing as she studied it, until the world became bright frilled petals and a saffron heart, a slim green stem and whirling universes inside the unfolding of a blot of crimson. The old woman's touch on her shoulder would wake her from a burning reverie, and the roses would explode with vigor, charmlight under the surface of the garden's blossoming all but blinding her.

The days were long seashore-curves of charming, with plenty of food to fuel the Potential. Round loaves of sweet or rye bread, spiced honey, apples, eggs always spun on the counter before being cracked into a bowl, wild rice, seeds and nuts, cheese tangy-yellow or mellow white. Auntie didn't eat meat, and Ellie didn't miss it. For once there was nobody watching every bite as if it cost cash, nobody bringing extra and pretending it wasn't charity.

Auntie herself only ate bread and honey. There were weirder diets, and Ellie had seen Laurissa on a lot of them. Besides, Auntie was old, let her eat what she wanted.

After lunch there was cleaning the cottage while Auntie

bustled through the garden, charming and weeding and snap-pruning. The bees followed the old woman, circling her white head while their hives near the back fence murmured a song Ellie didn't dare get close enough to decipher. She'd never been stung, and Auntie said the little buzz-cousins wouldn't, but why take a chance?

Auntie never gave a room the white-glove treatment once Ellie was done with it. She merely glanced about and nodded, mumbling in that odd way, as if singing along to music nobody else could hear. Once in a while she would smile, pleased, and that white V-shaped smile did something funny to Ellie. It made her shoulders clench but her chest loosen, and she found herself standing straighter every time it showed up.

The old woman never yelled or threw things or told Ellie she was worthless. Instead, she was downright *pleased*. Sometimes she even said the magic word, and Ellie's heart would get two sizes larger and several ounces lighter all at once.

Apprentice. There wasn't any paperwork to make it official, but that could come later. For right now, this was enough.

Juno was walking distance away, but why risk the Strep finding her there? Or risk the Sisters insisting she go "home"? Her schoolbag, broken and reknotted strap looped back on itself, hung in the closet. No homework, no Babchat. She rose when she felt like it and went to sleep when she was exhausted and charm-drained. It was a good feeling, to work hard and fall into the soft gray bed. No bruises, no scrapes, no flinching at every shadow or sudden movement. Auntie was halfway to apprenticing her already, and that would be enough to get Ell a license. More importantly, even half-batty as she was, the old lady could *charm*. Apprenticing with her would be *worth* something; Ellie learned more in a week here than she had in a year of Juno's careful, mind-numbingly safe classes, where you always had to wait for the slowest damn idiot in the room to catch on.

The early evenings were the best, because as Auntie made dinner Ellie practiced charm-symbols, looking through her battered thick paperback copy of Sigmundson's. The blue-jacketed scarecrow rustled, but she was used to it by now. The entire house was friendly and familiar, no sharp edges or cold stone. No screaming, no slaps, no steady drip of venom.

Sometimes she still heard Laurissa, though. *Worthless, lazy, stupid, slut, bitch, HATE YOU.*

Thinking about it made her hands shake a little, but she took a deep breath and the trembling retreated. It was getting easier. "Auntie?"

"Mh. Barley tonight, the soup must be thick."

Vegetables and barley. Toni would add meat. Had the cook found another job? There was no way of telling. Had Ellie been the problem all along, and Rita and the Strep now nice and cozy because she was gone? How was Rita dealing with the Strep's attention all on her? Did she like it?

We all have to swim on our own. Tentatively, Ellie tried a question. "Have you ever been afraid of Twisting?"

The old woman waved a wooden spoon, absently. "Why does the dove ask, hmm? Does Auntie seem tumbled-about to young eyes?" A flash of white teeth, and a small branch fell from her tangled white head.

"I'll comb your hair tonight." Ellie pushed her chair back. "And no, I just wondered. I've always been afraid of Twisting."

"Little Columba will not Twist." Auntie nodded, sharply. "Comb Auntie's hair with quick fingers, yes. *Sarbirin.*"

Ellie's hand leapt up, the tiny stick in her fingers sketching a fluid charm-symbol with eldritch light. Pale in the lowering sunshine through the kitchen window, it still fluoresced just fine, and the smile that filled her cheeks didn't feel like a mask anymore.

"Tripaltia."

Another symbol.

"Kepris."

It was so easy, like breathing. Potential shaped itself, and the symbols hung in the air, two stretching toward each other and the third—*Tripaltia,* repelling most of the Second List and all of the Third through Thirteenth *except* when used in subordinate position—kept them apart, straining, threads of Potential building a structure of reaction and chance around them.

You weren't supposed to be able to hold them in open air

for very long, but it was so *easy*. Or it had become that way, under the old woman's careful tutelage.

The longer she stayed here, the more she'd learn, and the better equipped she'd be to make some sort of living. Maybe even save enough to go overWaste. She had hazy memories of the train ride, Dad catching up on his law-journal reading as the sealed carriage holding their sleeper compartment hurtled through the night. Ellie dosed with a sedative pill to make travel easier, both of them not speaking around a hurtful absence that was her mother's shape and size—

She caught herself, swallowing hard, and willed the stinging in her eyes to go down.

Auntie's wide white smile sharpened. "Good." She nodded, and turned back to the bubbling pot on the sleek stove.

Ellie brought her hands together, the branch—sensitized now—trapped between them. The three symbols exploded in a cascade of harmless sparks, winking out before they hit the cinnamon floor. The sapphire glinted uneasily, swirling with charmlight, but Auntie didn't even notice. She just stirred the soup and reached for an earthenware crock by her elbow, cast a handful of pearly barley into the simmering pot. She paused, added another.

Ellie sank back down at her place at the table. She sniffed once, hard, and the tears retreated. The scarecrow rustled again, and a flicker of motion made her head turn instinctively, her pale hair moving in a smooth shining wave, longer now.

How long have I been here?

It was a relief to find out it didn't matter. If she kept moving steadily, working hard, being useful, Auntie would let her stay. After a while, the aching places inside her wouldn't matter.

The scarecrow's faded eyes were blue smears, its mouth a sad downturned line. Why Auntie had the thing stuffed into the chimney corner was beyond Ellie.

On impulse, she leaned over, tucking the scrap of wood under the scarecrow's faded denim sleeve. The twig was sensitized by the passage of Potential, sure, and a single strand of thistledown hair was wrapped around its smooth bark. The scarecrow was looking a little thin. It could use all the stuffing she could find.

"Bowls!" Auntie crowed, and Ellie leapt to her feet again. Funny, but she didn't mind serving dinner here. Especially since she seemed to get it right, the way she never had for the Strep.

The scarecrow rustled again, but there was the bread to slice and the bowls to fill, and Auntie's silver spoon to ladle the hot soup to her watering, waiting mouth while Auntie dipped her own in thick amber honey.

Outside, twilight deepened into night, and once Ellie made up her mind to ignore it, the world beyond the garden's fence didn't matter at all.

TWENTY-THREE

A STONE SPAT BLUE AND THE THING HISSED, ITS HUNGRY ancient face splitting in a wide V to show white, white teeth. The night around her was not dark but white, each edge laden with hurtful brilliance; creeping darkness threaded through with slim grasping fingers.

At first there was a sting at her breastbone, a pinching. Then a drowsy warmth all through her, a feathered nest, the safety of exhaustion.

The last time she'd felt protected had been with her head resting against his neck.

Avery? Slurred and heavy, a sleeptalker's mumble. If this was a dream, it was a funny one. A queer draining sensation spread through her dream-body; a brushing over her dream-skin, as if she was back in Ruby's car and the minotaur was chasing them. The streets warped like the minotaur's Twisting, ribbons of diseased Potential rising and twining around its bone-heavy head, and as she looked down her own arms were wavering corkscrews, bones painlessly warping. Her head was heavy, drooping forward as her neck shortened and her shoulders rose, and she tried to wake up but there was no air, she could not breathe, fish-gasping, her jaws working . . .

The thing crept away, and for a long time she didn't know if she was awake or asleep. Until finally her body became her own again and—

She jolted upright, clutching the sheet and coverlet to her chest, her entire body throbbing and the sapphire sending out tiny crackling sparks that painted the walls of the gray room, bleaching it to white with sharp-cut shadows. No moonlight braved the windowpanes.

Ellie fought for breath.

The cottage was still and silent, breathing to itself. Blinking turned the room into shutter clicks, an alien chiaroscuro. For a few seconds she couldn't remember just *where* she was, and the only thing that kept her from screaming was the hazy thought that the Strep might hear.

She's not here. You're at Auntie's.

Her heart quit trying to throw itself out through her ribcage. Sweat dewed her skin, but she was *cold.* Her teeth chattered, and for a second, there was the terrifying vertiginous feeling of being . . . invisible.

No, not invisible. Transparent. A clear pane of charmglass.

Why should that bother me? Her heart calmed down, and slowly, slowly, she warmed up. Her teeth stopped clicking together, the shudders coming in waves instead of constantly. The waves spread out, their peaks diminishing, and after a little while she could unlock her arms from around her knees and stretch, tentatively.

Her ribs ached. No, not ribs. A knot of pain high on the left side of her chest, and she rubbed gingerly at it. A bruise, maybe? What a weird place to be bruised. There wasn't anything here that hurt; Auntie never even touched her unless it was a brief brush while passing a plate or a small thing to be charmed.

When she could, she slid her legs out of bed and stood, shakily. Faint cityglow showed through the diamond windowpanes, dappled by leaf and branch shadows—though there wasn't a tree on this side of the cottage; it had to be a charm—and made blotches on her arms and legs. She tacked unsteadily for the door, opened it, and peered out into the hall.

I don't feel right.

For a hazy moment she contemplated getting her schoolbag and her uniform—Auntie had produced crisp white buttondowns and plaid skirts as well as kneesocks and panties, even a bra or two and several camisoles in Ellie's size, brushing aside her stammered attempt at gratitude, as usual—and creeping out the front door, through the trellis arch and the frilled roses, and sneaking to a phone box.

Who would she call? Ruby, who would probably just yell at her for disappearing? Cami, who would be so worried, so helpful, so fragile? Neither of them needed Ellie dropping more problems in their lap, especially Laurissa-sized problems.

Avery? The thought died as soon as it began. Another person who didn't need problems with the Strep-Monster, and who had probably forgotten all about Ellie and her annoying habit of not meeting him or calling when she said she would.

I'd forget me too. It would be a relief. Her shoulders sagged. Her panties were riding up, and she shut the door, standing and staring at the knob for a moment.

Wait. I locked this. Didn't I?

Maybe not. She didn't need to lock things here. Still, forgetting to do that was like forgetting to breathe.

A wave of exhaustion crashed over her, carried her across the floor, and deposited her into the soft gray bed again. She sank down, snuggling under the covers, and the leafshadows on the ceiling were skulls and bony hands until she blinked. Then they were normal, just branches dancing on the wind.

"I don't ever want to leave." Her furtive whisper took her by surprise, rippled the air like a pebble thrown into a still pond. "Not even if she throws me out." *I'm staying. I don't care what happens.* Ellie lay stiffly for a long while, watching the branches move as the hot tears trickled down her temples, vanishing into her hair.

I won't ever go back to Laurissa. I'll walk into the core first. The scary thing wasn't thinking that. It was the quiet, sure knowledge that once she started moving that direction, she wouldn't stop.

If the core didn't kill her it would Twist her, because of the black scratching thing she had flung at the Strep. A curse, almost as black as Laurissa's own work on a gaudy, loud-ticking watch. There was the wounded look on Cami's face, too, and Ruby's dismissal. *Let her go.*

Well, they had. Now it was her turn to let her fingers unclench a bit, and just let things go too.

When sleep finally came, there were no more dreams.

TWENTY-FOUR

"HOLD IT SO, LITTLE COLUMBA." AUNTIE'S SPIDERY fingers curled around a dandelion's stem. "Now, *pouf!*"

A symbol flashed blue-white and the plant shriveled, almost crying out as its leaves curled up and blackened. Under the flood of sunshine, Ellie shivered. "That looks unpleasant. Are you sure it won't Twist you?"

"No fear. See?" The stem, turning papery black, curled in a corkscrew. "A mirror does not Twist. Impossible."

Ellie's eyebrows drew together. "But that . . ." She studied the ripples of Potential spreading from the charming. *Is it really that simple? It can't be, or someone would have figured it out by now.* All it took was looking in the right place, and you could spin the effects of a nasty charm *somewhere else*. It would ripple through ambient Potential and the wave would die down, an ocean seamlessly repairing itself.

Is that even legal?

Who knew? A chill worked down Ellie's back as the bees hummed their drowsy song. She rubbed at the sore spot on her chest—there *was* a bruise, a small dark one, maybe from a button digging in while she leaned over the rain barrel to scrub off algae. Or maybe from thrashing around during nightmares.

Even in the sun, the breeze was suddenly cold. She didn't have a sweater, just her Juno blazer, which hung accusingly in the tiny closet. Right next to her dusty schoolbag.

I don't care if I ever wear it again.

Auntie creaked to her feet, leaving the blackened dandelion to shred itself into ash and dirt, making the garden richer. "No sunwheels, Columba. Spin, or pull the weed."

"Yes ma'am." *I don't know if I can.* She found another bright yellow flower, just sitting minding its own business in the middle of a riot of other things—tomato vines with hard green fruit swelling toward ripeness, leafy green potato plants, petunias, mandrake, and deadly nightshade crowding around each other with slightly embarrassing vitality.

Aren't you afraid of poisoning yourself, Auntie?

Auntie is not stupid, the old lady had sniffed.

Ellie began weeding, whispering a loosening-charm to get the juicy pungent taproot out of the dark, damp soil. The old woman hummed as she went around the corner of the house, and Ellie hunched her shoulders. *I saw how she did it.*

So what's stopping me?

The next dandelion was a tiny runt-like one, and she felt a little sorry for it. Well, honestly, either she was going to rip it up out of the ground where it was minding its own business, or she was going to charm it to death. It would die in slow agony, wilting in the compost heap, or it could be finished quickly.

Which was better?

Her fingers sketched the symbol. A bright blue-white spark, and she spun the twisting down the taproot, delicately.

The dandelion immediately shredded into a spiraling puff of ash. It was just so *easy*. The spreading ripples melted together, and Ellie examined her fingers.

Garden dirt under her bitten-short nails, a cupped palm, and long slim fingers. A blur of charmlight, because she was alive, emitting Potential like everything did. Even machines exuded *something*, any complex system threw off little bits of energy that melded into eddies and swirls that charmers tapped into. Maybe there was just a cosmic drain backed up somewhere, something falling in and plugging it around the time of the Great War, and the whole Reeve just the energetic version of a stuck toilet.

Which would make minotaurs . . . what? Torrents instead of swirls and eddies, or swimmers drowning in energy waste?

The problem with metaphors was that they broke down so damn *easily*. Ellie cursed under her breath. She pulled three dandelions for every one she charm-killed, and carried the wilting wounded to the compost pile at the back of Auntie's garden, a simmering mess of vegetable stew inside a white-painted cage. The hives off to her left hummed sleepily, and she cast them a nervous glance.

There was an elm tree looming over the fence, black-barked and shifting in a cool breeze, and she tossed the dandelions in with what probably should have been a whispered charm.

Instead, what came out was a soft "I'm sorry."

Apologizing to plants. I'm going to be as cracked as Auntie before long. That'd be just fine with me, too.

"She's talking to weeds," someone said, and Ellie almost leapt out of her skin. "Girl's crazy for sure." It came from *above*, and as she stared, the shifting branchlight hid him for a long moment.

"Mithrus *Christ*," she breathed. "What are you doing up there?"

"Looking for you. This was as close as I could get." Avery Fletcher crouched on a branch that looked too spindly to hold his weight, clutching grimly at another branch, this one dead.

"You're going to break your *neck*," she whisper-screamed. For some reason she couldn't get in enough air to yell at him. "What is *wrong* with you?"

"I could ask you the same thing. You never called."

You should be thanking me for not dragging you down with me. "Auntie doesn't have a phone."

"Auntie?"

"She lives here."

His nose wrinkled like he smelled something bad. Maybe he did, he was right above the compost. "And you do too, now, I guess? Do you know how hard it is to find this place?"

Which meant he'd looked. A traitorous little weed of hopeful heat rose inside her chest; she quashed it as sternly as she could. "Some charmers don't want to be found. Look, I thought of calling you, but—"

"But what? You decided I wasn't worth the effort?" He had twigs stuck in his gleaming hair, and his eyes were more gold than green now. For a moment he looked fey, his coloring blending into wood and leaf. "Your friends are climbing the walls. You could have let someone know where you were."

"Why, so Laurissa can drag me back and make a mint off . . ." She clapped her dirty hand over her mouth, trapping the secret behind her teeth.

He just nodded, not even looking surprised. "Yeah, I pretty much figured those weren't her work. They sold fast, though. And they dried up when you disappeared. No more Choquefort-Sinder work on the market now."

Yet another reason to stay as far away from Laurissa as possible. If Fletcher had found her, someone else could—and would Auntie still want her if there was trouble?

For a moment she thought of the Strep showing up here, and panic was a stone in her throat. What could she say? *Don't tell anyone?* Should she beg? Offer him . . . what? She didn't have anything.

Of course, he'd never know what she did to keep him safe. Nobody would believe her if she tried telling them Laurissa was a black charmer. She was respected, even if she wasn't liked, and she was an *adult*. She'd put on her sweet voice, the one she used with the boyfriends, and it would be all over.

Her arms fell to her sides. "What do you want?"

"I wanted to make sure you were okay." He had a deathgrip on that dead branch, tendons on the back of his broad capable hands standing out, and his charm-shined boots had black dirt and leaf mold clinging to them. "Also, to tell you something."

What would that be? She just glared at him, and he actually laughed, tossing his head back a little. Not too much, it would throw his balance off.

When he leveled his gaze back down at her, she had her hands on her hips, not caring that she'd have to charm the dirt out of the white button-down. She was always untucked and disheveled around him, for God's sake. It was like the entire world was conspiring to make her feel like an idiot whenever he was in sight.

"This year's Midsummer Ball is set for fullmoon." He shifted a little, very carefully, and there was a sharp groaning creak from the branch he perched on. "Three days from now, at the Fletcher estate. We won the bidding; my mother's happy as hell and the phones are ringing nonstop. I would like to invite you, Ellen Sinder, to dance with me."

That's impossible. "It's way too early in the season—" she began.

A flash of something like anger crossed his face. "It's the end of *Junius*, Ellie. You've been here a while."

Junius? But . . . oh, crap, I missed finals, and—had she really believed she was going back to Juno?

No. They couldn't drag me back. That was the trouble about being a teenager, though. They *could* drag you back.

"Seriously?" She searched his expression, her neck aching as she stared up. "Avery . . ."

"If you don't like me, Ellen, just *tell* me so and I'll quit bugging you, okay? I had the hugest crush on you at Havenvale but you never gave me a chance. And the funniest goddamn thing happened to me when I came home and saw you on the platform. I started thinking about you again, couldn't get you out of my head. I still can't, but I'll leave you alone if I'm not wanted here. Okay?"

Is he serious? What's in it for him? Everything she had ever wanted to say to him rose up inside her, hit a rock, and boiled. Charmsparks popped around her, and the feeling of his attention, as if her skin was alive again, poured over her in a wave. "It's not that," she managed around the obstruction in her throat. Now she felt guilty for thinking he was like the Strep, always looking for an advantage. "Really, Ave, it's not that. I like you. A lot." *You have no idea how much.* "I just . . . I have problems."

"So we solve them."

We? You don't know Laurissa. "That's awful sweet of you, but—"

"Are you coming to the Ball, princess?"

Oh, for God's sake. No. It's not worth her finding me there, and what do you want from me anyway? Not a chance, dammit. "Okay. If you promise not to tell anyone where you found me." *Wait, what did I just say?*

"Done, charmer's word. I'll be silent." The branch creaked sharply and he scrambled back with monkeylike agility. "Three days, Sinder. Don't forget!"

"Wait!" she called after him. "I don't have anything to wear!" *What are you doing here anyway? Why didn't you just come to the front door?*

He was already gone, and unless she climbed into the compost heap, she wouldn't be able to yell after him.

Oh, Mithrus Christ. What now?

Now, she told herself, staring at the wilting, slaughtered dandelions, she should probably talk to Auntie.

TWENTY-FIVE

". . . So it's in three days. And I should maybe go."
She tried not to bite her lower lip.

Auntie had gone still, the pot on the stove bubbling. The
old woman's hair had grown thicker, longer, and more tangled,
if that were possible, and the twigs and leaves caught in its wild
mess struggled to poke free.

If I go, maybe he won't tell. Or maybe . . . I don't know. She
did know, that was the trouble. She wanted to go, to see him.
"I don't have anything to wear, but I can fix that. I might go
to Southking and get a bolt of something, make a dress. I can
charm . . . Laurissa's a *couturière*, so I know how to do cloth and
shoes. What do you think?"

Her words petered out. A pounding in her chest echoed in
her wrists and ankles, and why was she sweating? Auntie wasn't
like Laurissa.

"A fête?" The old woman sounded puzzled. "But Columba

will return, yes?"

"Of course." *Like I have anywhere else to go.* "I wouldn't leave you, Auntie. I just don't want to bring *her* here."

"Wickedness will not follow Columba to Auntie's door." The old woman muttered, her head sinking forward as she stirred with a wooden spoon. Fragrant steam rose—it was spaghetti, though the tomatoes in the garden were all still green. "But a promise, a promise to return."

The scarecrow made a sharp crackling noise, and Ellie almost flinched. It was just a pile of stuffing, though. Even if its painted mouth was a grimace, even if the smears of blue paint that were its eyes almost seemed to follow her as she pushed her chair back and moved restlessly into the kitchen.

"I *promise* I'll come back. You need help in the garden." She stared at the smaller cheese press on the counter, where a block of creamy, crumbly white was being pressed. The cinnamon kitchen was too bright; her eyes stung a little. "I can work, I want to stay and work with you. If you'll have me." *Don't get greedy, Ell.* "Maybe I can do some marketing too, now that I've been here a while. Anything."

The spoon splashed in rich red tomato sauce. "Oh, Auntie markets in her own fashion. I shall find you cloth, and conveyance, little Columba. And when the dancing is done, you shall return."

"Well, yeah." Her heart ceased its wild pounding. It was a

good thing, or she might have been sick. Her fingers, digging into the countertop, relaxed little by little. "I'm scared. I really . . . really just . . ."

Before she could help herself, she'd taken the few steps to cover the space between them and thrown her arms around the old woman. Auntie stiffened—some charmers didn't like to be touched—and as Ellie squeezed gently she got a sudden strong whiff of rotting copper. Sour sweat and dirt, and that nasty scabby breath.

Well, no old lady smelled sweet, right? She worked all day, just like Ellie did.

"You're amazing," Ellie finished. *Because I know you don't like to be thanked.* "Really *amazing*. I wish I was your apprentice, you're the best charmer I've ever known. You saved my life, and you're just so . . . amazing." *Lame, Ell. Really lame.*

"Auntie is merely Auntie," was the grumbling reply, but the brown, creased face broke into its wide white V-shaped smile, and this close Ellie could see a fine sprinkling of iron-grey and black hairs among the white thistledown.

Maybe she wasn't *that* old. Her skin was fine parchment, and this close it looked fresher, somehow. The wrinkles weren't that deep.

"You look good." Her grin didn't feel like a mask, again. Maybe soon she'd be able to smile naturally. "Having some help around is really good for you."

"Yes yes. An apprentice, a young apprentice for an old woman. Yes, little Columba, little apprentice." A faint frown crinkled the old woman's face.

Her heart almost stopped. "Do you mean—"

"Auntie needs apprentice, but only if Columba returns." Auntie shooed her away and went back to stirring, and Ellie picked her jaw up off the floor, whirled, and ran down the hall past the three other doors that never opened. One of them had to be Auntie's bedroom, but which?

It didn't matter. The stairs were old friends now, she knew all their creaking voices, and the grey room welcomed her with soft light.

Her shabby schoolbag, thrown in a corner of the tiny closet, was actually *dusty*. End of Junius already; she'd been here a lot longer than she thought. Her High Charm Calc notebook was stuffed inside, and she tore out a few pages and grabbed a pen.

Her breathless arrival back in the tiny dining room almost made black spots dance in front of her eyes. "I'm going to design a dress," she announced. "And shoes, I need to charm some shoes. I'll have to have a couple charms ready for throwing and showing, and . . ." *What if Laurissa's there?*

Well, what if she *was*? The thought was terrifying and intriguing in roughly equal measure.

Who am I kidding? Terrifying wins out. Still, she'd fought Laurissa to a draw, hadn't she? And escaped. In front of the whole

charming community, what could the Strep do? All her nastiness was done in secret, at home.

The strength ran out of her arms and legs, and she sat down
hard. The chair groaned sharply, and the scarecrow rustled.
Auntie peered at her, so Ellie essayed a weak smile. "I'm fine. I
just thought of something, that's all. What if *she's* there?"

"Thinking too much. Little Columba is strong now." The
old woman made a sarcastic little noise. "Come, the long strings
are ready."

Which meant supper was right around the corner, and it
was time to collect the hanging fingers of egg noodles from the
drying racks. There really wasn't much better than homemade
pasta, especially with the pale unsalted butter left on the translucent stone front step every morning. Auntie now ate a *lot* of
butter to go with her bread and honey, but you wouldn't think
it to look at her.

"I'm on it." But it took Ellie two tries to stand up. "I'm
going to have to go marketing."

"Leave it to Auntie, little one." She sounded odd, a little
strained . . . but it could have been because she was lifting the
heavy pot of simmering tomatoes. "Leave everything to Auntie.
A dress will be had, and shoes, and pretty pretty things for Auntie's
apprentice. Who will return to old Auntie, yes."

Her heart made that funny lifting thump again. It was as if
leaving Perrault Street had been the last gauntlet to run through

before things finally started to be *good* again. "I can make the shoes—"

Now the old woman's face turned grave, but there was a twinkle in her dark eyes. "No, Columba. For the ball, Auntie will bring her apprentice shoes."

The next morning dawned overcast and warm, and the cottage was empty. The kitchen was spotless but dark, and the scarecrow had fallen sideways out of its place. It took some doing to heft it back up—it was a lot heavier than it looked and weirdly warm too, as if full of heated sand. It crackled as she settled it back down, and she rearranged his hat, more gently than she probably had to. *Nothing's ever going to make you look better, friend. But at least you're right-side-up now.*

His grimace suggested he didn't agree. This close she could see his hair was corn silk among the straw poking out from under the antique hat, dry and raveled but still golden.

Ellie yawned, scratching at her ribs. "Auntie?"

The antique icebox, under a heavy layer of seal-and-cool charming, hummed quietly to itself. The back door was slightly open, so Ellie stepped out barefoot, teetering on the threshold. "Auntie?" Her tentative call fell into a breathless hush. "Are you out here?"

The garden held itself still under a cloudy sky. There was a faint sweetish smell, like the breath of choco-beechgum that followed Ruby around. The weather had changed overnight, and maybe late-summer storms would start sweeping in from the bay. Salt breeze and thunder, and warm rain on the thirsty earth. Now that the rain barrel was clean, it would be a good thing. Auntie said bathing in rainwater would give a girl good skin, but Ellie shuddered at the notion. She'd scrubbed at least three inches of algae out of the oak cask, stinking green goop that Auntie wanted in charmed sacks. If you dried it out, maybe it was worth something, but still.

She rubbed at the tender spot on her chest. She hadn't quite *dreamed*, precisely, but she'd woken up tired, as if she'd thrashed around a lot. Probably the change in the weather.

Ellie rocked back and forth on the threshold, uncertainly. *It's not like her to leave.* A horrible thought took shape—what if she'd gone out into the garden last night and something had happened? She was an old lady, and . . .

It was enough to get her out the door and onto the back path, the paving stones warm, glossy licorice-black holding the sun's veiled heat. She checked the herb beds and the vegetable garden, even venturing close to the domed, cheese-yellow beehives and their drowsy mumbling.

She circled the house, hopping over the crushed-shell walk—that sugar-white stuff was *sharp*—and found a broken-down place in the gleaming white fencing, but no vivid splash of Auntie's housedress. Finally, wet to the ankles—the grass was long and dew-heavy—she came around the far edge of the house and made it to the back steps again, where she sank down and hugged her knees.

Well, I've been wandering around a charmer's garden in my underwear. She shivered, picking little bits of grass from her tanned calves. *No wonder we end up eccentric.*

Auntie was really no weirder than Laurissa, or even the Fletchers—Avery's mom had a bad allergy to seafood and avoided even fish-shaped Beltane candies, and it was common knowledge Mr. Fletcher hated rust because of his Affinity. The head of the Tharssman clan, old Benito himself, always whistled while charming, high piercing notes or nostalgic tunes popular on the kolkhoz he was rumored to have grown up on. The Hathaways had taboos against lemons and leeks, of all things.Scratch a charmer, find a weirdo. Potential gave you funny hypersensitivities, even if it didn't turn you into a jack or Twist you.

She found herself rubbing at her chest again, high up on the left side, an inch or two down from her collarbone. There was a slick dampness, and she blinked at her fingers.

Bright red. "Oh, Mithrus *Christ*," she said. Maybe something had gotten stuck in her camisole and poked, since she'd spent all that time in the bushes looking for Auntie. "Great."

Inside, the cottage was just as neat, just as clean, just as dark and empty. And the stupid scarecrow had thumped down on the floor again, its limbs spilling anyhow. For a second, a trick of the dimness made it look like it was *moving*, but as soon as she snapped the switch and the overhead fixture flicked into life it was just an inanimate lump of stuffed denim and velvet again.

"Anyone else would keep a scarecrow out in the *garden*." She hefted it back up, straining as its bulkiness slipped and slid, her bloody fingers wiped clean against the torn velvet jacket. "But oh *no*. Of cour—" The thing slipped again, for all the world as if *fighting* her, and she snapped a weightshift charm to help lift it. Sparks cracked blue-white, and it settled back in its place on a low chocolate-varnished wooden shelf, curiously carved and with rotting leather straps dangling from it. She'd never been close enough to see before.

Looks like something chewed its way loose there. She blew out between her teeth and had to sit down, glaring at the scarecrow. Its blue-painted eyes returned her stare, insouciant.

"Don't look at me like that. What, you *want* to be on the floor all the time? Auntie would be mad." It popped out before she thought about it, and that was curious too.

She had to take a deep breath and find a sticking-plaster for whatever she'd scraped herself with. Just because Auntie wasn't here didn't mean there wasn't work to be done.

"Maybe she's marketing? For stuff for the Ball, and she didn't leave a note. Maybe she just didn't think about it. She never writes notes." Her whisper took her by surprise. "If she's at market, she'll be tired when she comes home. I should have lunch ready, and the rue's ease weeded, and the hollyhocks trimmed and charmed."

What if she doesn't come back? The scarecrow's piercing gaze was uncomfortable, to say the least.

"Then it's just you and me, right?" It can't be that hard to survive here. Auntie's done it for a while now. Nobody even has to know.

How would she pay for the grocery deliveries? She didn't know where Auntie kept her credits. Or maybe it was automatic, but that was no guarantee that it would continue. Still . . . it was a thought.

The old woman had said the magic word. *Apprentice.* This was also Auntie's home, of course she'd come back. Home was the place where they had to take you in, but Auntie didn't have to. Ellie was on sufferance here, just like everywhere else.

Still, this was a better sufferance than most.

The scarecrow sagged. She kept watching to make sure it didn't fall again, and finally hauled herself shakily to her feet. "She's coming back." The words sounded flat and unconvinced. "She has to. I'm her apprentice."

But the calm, iron voice that she used for planning was back, and it would not be silenced. *If she doesn't, I'll figure something out.*

TWENTY-SIX

BY THE TIME AUNTIE DID COME HOME THE NEXT AFTER-
noon, Ell was pretty close to climbing the walls. She'd cleaned
everything that could be cleaned, weeded everything that could
be weeded, charmed until her head was empty and her stomach
ached, and set out the morning milk bottles not just rinsed but
sparkling. She'd even cleaned the old ash out of Auntie's kitchen
fireplace, and when the old woman waltzed in with an armful
of packages wrapped in rough brown paper, Ellie was up to her
elbows in soapsuds, having taken every painted dish and bright
copper pan out of the cupboards. She was on her last load,
Auntie's mismatched silverware and some odds and ends, like
the butter dish and the red-lacquered serving platter shaped like
a leaf, a sort of cross between oak and maple.

She looked over her shoulder, blowing pale hair out of
her face—it was longer now, and lighter with all the time she'd
spent in the sun—and the relief blew her heart back up like

a balloon. "You're back!"

Auntie's housedress was a vile fuchsia, her thistledown hair combed and pinned atop her head. The old woman looked thinner and oddly radiant. Maybe it was just that Ellie was seeing her afresh after an absence. Auntie's face was smoother, and her smile did not make a mass of wrinkles on each cheek. Even her hands looked better. She was middle-aged instead of *old*, and the streaks of iron-gray in her hair had widened, each with a thread of pure black at its center, vital and growing.

"And you look good," Ellie finished. "I missed you. Have you had lunch? I made bread, not as good as yours but it's okay I guess. I've been weeding, and the hollyhocks are fine. You must have seen them, right?" She had to stop for breath. "I tried to do everything, I really did."

"Good little apprentice." Auntie's white smile widened. "The house is happy. Auntie is happy. Come, see what she brings thee."

The table was freshly wiped, so Auntie set her cargo down on it with a theatrical sigh. Ellie, drying her wrinkled hands with an embroidered dishtowel, edged into the teensy dining room. The scarecrow was no longer twitching, Auntie's presence nailing everything in the cottage back into its normal dimensions and usual cheerful glow. The ghost-scent of the bread baked earlier strengthened, too.

Auntie made a quick movement, and a tide of moonlight spilled over the table.

"Oh . . ." Ellie's breath rode out in a gush of wonder. "Is that . . . is that what I *think* it is?"

"Does Auntie's dove like it?" Did she sound *uncertain*? Why?

The dress was silver, but not *just* silver. Glittering beads hung on strings, as if a post-Reeve flapper-girl had just stepped out of it. Spaghetti-strapped and low-waisted, a small tinsel flower at the left hip, it shimmered and shone. That flower was sharp-petaled, with that same strange grace the frilled roses planted along the garden's borders showed. At its heart, trembling crystal raindrops shimmered with charmlight.

"It's *beautiful*," Ellie breathed. "It looks like fey work."

"And here." Work-gnarled fingers undid the string around another parcel. "Delicate hooves, yes."

Low-heeled slippers, a net of silver suspended in their sheer crystal sides, with the same charmlight glow caught in the heels. They quivered, ready to dance, and Ellie saw how the charming had been applied, fluid beautiful work that held no hint of Sigil, or even a breath of the charmer's personality.

Definitely fey work. "Wow." She touched them with one trembling, raisin-wrinkled fingertip. "Oh, Auntie. They're *incredible*. How did you—"

One finger wagging and a broad white smile. "No asking, no telling." The third package was tiny, and it opened up, flower-like, to show a silver-beaded headband with a pale feather uncrumpling itself, growing like a fern under a plumping-charm. There was also a tiny silver key, hanging from a thread-fine chain. "Conveyance, for my scorched dove. Full moon, so very difficult. From moonrise to midnight, Columba has a fine silver carriage. Afterward, Auntie cannot promise."

"That's more than enough." *I just need to dance with Avery, that's all.* The thought that she didn't precisely *need* to was shouted down by a hot flush staining her cheeks and making her palms sweat. *And stay away from Laurissa if she's there,* she reminded herself sternly. Although that bit was likely to be the most difficult. "I can't . . ." *She doesn't like those words.* "Auntie, you're amazing. You're really, truly, incredibly amazing."

"Little apprentice." Auntie beamed. "Flattering poor old Auntie."

"You aren't so old. Sheesh." Ellie held her breath as she picked up the dress, delicately, afraid that even breathing on the bead strings would break them. "Actual fey work. Wow."

Maybe if Laurissa thought Ellie had connections with the Children of Danu, she'd leave her alone? Those sorts of connections never really worked out well for charmers; it was all over the old stories. Flighty, fickle, some fey were really nasty tempered, too. Maybe Auntie knew how to visit the goblin market—you couldn't find it unless someone took you there the first time, but after that it was pretty easy. Or at least, that was the story. Maybe that was why she'd been gone so long?

Tomorrow night. Her heartbeat settled into a thin high gallop, and the scarecrow rustled. Ellie glanced up in time to see Auntie dart a venomed look into the corner, and her breath caught again.

For a flashing second, the old woman's familiar dark eyes were *black*, from lid to lid. Just like the Vultusino house fey's. Only Marya never looked this . . . dangerous, lips skinned back and that black gaze hot with rage.

Then Auntie's face smoothed, her eyes were normal, and she blinked at Ellie. Strands of her fine thin hair were coming loose, and they floated into springy curls. Yes, there it was again. She *did* look younger, Ellie wasn't imagining it.

Well, good. Maybe it helps having me here. The thought made Ellie's heart blow up another size or two, and she actually hopped with delight, her hair bouncing and her skirt swinging. The beads made delightful silvery music as they slid against each other, and when she walked in this dress, it would be easy to throw soundcharms to impress an onlooker.

"Take them upstairs, little dove." Auntie shook her housedress, pulling down the sleeves as if they had become ruffled. The blots of blue flowers on the fuchsia widened as she turned, trundling into the kitchen determinedly. "Auntie will make dinner, and butter to be churned, yes. Yes, yes." She mumbled as usual, and snapped a drying-charm at the butter dish.

Even if she was fey, or part-fey, she wasn't harmful. Maybe she was like Marya, housebound unless she had a stone in her pocket to anchor her. Or maybe she'd been fey-touched, or who knew? She'd been better to Ellie than anyone else, really.

Her conscience pinched. *Better than Ruby? Or Cami?*

Well, they'd probably found someone else to be their third wheel. Plenty of Juno girls would have been glad to fill that vacancy. Whoever they picked wouldn't have gigantic black problems looming over them. It was for the best, really. She had no business talking to Avery, even. She was just going to contaminate him the way she did everything else.

You're poison, Ell. Except maybe to Auntie.

That particular bit of knowledge burned inside her chest, but she said nothing. Maybe the Strep hadn't been that bad, but something inside Ellie had turned her rotten; maybe she hadn't really given the woman a chance. Laurissa was probably relieved she was gone, and Rita too. They could have each other, they didn't need her.

Nobody did except one batty old charmer. What did it matter? She scooped up her prizes carefully, holding them away from her dishwater-sodden shirt, and left the embroidered towel crumpled on the table, retreating so, so cautiously, stepping gently and almost holding her breath so she didn't inadvertently damage the beautiful, beautiful things. The oddest thought filled her up with sparkling charmlight, and managed to make her feel a little less toxic.

Wait until Avery sees this.

One dance, because she'd promised. Then she could come back, and work so hard Auntie would be proud to give her an apprenticeship.

TWENTY-SEVEN

THE NEXT DAY PASSED IN A FEVERISH BLUR. STILL OVER-cast, with thunder rumbling in the distance and breathless heat, and Auntie's fussing all day. There was butter and beeswax and rosewater, various potions and charms to make Ellie's skin glow and her pale hair behave. There was clove-water for her feet and shaving-charms during a lukewarm shower to make her legs and underarms smooth. Non-charmers had to buy them wedded to razors, with all the attendant risks of nicks and rusting. Having Potential to burn was good for *some* things.

There was lemon juice to bleach some of her freckles, and crumbly kohl worked with beeswax to line her eyes. A berry-red tincture to blush her lips, deodorant charms, a pack of moss and hot clay for her much-longer hair now—it brushed her shoulders, and she would be glad of the headband, she supposed.

There were long shivering silver drops for her ears, and the thread-thin chain for the tiny key was pretty long. Auntie had thought of everything, including underthings fine as a sylphire whisper.

Getting ready for a Ball, Charmer's or Midsummer, was always an all-day event. When her mother was alive, it had been full of giggling and warmth, and her father had despaired of ever arriving on time. *You're beautiful*, he would tell them both, *two beautiful girls, now let's* go! Later, Ruby and Cami had all crowded into Gran de Varre's tiny cottage or Cami's white bedroom in the Vultusino fortress, taking turns in the bathroom and elbowing each other in front of mirrors, sharing lip balm and powder and scented creams, fixing each other's dresses and . . .

Ellie shook herself out of the memory. That was in the Past, and she was concerned with the right-fucking-now. She would have to be on her toes tonight. One dance, and she'd hurry out the door. It might be rude, but at least she could pay Avery back for being kind. Then they would be even, and she wouldn't have to worry about him ever again.

Right? But nothing in her answered. She was too busy trying not to panic.

Auntie stepped back, sharp white teeth catching her upper lip gently as she surveyed her apprentice from top to toe.

Finally, Auntie nodded. "Yes," she said softly. "Yes, Columba."

She let out a long breath she hadn't even been aware of holding. "I look okay?"

"More beautiful than the Moon, my dove." Auntie's smile held all the softness in the world. "See?"

She stepped aside, and the mirror in the corner of the small gray room shimmered. Waterlilies carved into its dark wooden frame bent toward a slim, long-legged shape sheathed in fluid silver, pale hair curling over her ears and the feather tickling one side of her soft flawless cheek. Wide catlike gray eyes ringed with kohl sparkled, and the girl's berry-red lips stretched into a disbelieving smile.

The dress clung like solid water, and the charmed shoes twinkled as she took a step forward. Her knees peeped through the beaded fringe, shy satiny glances, and her smoothly muscled calves needed no stockings. Her bare arms almost crossed defensively, but then dropped and hung gracefully at her sides, her chewed-short fingernails blushing palest pink and smoothed to perfection.

That's not me. The girl in the mirror moved as Ellie did. She even frowned as Ellie did, with a vertical line between her eyebrows, their thin curves much darker than her hair. There was the same line to her jaw, and Ellie's high, wide-spaced cheekbones.

"Oh, Auntie. Wow." The girl's lips shaped Ellie's words, and it was still her voice. "*Wow.*"

"Sun's downing, soon," Auntie replied, pushing back strands of fine, sweat-soaked iron-gray hair. There was almost no white left on her head, and her cheeks were even smoother, if that was possible. "Until midnight, yes, when the Moon is at Her highest."

"I know. After that I'm on my own for travel." *You keep saying it, I've got it. Really. I'll be back long before then. Back . . . home?*

Did Auntie really, truly want her to stay? She seemed to.

"Look into the mirror, little apprentice. Promise Auntie."

"I'll come back, I promise." Ellie stared at her own familiar-strange face in the mirror. The reflection rippled like clear water, Potential from Ellie's skin filling the dress, the shoes, and the painstakingly applied layers of charm that would dazzle onlookers. "I prom—"

The girl in silver stood mannequin-still, her head tipped back. The mirror blurred, refusing to hold the shape crouched before her, the beads of the dress filling with indigo shadows as its head nuzzled at her chest.

A puncture, a glass needle driven into the heart, and the feather against her hair trembled, trembled. A draining, swimming sensation, not enough breath to fill slack lungs, a sapphire cracking violent lightning-sparks again and again as it struggled ineffectually. The thing's ancient bony hand was around her wrist, holding the ring and its deadly light away; it suckled greedily, its iron-gray head moving. Its other spindly, too-strong arm nipped around her slim waist, holding her up, and the

choking sound as the girl struggled to breathe was muffled by dead gray
feathers, fallen plumage packed tight around a tiny ticking thing.

Ellie shook her head. There had been a curious skip, as if a
phonograph needle had jumped from one groove to the next,
and she swayed. Auntie held her wrist, solicitously, and the
gray bedroom was full of a low rubescent glow.

Sunset already? She'd lost time. "What . . ." Slurred as if she
was drunk, or just now sobering up. "Auntie?"

"Must hurry now, little one. Come." Auntie stepped back,
and her eyes were black from lid to lid. She blinked, gray eye-
lashes sweeping down, and they were human again, the whites
as pearly as her teeth.

Ellie's left hand ached, her throat was dry, and her chest
throbbed. Her legs refused to hold her for a moment, knees
buckling, but she righted herself with an effort. "I feel weird."
Why was her tongue suddenly so huge? Her throat was full of
a metallic taste.

"She will recover, yes. Come, hurry. Sundown, little dove."

The stairs unreeled underneath her, and Ellie floated into a
dream. The front door opened like a flower, the good smells of
Auntie's house falling away and the heady spice of the garden a
cool draft, taking away the metal tang choking her.

Under the rose-weighted trellis it was dark, but when she
stepped outside Auntie's garden for the first time in forever,

there was a familiar elm-shaded street full of dusk's whispering shadows. At the curb was a moonlight-colored limousine, its driver in a gray velvet suit, his pinched ratlike face sending a stab of fear through her before she thought, *Well, Auntie must trust him.* The car door slammed, enclosing her in a soft burnt-orange interior that smelled of spices.

I'm dreaming. This is a dream.

She settled back against the buttery leather upholstery and half-closed her eyes.

TWENTY-EIGHT

SHE'D ONLY BEEN TO THE FLETCHER CHARM-CLAN'S main house twice, and both times she'd avoided Avery like the plague. She had a hazy memory of him throwing dirt clods at her in one of the ornamental gardens, and of her throwing one in return, splatting against his tailored party garb. It had felt good to get a little revenge.

Now, though, the limousine halted and a valet stepped forward. He was in the Fletcher clan's blue and gold, but he was party staff hired for the week—if it took a day for a girl to get ready for the Ball, it took a house a couple weeks, and the clan had to work on the whole thing for at least a month. Plus there were the bids, which meant the clan had to get a certain amount of support from all its subsidiaries *and* its allied clans, as well as outmaneuver rivals. No wonder they'd needed a whole bank of phones to keep up with arrangements.

The rat-faced driver said nothing the entire way, but his

dark gaze had drifted over her more than once in the rearview mirror, the smoked-glass partition between the front and back of the limo lowered all the way. She didn't even think of raising it, just stared back, willing the trembling all through her to die down.

By the time she stepped out, her numb fingers against the Fletcher valet's crisp white glove, she was a little better. Her head still swam, and she had to take deep breaths. The valet, a weedy-looking kid with ghostly acne on his cheeks and slicked-down dark hair, gave her an encouraging smile, and Ellie smiled back. A blush rose up the boy's throat, but she was already past him, climbing the granite stairs to the white colonnaded front of the Fletcher clan's beating heart.

The Fletchers had been charmers since the beginning of the Reeve, and it showed. The house was a gracious, spacious white chateau, its lines beautifully restrained but the white dingy compared to the glow of Auntie's fence. Everything about the outside world looked worn down and a little shabby now, and she supposed it was because she'd spent so long swimming in a sea of bright, active charming.

Shouldn't it look the same here? She pushed the thought away and it went quietly. She was occupied in getting up the stairs anyway.

The doors were open, and she was fashionably late, perhaps, because the sky had darkened and there was no crowd waiting

for entrance. She stepped into the front hall, and followed a
pointing hand—was he a butler, this black-masked man in a
black suit with strings of hair combed over his bald dome?
Maybe. The Fletchers could certainly afford one.

The doors to the ballroom were flung open as well, and
she floated toward them on a tide of silvery tinkling music.
Her heels chimed, and the strings of silver beads on her dress
each held a thread of indigo at their hearts. An active blanket
of charming followed her, fluttering and swirling—she couldn't
remember half the ones Auntie had applied, and the rest were
standard Ball fare. Light refraction, sweet smells, a subtle glow
around her; the remaining radiance was the dress itself, perking
up and singing louder, feeling the vibrant Potential rippling in
the air.

She stepped through the doors and into a warm bath of Potential thrown off by a bunch of active charmers all in one place
and in a heightened emotional state. The wall of dreamlike calm
around her threatened to crack as a hush fell under the tinkling
crystal chandeliers.

So bright. Laurissa would hate it. The smile on her face was a
mask again, familiar and hateful. *Is she here? Is she?*

The crowd parted. They were staring. Charmers in fantasti-
cal dresses, like Amy Bolletta in a flaming-red handkerchief-hem
skirt and a sweetheart bodice, Tintoretto shoes and a look of
absolute thunderstruck awe on her nasty blonde face. The head

of the Valseth charm-clan—they did protection work, mostly, and buffering for Babbage components—with her hennaed hair piled atop her head and a glittering-blue Auberme sheath that Laurissa would have *killed* to wear, stared as she clung to her husband's arm. The men were all in black and white tails, since it was formal, so they had to charm more intensively to stand out amid bright female plumage.

The high-ceilinged ballroom, its wooden floor a mellow glow, was the throat of a whale. It was too bright, and the chandeliers tinkled madly. There would be no suppressors for this party— if you couldn't handle charm being thrown, you shouldn't be here, and the staff had all signed waivers and would be paid quadruple for the risk. You couldn't stint when you threw a Midsummer Ball, that's why it took a whole clan to do it.

Is he here? Is Laurissa? Ellie couldn't look everywhere at once, and they were staring. All of them.

The terrible feeling that she might look ridiculous un-hinged her stomach, and she suppressed a sour flood of bile at the back of her throat. *I'm going to throw up. I'm going to—*

"Ellie." Very soft, at her elbow.

She turned, her entire body leaden with terror.

Avery's smile was a warm bath dispelling the fear, sunshine through fog. His hair burned with golden highlights, and he seemed impossibly tall. He looked just as vivid as everything in

Auntie's house, and her sigh of relief made one of the sweet-smell charms fill everything around her with cinnamon.

"Hi," she managed, weakly.

"You look . . ." His pause was the stuff of nightmares, but he was *smiling*. He wouldn't look at her that way if she was hideous, right? His tux was impeccable, and he held out a hand—his skin was warm, and the instant his fingers closed around hers she felt like she could breathe again. "You look *incredible*, Sinder."

What a relief. "Thanks. I was beginning to be afraid."

"You? Never."

Not now that you're here, no. Just one dance and she would leave. But it was nice to feel . . . what? "They're staring."

"Because you're beautiful." His free hand flicked, and charm-flitters sparked into being, like the fireflies that filled Auntie's garden. "I mean, you're always beautiful, but you're . . . oh, *hell*."

A laugh jolted out of her sideways, and the charmflitters flashed blue, blinking in almost random semaphore. Her skin was alive again, every inch of her sparking. "Are you kidding? Every time you show up I'm *en déshabillée*."

"Speak some more French, and you'll get there quicker, too." He hadn't let go of her hand. The flitters made thin crystalline singing noises. It was a nice trick. "You want a drink? Or . . . I mean, there's food, or . . ."

"I promised you a dance." *I have to go back to Auntie. This isn't what I wanted.*

Wasn't it? Why go to all this trouble, run the risk of the Strep seeing her, if she hadn't wanted to be right here, looking up at Avery Fletcher and feeling every atom of her body completely awake, for once? Suddenly feeling a little less ugly and threadbare? "Is Laurissa here?"

"I haven't seen her." He looked uneasy now, a faint line between his eyebrows. "You're pretty pale. Is it a charm?"

"Nope. Just me." *I've been working in the garden, I should be brown as Ruby in the summer.* A pinch under her collarbone—when Dad was alive, she'd always brought Ruby and Cami to the Ball. The three of them would sneak honeywine coolers and find a corner, giggling and mocking the glittering whirl of fashion *sotto voce.*

Was there another girl taking her place in Juno's halls? And Rita, had she been taking Ellie's place on Perrault Street?

Well, that was what she wanted, wasn't it? That was what everyone wanted once Dad was gone. Stick me in a corner, rub me out like a stain, make me behave. Or just make me vanish. Same thing. "I've just been . . . well, you know. Learning a lot. Working in the garden. It's nice. You?"

"Job offers. Some good ones since I'm settled. Deciding what I want to do once I finish summer vacation. Mom's still hoping I'll Sigil." A shrug, disturbing the line of his suit, and the buzz of conversation had started around them again. Maybe he had some sort of charm to make people stop looking at her so funny. "Hope springs eternal, you know. Are you going to go for your boards?"

"I can't just yet." *Let's just leave it at that.* "You want to dance, or—"

"Actually . . . I want to apologize."

"For what?" What could *he* have to apologize for?

He glanced up over her shoulder. "Well, I did want you here. That was the biggest thing."

A soft hand touched her bare arm, fingernails scraping slightly. Ellie froze. But it was only Cami, the Vultusino girl's ivory silk slip-dress fluttering a little around her knees. She wore a crown of silvery charmed tinsel-flowers, her hair was a blue-tinted waterfall of ink, and the transparent relief and naked hope on her pretty face was a knife to the heart.

"*There* you are." Ruby was on Ellie's other side, vivid as usual in a deep crimson del Paco dress, halter-backed and subtly sequined with tiny sparkling crystals. "Mithrus, we've been looking *everywhere* for you. What have you done to your hair? And my God, that dress is killer. You *could* have called, you know."

Ellie stared. She could find nothing to say.

"I'm sorry." Avery's hand tightened on hers. Was she trying to pull away?

"Mother H-heloise is w-w-worried." Cami's blue eyes had filled with tears. The stutter had returned, just like a bad habit. "She called the p-police. The Strep s-said you'd r-run away.

N-n-nico has a r-r-reward out f-for information about you. I th-thought—"

"Auntie doesn't have a phone." *I sound dazed.* "You invited me so everyone could see I was still alive, right?" He must have invited Ruby and Cami, because they couldn't attend otherwise.

Not because he wanted to see her. The nausea was back, filling her throat with hot sourness.

Avery actually had the grace to look ashamed. "No. I mean, yes, but no. I wanted to—"

"Just what *did* you want?" The constriction in her throat didn't let the shout out. Instead, she sounded like she'd been punched. If she talked any louder she was going to spray whatever she'd had to eat today—probably the morning's bread and honey, since she'd been too nervous for lunch—all over his tux.

He wouldn't let go of her hand, even though she tried to pull back. "Look, Ellie, I worry about you, okay? You just vanished, and when I found you—"

"Yeah, let's talk about that." Ruby, as usual, wasn't going to sit around and let everyone be in suspense about how she felt. "You ran right off school grounds and *disappeared*. Mithrus, Ellie, why didn't you at least call? I went to Gran and the cousins scraped the city; we couldn't find you. Where have you been hiding? Are you okay? You look . . ."

Ridiculous? Stupid? Afraid? "What do I look like, huh? Tell me." Her throat still wouldn't work right. She tried to jerk her hand back out of Avery's, but he wasn't giving up.

"Ellie—" He almost pulled her off balance. "Please. Please just *listen.*"

"I think I've heard enough." She tried to pull away again. "Stop it. Just *stop.*"

"You disappeared for m-months." Cami didn't let go of her arm, either, and the humming preternatural strength of Family just under that soft grasp made Ellie freeze. "He's been trying locator charms. So have the p-p-police. The S-s-strep's h-holed up in that h-house, and there's been a m-magistrate inquiry—"

"An inquiry?" *Because I was gone, but they didn't have a body or any evidence. Oh, God. She'll be furious. Especially if they searched the house. How did she cover up the black charming? Oh, you know she's got her ways.*

The dreamlike feeling was back. The beads on her dress shivered, chiming musically. *Oh, God. I'll never get a license. I can just stay with Auntie, though, right? She'll teach me everything and then . . . and then . . .*

Then what? Spend her entire life tending Auntie's garden? It didn't sound too bad, but still.

"There wasn't enough proof—of *anything*—to indict." Avery glanced over Ellie's shoulder. "Oh, boy. Incoming."

Oh, God, what now? She tried to take her hand away, but he wasn't having any of it.

The crowd of brightly colored charmers parted, and a slim dark-eyed woman appeared. She had Avery's cheekbones and a fantastic leaf-green Armaio gown, veined with glittering charmlight. Avery had obviously learned the charmflitter trick from her, because she was attended by a swarm of bright green dazzles moving around her head much as bees or fireflies did around Auntie's. It was odd, but something else about the woman reminded her of Auntie, too—a tilt to her head, maybe? Or the shape of her jawline?

"The mystery girl!" she said brightly. "Ellen, right? Avery can't say enough about you."

"Mom." He still wouldn't let go of her hand. "This is Ellen Sinder. I told you about—"

"About that terrible woman passing off another charmer's work as her own. Yes. Which reminds me, the Council has her under review. If you could charm a piece in front of us for comparison, Miss Sinder, it would be proof of a very grave offense indeed." Avery's mother paused, and it struck Ellie that she was moving cautiously forward, as if she thought Ell was going to bolt.

Which was a distinct possibility.

"There's also the matter of your Sigil, clearly visible in the charmed pieces now that we know Ms. Choquefort-Sinder did not perform them." Mrs. Fletcher folded her arms, sternly. "I can't understand why Juno didn't have you registered, really.

And your work is so exquisite, well, we'd offer you a place in the clan. If you want it."

"*Mom!*" Avery's cheeks had reddened. Did he look . . . yes, he did. Sheepish. And embarrassed.

"What?" She almost rolled her eyes, a startlingly young movement in a parental adult. "She's a better charmer than you, Ave, if those pieces are any indication. You'll be lucky if she teaches you a few things." Her smile stretched, and she actually looked *mischievous*. "He's had the maddest crush on you for the longest time. You can't imagine."

"*Mother!*"

"This is really weird," Ruby muttered. "Does anyone else see how weird this is?"

Ellie struggled to think. The world had taken a screeching left turn, and maybe it was being at Auntie's that had robbed her of the ability to keep her balance.

Once you relaxed, the world just threw something else at you. There wasn't any way to win, ever.

Laurissa. He told his mother Laurissa was passing off my work as hers. "You told her?" The nightmare just kept getting worse. "She's going to *kill* me."

"Ellen . . ." Mrs. Fletcher's smile faltered. She glanced at her son, at Cami's set, pained face, and at Ruby. "Tonight we'll take you to the police station. There's nothing to be afraid of. Your stepmother . . . well, let's put it this way: Her business practices are not really what they should be." She took another step closer, and Ellie twitched nervously. "There's been disturbing rumors about her for quite some time. But your father . . . well, he had diplomatic immunity, so—"

"My father?" *Oh, sure, let's blame him.* "What about him?"

"Olivia?" Avery's father appeared from the side. Absolutely nobody was now paying any attention to Ellie, because a tinkling flood of music had begun to thread through the air. The best part of the Midsummer Ball was about to start. "You're not going to believe this." He leaned down, murmuring in her ear, and the sight of them together—a mother, a father, the way he stooped a little as if being close to her was the best and easiest thing in the world—spilled terrible heat into Ellie's stomach.

She finally succeeded in getting her fingers free of Avery's. Cami's hand fell away from her arm as well. "S-s-see?" the Vultusino girl whispered. "His m-mother's on the Council. You can show them the Strep's been using your work. And we can go to the p-p-police, or to N-n-nico if you—"

Ellie darted a venomous glance at Avery. Was there *anyone* he hadn't told about the Strep using her for a workhorse?

Next he'd say something about Auntie, and if there was trouble, there would go Ellie's apprenticeship to the best charmer she'd ever known. The old woman hadn't done anything other than *help* her, and Ellie, just by breathing, was going to drag her into Laurissa's sights.

I'm poison. The sudden burst of knowledge was copper-edged, sickening. "Mithrus *Christ*," she hissed, "*stop* it. Don't you see?" *Of course they don't. Nobody does.*

"You don't have to be afraid." Avery kept trying to grab her hand again. "Ell, my mom, she knows about Laurissa—"

"*Nobody* knows about Laurissa," she snapped. "She's gotten *this* far by making people do what she wants, she's just going to run right over anyone who gets in her way. Even the Council, for God's sake. Even an inquiry, since I'm *obviously* alive." *And now your mother is right in front of her, and so is Auntie. If something happens it will be my fault, as usual.* "I am not a *charity case.* I do not need *help.*"

"Don't be an idiot." Ruby tossed her head. "Of *course* you need help. I mean, you're practically *homeless,* and you're not even in *school.* You missed finals, and Mother Hel gave Cami and me talking-tos for weeks as if we knew where you were. You ran off in front of *everyone,* Cami's been crying her eyes out thinking you might be dead in a ditch somewhere—"

"I get it, Ruby. I'm a huge problem, and someone needs to solve me, right? And *you*—" She rounded on Avery. "You think you're the charmer who's going to break the Unspeakable Riddle, right? Just ride in with your mother and your nice little charm-clan and save me, right? The real world doesn't work like that, Fletcher."

There was a spark in his gold-green eyes now, and it flared.

"Yeah, well, you're a whole, what, sixteen? You don't have that hot a grasp of the real world either. What are you going to do, go charm on Southking to make ends meet, and let Laurissa get away with all this?"

"Southking?" Cami was having a little trouble keeping up. It wouldn't last. "Ellie—"

"*Just stop!*" she screamed, and the chandeliers swung, chiming. The sound was a nightmare echo. For a moment the lights dimmed, and she expected to see the stairs again, Laurissa's body tumbling down—and that was really all the Strep had to do, right? Accuse Ellie of trying to kill her, and use Rita to back it up. That girl would swear to anything to get the Strep off her back or keep the peace, because *she* had to live in that stone-towered house on Perrault Street, too.

Goodbye Auntie, goodbye apprenticeship, goodbye to everything. She'd be lucky if she was sent out to a kolkhoz and worked to death if she was convicted of trying to kill another charmer. All because she'd stupidly, foolishly believed she had a chance.

The beads on Ellie's dress clashed and slithered. She skipped back nervously, avoiding Avery's hand. He was *still* trying to hold onto her, the idiot. "I don't need charity," she informed them all. "From *anyone*. Thanks, but no thanks. I was stupid to come here. You can *all* go to hell."

She turned, staggering a little as the low heel caught a bit on uneven flooring. They could all dance right over it, but of course *she* would trip. It was the same old story. The music swelled again, and Avery's father said something that rhymed with Ellie's name, but she was already moving.

"Ellie . . ." Cami, as if she'd lost all her air.

"Let her go," Ruby answered, pitilessly. "At least we know she's alive. If she's going to be a bitch about it, let her go."

Exactly, Ellie thought. *Thanks, Ruby. Thanks a bundle.*

She walked quickly, with her head held high.

Nobody stopped her.

TWENTY-NINE

THE RAT-FACED DRIVER DIDN'T SAY A WORD, JUST closed her into the eggshell limousine and walked steadily around the front to the driver's door. When he dropped down into his seat, his gray-gloved hands closing around the wheel, Ellie summoned up her courage.

"Perrault Street," she said. "The 1800 block. Do you know where that is?"

A single nod. His hat brim had begun to droop a little, and there was a shadow on his cheeks. Stubble, maybe.

It didn't matter. "Take me there. Please."

Another single nod. Ellie sagged against the pumpkin-colored leather, and the shaking weakness was all through her. *I should have known better. I know I should have known better.*

Streets slipped away underneath the limo's tires; the pale car threaded a needle's eye between the charm-clan estates, their gates closed and secretive. New Haven twinkled with lights, the diseased glow of the core rising like a beacon and staining the cloud ceiling. The moon was hiding, and everything had turned sticky-sultry. Thunder muttered restlessly, a giant sleep-talking animal in the sky.

What are you going to do, Ellie? You need a plan.

The trouble was, her plans never worked out. She did better when she just ran blindly, didn't she? Right now it was Rita she was thinking about. Pale, pudgy Rita. Who was just about Ellie's age. Who threw her arms around the Strep and hugged her. Who slammed doors and crept around and sneaked and spied, but who also dropped a bottle of sylph-ether when she didn't have to.

I know what you're doing . . . acting friendly . . .

There was a black suspicion in the very back of Ellie's head, not quite formed and, she supposed, more terrifying than it would be if she just let herself think it out. Instead, she tuned her brain to a blank, formless hum, and her mother's ring glowed a little as she stared at it.

It was restful in here, the soft upholstery and the shushing tires and the world going past outside. It wasn't as nice as driving with Avery—

Don't think about that.

It was useless, because he was creeping in, filling up the formless buzz inside her head.

I hate him. He broke his word.

He'd kept reaching for her hand. With his mother standing right there, practically inviting Ellie into the clan. Wouldn't that be something? With a charm-clan behind her, she could get a decent job; she would be assured of an apprenticeship and a license. . . .

But there was Laurissa. Spreading like a stain between Ellie and everything that might have given her a break. She could make Avery's mother sorry, *plenty* sorry, and that would make Avery sorry too. Auntie was old, how much damage would the Strep do to *her*? Laurissa wasn't in a buffered jail cell, so they hadn't found any evidence of black charming at the house if they'd searched it. She was free to walk around and be just as soft and dulcet and treacherous as she could until she struck, and there would be no evidence afterward, either.

It was all so ridiculously clear now that she'd thought about it. The Strep could accuse Ell of attempted murder, Rita would back her up, and then what? A kolkhoz somewhere, if she survived transport through the Waste.

Would that be so bad? Yeah, there would be the Waste pressing against the sinkstone and electric-wire fences, and backbreaking work, and the weather, and probably jacks like Cryboy and his gang. They'd send her to a Twist-free kolkhoz, at least, and she'd die before she was forty, worn out by the work and the weather.

So why was she thinking about Rita, then? Was it just

self-insurance? Did it matter if she got the girl away from the Strep?

Yeah, you're going to ride in and save her, just like you helped save Cami. Remember how good that felt? Like you'd finally done something right. Something nobody could argue with, and you'd earned all that charity they've been handing out ever since the Strep got nasty.

A long frustrated sigh, and the feather scraped against the side of her face. She carefully worked the headband free, and her hair wasn't drooping, at least. The dress was just as gorgeous, even if the beads were a little uncomfortable to sit on.

It's not mine, though. Even Auntie's charitable.

At Auntie's, Ellie *earned* her keep, didn't she? She weeded, she cleaned, she cooked, she learned everything the old charmer could teach her. Surely she wouldn't have let Ellie stay so long otherwise? She was Auntie's apprentice.

And what? You bring Rita there and all of a sudden there's someone else to help Auntie.

Rita wasn't a charmer. Even thinking about her in the tiny little charmer's cottage, feeling the stab of worry and bleak black almost-jealousy, made Ellie's stomach flip. It wasn't right to feel that way about someone caught in the same trap you'd just escaped. She was going to save Rita and earn a little peace.

Didn't she deserve some? Maybe not, since she ruined everything she came near.

Down Severson Hill, a left onto Colsonal Avenue. The estates were no more; instead it was narrow middle-class homes with fenced backyards, some with charm-burning globes over narrow, cracking driveways that had been laid in the big boom of the seventies. A decent neighborhood, a *nice* one, away from the core.

What if Dad had been something other than a lawyer, and Mom something other than a high-powered textile charmer? The kids around here would go to Hollow Hills, not as high-crust as Juno but certainly not *public*. The public schools were for kids who were both poor and didn't have enough Potential to snuff a candle.

Would things have been better, maybe, if she'd been at Hollow Hills? No Ruby, of course, no Cami. No Avery throwing sand at her or being so . . . whatever he was.

Maybe no Laurissa, either. Did it balance out?

The houses got larger and larger. These weren't the charm-clan estates, but they began to have walls in unconscious (or very conscious) imitation. Right after the Reeve, any place that could afford a wall built one, and now it was tradition. If you suddenly gained the money, you went for walls. *Nouveau riche*, Mom had said once, her mouth twitching, and her father had frowned a little. *Nouveau murs*, he had replied, and they had laughed together, and oh how she missed that sound. She had laughed as well, too young to understand the joke but loving the sound their voices made together.

The walls rose, and Ellie began to shiver. A sullen flash of lightning, probably over the bay; she held her breath and counted.

Before she finished counting, though, the limousine slowed to a crawl. How was it possible? She hadn't even noticed the four turns and the long stretch through Heathline to get to Perrault.

Nothing's moving like it should.

The thought sent ice cubes trailing down her back. When the rat-driver brought the car to a soundless stop in front of the iron gates with the Sigil of high-heel shoes warped and glowing dull red, she wasn't even surprised when a patch of darkness on his neck took on a sheen like fur. He lifted one wrist and tapped it with a point-nailed finger.

Close to midnight? It can't be. But then, dusk is late in summer.

"I know," she murmured, and slid toward the door. He didn't move to open it for her, and she wasn't really surprised either when she shut it behind her—quiet, or as quietly as she could—and the car roused itself, creeping away down the street. Maybe he'd wait under a tree, but she doubted it.

THIRTY

THE BACKYARD WAS A JUNGLE NOW, AND LAURISSA HAD evidently fired the landscapers for the front too. There was a breath of something rotting, foul and rank and wet, probably the pool behind the tangle of black-spotted rosebushes, their leaves dropping early. Withered but strangely juicy, their long thorny arms stretched and shivered as she glanced nervously at them.

The kitchen door was locked, but she stretched to reach overhead, standing on tiptoes, wishing the beads on the dress didn't clash and shiver. The key was there, another of her little secrets, and she had a moment's brief burst of hope before the knob squeaked.

She stepped back, almost catching her heel on the edge of the stair, and the door ghosted itself open. A pallid, haggard face under a mop of dirty hair stared out, and for one heartstopping second Ellie teetered on the precipice, because it was Laurissa's face, the dull rage-hot gaze and the sharp nose, the high cheek-bones and the long elegant fingers as she reached out.

Intuition coalesced, and she finally understood what she had always seen in Laurissa's "sister." *Oh, wow.*

Rita's hand closed around Ellie's upper arm. "What are you *doing* here?" the girl whisper-hissed, and Ellie's heart attack turned into an acid burp.

Well, isn't that embarrassing. "Rita?" A croak, she tasted the bile in the back of her throat.

"If *she* wakes up she'll kill you." The other girl's fingers dug in. "Leave her *alone*. She's been doing poppy to keep charming, and I dosed her double tonight so she'd stay away from the Ball."

Poppy? It'll eat her up. "Mithrus Christ." Ellie blinked. Another flash of lightning, somewhere overhead. "You look *old*." A torpid mutter as the sky overhead twitched its cloudy skin again.

"You look like a skank, so we're even," Rita whispered fiercely in reply. "You have got to get out of here. If she wakes up—"

"I came to get you." Her lips were numb. "Look, Rita . . . I've found a place. A safe place. You and me, we can—"

"Dressed like that?" A low, contemptuous laugh. "Did they throw you out of the Ball? They would, you know. They're all like that. *Charmers.*"

What do you have against them? Then again, the Strep was

plenty to have against *anyone*. You could hold her against the whole human species. Ellie tried again. "I came to get you, Rita. She . . . you don't have to stay here. You don't have to . . . to get hurt."

"What do *you* know?" Another bitter little laugh, and another flash of lightning showed the kitchen behind Rita's slim shoulders. She was just as thin as Ellie now, but still wearing that goddamn peach sweater. It hung on her now like—

. . . a scarecrow . . .

—like a stretched, borrowed skin. Was she molting? Turning into a smaller version of Laurissa, talons, scrawny angry neck, and all? Was it even worth trying to save someone like that?

It has to be.

"I know she's not your sister." Quietly, but that numbness in her mouth was an enemy. She had to fight it, probably like Cami fought her stutter. "She's a black charmer, she's been one for *years*, and she's been hiding it. She used up all your charm too, didn't she? She took your Potential."

The blackest charming of all, one the hedge of restrictions and protections around Juno was built to avoid. Before Potential settled, you could do a lot of things—like take it, especially from a blood relation.

Rita's head snapped aside, teeth bared, as if she'd been slapped. She let go of Ellie's arm, and it was Ellie's turn to lean forward, grabbing blindly. She got a handful of the peach sweater, and found the material was surprisingly soft. It crumpled in her fist, and Rita's immediate flinch was terrifying.

Because Ellie didn't mind if the girl cowered, as long as she *listened*, and who did that remind her of? Did it soothe some broken thing inside the Strep when she made someone smaller cringe? Maybe.

Now all the charmweed benders made sense, and all her boyfriends sent home drained. Feeding off other people's Potential to stave off Twisting for a while, scrabbling to get as much money as she could—another intuition blurred under Ellie's skin.

Hadn't Ellie herself been looking for credits any way possible, too? Was there something the Strep had wanted to escape . . . and had Dad been her way out, just like Avery might have been Ellie's?

What did that make Ellie, then? Not a physical copy the way Rita was, but similar all the same. Her skin crawled, and the itchy nasty sensation was all over her.

I'm not like her. I'm not. But the sneaking suspicion just wouldn't go away.

"Listen." She forgot to whisper. "There's a safe place, where she can't find us. I'll take you, and however much you hate me is fine, I don't care. If she's on poppy it's not going to end well, and you'll catch the worst of it. Let's just *go.* You can escape her. You really can." She groped for words, found them. "You don't have to put up with this. And . . . I *owe* you."

Even if you are a bitch. Was Rita really that bad? Hadn't Ellie been secretly relieved someone else would get the short end of the stick? Relieved that Rita was getting the random slaps and hissed insults—after all, there was plenty to go around, wasn't there.

She realized, miserably, that she could scrub and scrub, but she was never going to feel clean again.

"You? Owe *me?*" Rita slapped at her hand. "Get *off.* You don't owe me *anything.* Leave me alone."

"I'm trying to *help* you, you idiot—"

Rita shrank back, her dark eyes suddenly swimming. She cocked her head, and Ellie froze. She heard nothing but the rumble of thunder. Even the faint tinge of color drained from Rita's gaunt face, leaving her chalk-cheesy in the dimness. A hot breeze touched Ellie's bare calves, and there was a tinkle as some silver bugle-beads, shaken free, hit the back step.

"Sssssweethearrt?" A long, low, slurred word, breathed from the kitchen behind Rita. "What's haaaaappening out heeere?"

It was the Strep, but the shape was . . .

Mithrus. What's happened to her?

Hunching, its belly thickly distended, and Potential rising in corkscrew-invisible scarves of charmlight, subtly *wrong.* Ellie blinked, inhaling sharply, and the fear was a sharp silver icicle nailed all the way through her, crown to soles.

She looks like a—

Fabric tore. Rita shoved her, *hard*, and Ellie's left shoe flew off as she pinwheeled her arms, trying to keep her balance. The door slammed and she hit the pavers, a starry jolt of pain as she lost consciousness for a bare second. Beads scattered, rolling, and when she surfaced again she had scrambled to her feet and was limp-running, halting only to peel off her right shoe and hold it like a weapon as she fled.

The windows were suddenly full of golden electric light, and the entire stone pile of the house resonated like a plucked string. The kitchen door was wrenched open again, and there was a long, cheated howl.

The beads dropped, one after another, like the warm rain splattering dry gardens and dusty pavements in half-credit-coin drops. Thunder wallowed, splashing in the sky again, and New Haven took a breath before it plunged into the storm. Through that endless inhale ran a shivering girl, her dress steam-melting like soaked tissue paper. Her hair fell in wet strings, and behind her the thump-dragging footsteps of a nightmare beast with heavy shoulders and a terribly swollen belly grew louder and louder.

There was the limousine, its paint pitted and scarred by the rain, its taillights a dull glare. Ellie fumbled at the back door, managed to tear it open though the hinges gave a scream of protest, and threw herself inside.

The engine knocked, and the pale car leapt forward as if it

never intended to stay still. Lurching and squealing, the driver's thin shoulders under a motheaten jacket and his hands shrinking and turning clawlike at the wheel, the limousine ran as limpingly as she had. The rain drummed the roof, and soon it would eat its way through.

Oh Mithrus. Mithrus Christ, please. Great shudders gripped Ellie's body in waves. She stared at the car's roof, wondering if the entire thing was going to melt around her like Harvest Festival cotton candy. She lay curled on the floor, and the pumpkin-colored leather spread with rotten mildewed staining. The patches were growing, slowly but surely, and the seat sagged.

Charmwork, it's all charm. Fey, maybe. The trembling wouldn't let her think straight. Worn down, hollowed out, emptied by terror, she lay and felt the beads trickle slowly away, her rain-damp warmth eating at the fabric.

At least it was pretty when it mattered. Her throat stung, and her heart hurt, pounding in her head. She couldn't get her lungs to fill up, and her mother's ring was dead and dark, weighing down her entire leaden arm.

Her heart labored, and she had a sudden image of her veins as a roadmap, a collection of dusty highways winding through a desert, heading nowhere. Just a thin trickle of red dust where once there had been precious liquid. The Waste around New Haven was deep forest, but there were old dry glass negatives of desert-Waste to the west, sand and cactuses torqued into weird shapes, their begging fingers reaching to snare the unwary and herds of minotaur-shaped cattle roaming. Out west the cities had permeable borders, and curfews, and the Night Watch rode the streets between dusk and dawn to hunt down anything that straggled in from the dangerous wilderness outside.

Maybe Ellie could even run that far, one day.

But everything inside her was dry as dust. Her throat was slick sunbaked glass, and the shuddering jolting of the limousine drew away, as if down a long tunnel. Diamond lightning flashed, and her eyelids fluttered.

Laurissa's on the poppy. I wonder if she's firing it with charged sylph-ether.

It didn't matter.

Cold little kisses all over her body. Ellie stirred, flinched as a dead-white glaring flash speared her brain. The grass underneath her was slick and crushed, and there was a familiar trellis overhead. Frilled roses closed themselves tightly against the lashing rain, and Ellie blinked as she realized she was almost naked, icy beads melting from her clinging dress. Her feet were bare, and there was moss wrapped around her right hand, where she had been clutching a shoe.

Thunder roared, and she sat bolt upright. It took two tries for her to get to her feet, and as she edged under the trellis and onto the crushed-shell path she had to move gingerly. Not only were the shells sharp and her soles tender, but the rose vines stretched too, their thorns long and wicked. One striped across her upper arm, and Ellie cried out thinly, icy water threading down her back.

Vapor lifted from her skin in tiny traceries, fueled by her shivering warmth, and she sucked in sharp breaths as she tried to step lightly. After a little while she could move aside onto the lawn instead, but she still had to pick her way carefully.

Another shutterflash lit the garden, and the rain intensified into a silver curtain. She raised her head, blinking, and for a moment it looked like Auntie's trim house was steaming and melting too, bricks scorched and pitted, the quartzlike front step runneling, its chimney sagging.

Was something happening to Auntie?

No! Please, no! She picked up the pace, and the steps were sticky. Her feet stung, leaving dark prints on the softening mass.

The warped, rotting door swung wide. "Auntie?" Her voice sounded very small. "Auntie, please be okay . . ."

If she's not okay, it's your fault. You shouldn't have left. You messed everything up. Of course you did. Ellie Sinder, the charity case. Poison. Eating everything up, just like Laurissa.

She heard Mother Heloise's voice from a long time ago, on some other interminable chapel morning. *For Mithrus said, lo, thou becometh what is despised.* Cami's welcome warmth next to her, and choco-beechgum scent from Ruby on her other side.

All that was gone. She had probably fucked *them* up royally too. Just like everything else.

The walls sagged, and from the kitchen came a rustling, dry cornhusks and straw. Ellie grabbed at the wall, her heart suddenly a dry throbbing chunk of gristle in her throat. "Auntie?" The cherry parlor was a dark cave full of skewed shapes. The whisper made the entire hall ripple, as if her very presence was disturbing the knotted, snarled tangle of energy that lay below everyday reality.

It probably is. God knows you're a disruption everywhere else, Ell.

The rustling filled her head with the image of cornfields, and a blue velvet jacket. She almost *saw* the scarecrow jerking and twisting, something inside its stuffed-heavy body flopping and twisting desperately.

"Little Columba."

The world thudded back into place, and Ellie let out a half-sob. The last beads spilled away; the dress was a cobweb, clinging to steaming, living skin.

Auntie stood on the stairs, a smear of gray and black. Thunder rattled again, shaking the roof, and Ellie let go of the wall. The cottage looked just as it had for the past months, solid and real, the stairs straight and square, the walls creamy white, a gleam from the cinnamon kitchen down the hall. The cherry parlor exhaled a breath of sweetness, its fussy overstuffed furniture grinning. The rustling faded, like a train whistle vanishing into the Waste.

She's fine. Everything's going to be okay.

"Auntie!" She tacked away from the wall, grabbed the licorice banister. It was warm and comforting under her palm; it had helped her up the stairs so many times before. "I'm sorry, the dress—Auntie, I thought you were . . ."

The old woman smiled. Her hair was a river of ink; her white, white teeth gleamed. "Little singed dove, come back to the nest with her fiery self." Little speckles of foxfire revolved around her head. "A good apprentice for Auntie."

Wait. She's beautiful. Ellie blinked several times, squeezing hot water out of her eyes. "I had to. Auntie, she's . . . everything's *wrong*, everything's messed up—"

"Shhhhh." She beckoned, and her eyes were black from lid to lid. There on the stairs, she was suddenly taller. Instead of a violently colored housedress, soft black motheaten velvet fell in heavy folds. Tiny holes pricked in the folds of night showed white skin, and Ellie's heart gave another galvanic leap.

She's younger. She was old before, now she's not.

"Come to Auntie, sweetheart." She held out her arms, and the pain was a river. It shook Ellie from top to toe and filled up her nose with snot, slicked her cheeks with wet heat and pulled every tight-strung nerve in her tired, drained body.

It shouldn't hurt this much to live. But really, what did she have to live *for?*

Thunder again, shaking the cottage. For a bare moment,

Auntie recoiled, her teeth showing. Long, curved needle-teeth flashed like the lightning, so, so white. Then she recovered and held out her long arms again, not bony anymore but smoothly muscled and young. "Come," she whispered, and her face ran like clay under moving water.

The sobs came continuously now, shaking Ellie back and forth like a small animal in a terrier's teeth.

Because the face that surfaced from that running-clay formlessness was terribly, softly familiar. The ring on Ellie's right hand woke with a cascade of blue sparks.

"Sweetheart, little girl." Her mother smiled with razor teeth, standing on the stairs. "Come upstairs. Let me hold you. Nothing will ever trouble my little dove again, no. Come. There is a room prepared, with a door to lock. It is soft and pleasant here, is it not?"

More thunder, and a sound Ellie couldn't identify. She stared, her neck cramping as she moved forward, dreamlike, the bruise high up on the left side of her chest flowering with sweet insistent pain. A rhythmic thudding, interspersed with crackles.

"Mommy?" It was a child's voice, small and questioning. The ring seized her finger in an iron grip, but the thing that wore her mother's face hissed, baleful sparks lighting in her black eyes, and the circle of charmed silver loosened, sliding free. Laurissa had eyed it hungrily, and now it fell from Ellie's finger without struggle or qualm. It chimed as it hit the floor, and she put one bare, bleeding foot on the first stair.

"That's right," Auntie-no-more cooed softly. "Come to me, little Columba. Little apprentice. Come to me, let me take away the pain."

Charm it free, Ellie thought, deliriously. *She wants me. At least someone does.* Fever all through her, chattering her teeth, wringing sweat from her hot, living skin. So what if Auntie looked like her mother? It didn't matter.

What mattered was the wanting. And the end to all the pain and thrashing and poison.

Give it up. It's all you have left.

"Come," Auntie whispered. Ellie halted, gripping the banister. It gave slightly under her fingers, spongy, resilient.

"Ellie!" Someone screaming her name, desperately. A familiar voice. Growling, thundering lightning flashed again. A high crystal note, like a wet wineglass stroked with a heavy finger, the ridges and whorls that made up identity dragging along a thin rim. *"Ellie! Please!"*

She took another step. Her mother smiled encouragingly. "Come up, my darling. Come." Beckoning, telling her to hurry.

Her feet stung. Everything in her was lead, weighing her down, dragging on her. She stared at her mother's black, black eyes, and the sparkles over her mother's head were *almost* making a pattern. If she kept looking, she might find it, as long as she kept moving forward. That was the main thing.

Just keep moving. Another step. Her feet ached, but it was a

faraway pain. The frantic hammering was also distant. Then, she
had a curious thought.

*There's more than one way to drown. Ruby always told me I
wouldn't die while she found me amusing. Ruby . . . Cami . . .*

"*Ellie!*" Creaking, crackling, a snarling sound.

She was almost close enough, reaching out with one damp,
disbelieving hand. Her mother beckoned again, her wide eager
smile mirroring Ellie's own joy. It was all a terrible dream, and
soon she would be in her mother's arms where she belonged,
and everything would be fine. She would rest, at last, behind
a locked door upstairs in Auntie's wonderful, snug little house.
She would *belong*, and when she closed her eyes the twin needles
would drive into her chest and there would be nothing to worry
about ever again.

"Little dove," her mother whispered.

The front door, riven, exploded into sugary fragments. They
piled through, a flash of bright copper, a streak of gold, and long
black hair. Cami's teeth flashed as she grimaced, her sensitive
nose wrinkling, and Ruby, strangely, crouched on the floor, her
fingers spread against the melting linoleum as her red dress,
stippled with rain, pooled in a sodden mass. The wildness in her
flashed, a thrumming snarl under a girl's skin.

Avery, in a sadly battered and drenched tuxedo, dropped the
shoe he'd been holding, its flash of silver melting as it plummeted
from his fingers and shattered on the floor. He bolted up the

spongy, crumbling stairs and grabbed Ellie's wrist, hauling her backward while the thing above her champed its fangs angrily. It had changed yet again, her mother's face thin and graven, those black eyes huge under a snarled tangle of black, black hair. It crouched, and its shadow was full of writhing.

"Let me go!" Ellie shrieked. "I want to go! Let me go!"

The mad thing above them darted down a step, but Avery flung up his free hand. Blue-white Potential limned his fingers, and when he spoke even the sound of the storm drained away.

"I am of your blood, but iron is no bar to me." He yanked back on Ellie's wrist again, and she fell, barking her hip on a stair. Even then he didn't let go, though she tried to scramble upward, toward the snaking, crouching shape.

"*Coluuuuumba,*" it keened. "*Coluuuuumba . . .*"

Avery shook his golden head. The crackling on his fingers arced, Tesla's Folly on his fingertips as if he'd brought the lightning home. "No. *Ellie*. Ellie Sinder. Ellen Anna Seraphina Sinder. I know her name, spider, and *you do not*." He yanked on her wrist again, and Ellie tumbled down the stairs, crying out as their sharp edges bit her. Cami was suddenly there, and Ruby, and the preternatural strength in their arms just barely managed to keep Ellie contained as she erupted into wild motion.

"Don't hurt her! She's my mother! Don't hurt her!"

Avery stood, at once large and curiously small, before the hissing, thrashing shape on the stairs. The Potential sparking and crackling on his fingers intensified as he brought his other hand up. "How many have you lured here? I should burn your rotten web down."

"Noooooo!" Ellie almost, *almost* struggled free. Her scream broke halfway through, rasping and cracking just like the walls. Slivers of water runneled through. The whole place was melting, and a soupy mess of something sticky-sweet washed down the floor.

Ruby yanked her back down. "Oh *no* you don't," she snarled. "No way, no day."

It was Cami who wrapped her arms tightly around Ellie, stroking her hair and crooning a formless somehow-familiar song. It was Cami who quelled her last struggles and muffled her ears as the thing on the stairs came for Avery and screeched, Potential-lightning forcing it back.

"*You do not know her name!*" Avery yelled, and Ruby, as she held Ellie's hand in a bruising-tight grip and stared upward, did not have the face of a girl at all. Mercifully, the moment passed, and Ellie sagged in the cage of Cami's arms. The Vultusino girl's hair smelled of spice and warmth, and Ellie's bones, poking out through her thinness, sank into her friend's supple strength.

"It's all r-right," Cami murmured, over and over again. "We're h-h-here, Ellie. It's okay. It's all r-right."

You shouldn't be. And it's not. This is nowhere near all right. The strength to fight had left her. She stared past the mingled strings of her hair and Cami's, pale platinum and inky black mixing, as the thing with the writhing shadow retreated upstairs. Avery followed, step by slow step, his hands spitting sparks as he bore upward, his hair astonishingly full of gold even in the dimness.

Dreamy terror filled her. *It's not my mother. It just wore her face. It's . . . what is it?* "What is it?" she moaned, but the sound was swallowed by thunder. Rain sluiced instead of trickled down the walls now, they sagged like cardboard. The tiny sitting room was awash, and the sharpish stink of spoiled honey warred with rot and mildew.

The malformed, fanged thing on the stairs scuttled back into darkness. Avery halted, his head cocked, and agonizing fear filled Ellie like tea into a mug, hot and bitter and strong.

He retreated carefully, each foot feeling behind him in empty space. His gaze never strayed from the blackness overhead, where there was a sharp cracking as the roof sagged, and a cascade of rainwater poured down the stairs, foaming between the balusters as they were eaten away. Ellie gagged, and Cami did too, her blue eyes rolling as the smell grew worse.

"Whole damn place's caving in!" Ruby yelled. "Come *on!*"

He backed up, and it took Cami two tries to surge to her feet, carrying a sobbing Ellie with her. Ruby's strong warm hands were there too, and the two girls hefted Ellie between them like wet washing, her bare bleeding feet dragging as they hauled her for the yawing door. She tried to twist, to see

Avery behind them or to struggle free, but they carried her outside, where a tangle of long grass and overgrown thorny vines whipped wildly under the storm.

Lightning flashed, and Ellie hitched in a breath to scream. Thunder swallowed the sound, and the trellis archway had been blasted by something, still smoking against the falling water. It was *cold*, Cami's bare arms steamed and trails of vapor rose from Ruby's vital, healthy skin.

"Let me go," Ellie moaned. "Please God, Mithrus Christ, just let me *goooooo* . . ."

It was Ruby who replied. "No, you stubborn bitch, I am *not* going to let you go, and neither is anyone else!" She sped up, and Cami slipped on Ellie's other side, carried gamely on. "Not now, not *ever!*"

They lifted her bodily over the ruins of the trellis, and Ellie cried out miserably as something inside her snapped. It was the crunch of glass breaking under a thick silk blanket. She fled into merciful soupy unconsciousness for the second time that night as the elms towered above, their black bulk diverting some of the rain until wind tossed the heavy branches and pattering silver drops fell just like chiming, icy beads.

THIRTY-ONE

"THERE'S FEY BLOOD ON MY SIDE OF THE FAMILY." MRS. Fletcher pulled the counterpane up, tucking Ellie into the softness. Rain beat against the window, the summer storm wearing itself out. "It, ah, grants us certain . . . advantages."

Ellie blinked. Of course it would. "Unregistered?" she croaked, and the pained look on Mrs. Fletcher's face spoke for her.

The whole charm-clan could be legally dissolved if it could be proven in front of a magistrate that some of them had fey blood. Family or Woodsdowne—or fey—might be part-human, but the *other* attached to them disqualified them from incorporating. From other things, too. Like the Charmer's Ball, and the social season, and a whole hedge of legal and business advantages.

A clan of medic charmers might not have any clients left, even for free, if *that* happened. Ellie's throat worked dryly as she swallowed. "I won't tell."

"That's up to you," Mrs. Fletcher said quietly and laid the

back of her hand against Ellie's forehead. "Ave tells me it was an *arachna Portia*. They're dangerous." She hesitated. "You have a slight fever. If it gets worse, the clan doctor will come."

"S-s-sor—" Her teeth chattered over the word. *Trouble. I'm just trouble to everyone.*

"No, don't." She smiled, and it was a relief to see that she had blunt, pearly human teeth. "Something should have been done about your stepmother long before now, and no wonder the *arachna* snared you. You must have been very frightened, and very alone." Her long dark hair was pulled back into two braids, and except for the shadow of knowledge in her gaze she looked very young. Her cheekbones and jawline were half-familiar; they echoed the face Auntie had worn, but which had been the real one? Had Auntie really been the old woman, or had she been the ink-haired goddess on the stairs . . . or was the last face, the twisted hungry thing with white fangs and a writhing shadow, the true one?

Avery looked like someone else, too, but just then Ellie couldn't remember. She stirred restlessly. He had driven them to the Fletcher estate. The Midsummer Ball had been winding down, traditional sweetmeats showered on the charmers from the mezzanine while laughter and sharp cries of delight rang against the ballroom's roof. Bursting into that whirl of color, Potential, and crowding, Ellie had roused enough to be ashamed of the thin, dripping fey-woven rag she wore.

Mom! Avery had bellowed, and Mrs. Fletcher had appeared immediately. The confusion retreated before her bright gaze and imperious commands, and in short order Ellie was whisked upstairs, charm-cleaned, and tucked into this pale-blue spare bedroom, the dust scorched away from the pale birch vanity with a muttered snapcharm. The sheets were crisp and fresh, and the rain beating furiously on the diamond windowpanes couldn't get in.

"Just rest," Mrs. Fletcher said now, softly. "You're safe here, Ellen. Nothing can hurt you."

It was an empty promise—because there was plenty that could hurt anywhere you looked—but Ellie just nodded wearily. Her eyes half-lidded, but all her nerves were drawn tight. She could still hear the thing on the stairs.

Come to me . . . a locked room . . . it will all be made right . . .

Those other locked doors, what had lain behind them?

Ruby, her hair wrapped in a cerise towel, had a wrinkled, worried forehead. She stood by the window, watching anxiously. "Is she gonna be okay? Really okay?"

"Of course." Mrs. Fletcher sounded very sure. "You should call your grandmother. And, Miss Vultusino, perhaps you could let Mr. Vultusino know she's been found? I still don't understand how she slipped away."

"It was my fault." Ruby, uncharacteristically penitent, scrubbed at her hair. The scratching of the towel against her sodden curls was loud in the room's hush. "I didn't think . . . I mean, God. And the Strep."

"The what?"

"The Evil S-s-strepmother," Cami supplied, from her place near the door. She looked the least draggled out of all of them, but her blue eyes were wide and wild, and she was even more pallid than usual. "That's what we c-c-call *her*."

Mrs. Fletcher's unwilling laugh was bitten in half. "Laurissa? It fits."

"She's wasted on something, that's for sure." Ruby sighed, unwinding the towel. Her hair was springing back under the warm electric light. "She was out in the garden when we found Ellie's shoe—"

"Ruby!" Cami whispered, making a shushing motion.

"Ah, so that's where you went. And Avery?" She had the Mom Inquisition tone, but very gentle at the same time. You could imagine telling her *everything*.

"He wanted to find her. We found her shoe, and then he tracked her while I drove. I'm licensed!" Ruby added, hurriedly. "He's a good guy. Ave, I mean. He's not an asshole at all."

"*Ruby!*" Louder, Cami's shocked protest made the other girl grin.

Mrs. Fletcher's mouth twitched. "No doubt he's making a full confession to his father at this very moment. But a drugged charmer is dangerous. Do you know what she was on?"

I do. "Poppy," Ellie croaked, surprising them all. "Mrs. . . ."

"It's Livvie, Ellen. You might as well call me that."

Ellie dragged in a deep breath. If she was going to tell, it had to be now. "Rita. She's Laurissa's daughter. Laurissa stole her Potential." Her tongue stole out, a dry leaf trying to wet her cracked lips. There had been so much water, but she was parched.

"Black charming? That's a very serious charge." Mrs. Fletcher looked thoughtful, again. Her green gown sparkled, and Ellie shrank back into the bed. How was she going to escape from here?

Where did she have to go?

Still, she was compelled to speak. "She couldn't take mine, there's no blood between us." *Or sex. God.* At least the boyfriends would recover, once they got away from her. Rita might, with intensive long-term therapy from a charmstitcher. Expensive, and who would pay for that? Ellie's chest twinged, a sore, cracked egg. "But she made me charm, and charm, and charm. . . ."

"Rest." Livvie Fletcher had turned grave, a spark lighting in her dark eyes, so like and unlike Avery's.

"There's something else," Ellie whispered. "She gave Avery—"

"Dear God." The woman's hand leapt to her mouth like a white bird. "*That* horrible thing? We threw it out."

"Good." *So tired.* Ellie's eyes drifted closed. "I took the charm off it . . . she had . . . she had . . ."

"She had *what*?"

Ellie whispered what the charm had been meant to do, and the three horrified gasps they made in unison might have been sort of funny, if she hadn't fallen asleep.

THIRTY-TWO

THE STORM, ITS TATTERED WINGS FLAPPING, SPED AWAY *from New Haven, inland over the Waste. Restless, the girl tosses in a narrow bed, just like the cot at the orphanage. The bucket of steaming water, full of grit from the floor, and her mother's face as she turns to leave. "Keep it for me," the golden-haired woman says coldly, and she only knows her mother is leaving because the little girl has nothing more to give.*

The water sloshes, back and forth. It becomes an algae-choked eye, and the girl . . .

The girl . . .

The girl in the water.

If she isn't dead, she soon will be. Limp and boneless, she makes herself as heavy as possible. Blue ice and green slime closing overhead, crackling and creaking as it shudders and grinds. A false friend, the ice numbs her while it obeys her enemy's raging shrieks.

The dream comes back for several nights in a row, then hides for a while. Just when she starts to relax, it jumps on her again. The ice stinging every inch of her, her shoes too heavy, sodden clothes dragging her down.

She had tried so hard, but Mommy had left her behind. Then the letter came, with money, and the train through the Waste rocking and rollicking. Another chance to try, but it was just a chance to drown.

Again.

A splash, a scream, and frozen water shatters above her. She is sinking fast; the oddest part is how it doesn't hurt. Her lungs burn, but it is a faraway sensation, disconnected. All she has to do is choke, and it will be over. The water will rush in, suffocation will start. Already the blackness is creeping around the corners of her vision. This far down the water is darker, twilight instead of spring noon, and there is a shadow over her.

Fingers wrap in her hair, and now it is the time to struggle. Because if the murderer pulls her out of the water she'll have to go on living with her, and that is one thing she is determined not to do. There's a single route of escape, and all she has to do is blow the air out, watch the silver bubbles cascade up. Then icy water will flood in past the stone in her throat, fill her lungs and heart and every empty part of her, and there will be darkness.

In that darkness, peace.

The hand in her hair gives a terrific yank, a spike of scalped pain spearing her skull, dragging her toward the surface of hell once more . . .

• • •

Ellie sat up, gasping, one hand at her mouth to catch any betraying noise. For a long terrified moment she had no idea where or who or *what* she was, and she thrashed against sweat-soaked covers.

The pale blue shell of an unfamiliar room closed tightly around her. Her hair, damp-dried and curling with rainwater, whipped as she tried to look everywhere at once. Condensation frosted the diamond windowpanes, and faraway thunder was a mutter instead of a crashing overhead.

Storm's past, she thought, but she knew it wasn't true. Something was wrong, and it had to do with . . .

No, please. I'm tired.

She couldn't shake away the urgent feeling. So she took stock.

Her chest felt savagely bruised, so did her arms. She was dizzy, and weak. The ringing emptiness in her head wasn't the aftereffect of charming. Her feet throbbed, crisscrossed with harsh slashes.

This isn't going to be fun. Compelled, she slid her feet out from under the covers.

It wasn't the blue bedroom on Perrault Street. It wasn't her safe little hidey-hole either, though it hadn't been so safe, had it? Neither was it the tiny gray nest with its water-clear mirror, but that was funny—her memory of the room warped at the edges, fraying as if she couldn't . . . *quite* . . . grasp it.

Arachna Portia, Avery's mother had called it. Relief as she finally figured out where she was: inside the Fletcher charm-clan's main house, safe and sound.

No place is safe. You know that. You have to go, now.

Why? What was going to happen?

You have to go. Now. Right now. An image rose inside her head, a gray pile of stone with its gate warping, glowing dull red as something nasty bit and ate into the metal. The weed-choked pool in back, its surface green with fast-growing algae. The thought of the pool filled Ellie with unsteady dread.

She hobbled to the small door she'd glimpsed white ceram-ic through, and was rewarded with a stinging-clean bathroom, every inch charm-cleaned and rippling with the hurried focus-ing of Potential used to scour and scrape.

A hollow-cheeked, pale-haired girl greeted her from the mirror over the lily-shaped sink on its graceful stem. The bath-tub was a cast-iron claw-foot, and the towels were sky blue and obviously little-used. There was no shower curtain, but the thought of more water made her flinch anyway.

The girl in the mirror had been bleached. Her hair was platinum, and slightly wavy instead of sleek. It was longer, too. Her cheekbones stood out, startlingly, and her eyes had been drained of color. They were ice- instead of storm-gray now, as if a puddle of ash had frozen.

I look like Mom. For the first time, the thought didn't warm her. Her arms ran with fresh bruises, and she carefully pulled aside the ragged gray threadbare silk, all that remained of a beautiful fey-woven dress hung with glittering beads.

Why did Auntie let me go at all? Just to show me I ruin every-thing I touch? Ellie shook her head. It didn't matter. Her fingers trembled.

There, right over her heart, was the deepest bruise of all. At its middle, two holes, their edges white and ragged.

Fangmarks.

It came back to her in a crashing wave—the gray head clasped to her chest, the draining sensation, the thing's ancient face . . . and the sucking sounds.

Ellie found herself on her knees, clutching the toilet as she heaved. There was nothing in her stomach to come up, but she still retched at the memory. Finally, weak and fever-cheeked, she made her hands into fists. Rocking slightly back and forth, she reached for strength, found nothing, dug deeper.

Something's going to happen. Something I have to stop.

She had nothing. Her hand was naked, only an empty indent in the flesh where her mother's ring had nestled. Her schoolbag and uniform were at Auntie's, probably upstairs where the . . . the thing, the *arachna*, had retreated.

She forced her bare legs to straighten. She had nothing but this rag that showed almost everything she'd been born with, and she had to get out of here. She *had* to make it to Perrault Street, again, because something bad was going to happen.

No, not just bad. Something terrible.

It's probably Laurissa. Why should I care? Now that someone on the Council knew about Rita, they'd intervene, right? The grown-ups should handle this. Finally, someone else could do it.

They'll be too late. Her own sudden certainty was chilling. She shivered and looked consideringly at the towels. Not big enough. She rinsed her mouth with mineral-tasting water, shuddering as it went down the drain with a gurgling, sucking sound, and paused in the door, staring over the room.

Nothing. The curtains were too heavy, the bed . . .

Huh. It was an interesting question—would she look more ridiculous wandering around half-naked, or wrapped in a pale-blue sheet? Like an old Greek ghost, a revenant dragged up and wandering the streets of New Haven. *Hilarious*, as Ruby would say.

She winced at the thought of her friends. They'd rescued her, right? Except maybe they just should have left her alone. At least Auntie would have made sure there was no pain.

Or would she? What was behind those three locked doors upstairs? Rotting rooms festooned with thin strands of gossamer foulness, each with a narrow bed holding a cocoon of . . .

Don't think about that. You have other problems.

Rube and Cami would be home now, safe and warm. It would take too long to call them out again tonight. Something horrifying was going to happen soon, and the thrumming urgency underneath her laboring heartbeat just would not *quit*.

Ellie heaved a deep sigh and set to work.

The hall outside was dark and quiet; the toga-sheet wrapped around her brushed the soft carpet. It was way too big, and there was nothing she could do about her feet. Ellie crept in the direction she guessed a flight of stairs was most likely to be in—she barely even remembered being hauled up here. Getting outside would be a chore and a half, and sidewalks and roads were going to be a bitch, as well as filthy against her wounded feet—

A warm, strong hand closed gently but irresistibly around her left arm, and Ellie swallowed a scream.

"What are you *doing?*" At least he kept his voice down.

Her heart tried to hammer its way out through her ribs, and Avery pulled her forward. He wasn't in the battered tux anymore; instead, he wore a deep-green jumper and worn jeans, and a pair of battered trainers she would have been jealous of if she hadn't been choking with panic.

"Shhh," he murmured into her hair. "Sorry, I didn't mean to scare you. Shhh, it's okay. Really, Ell, it's okay."

She balled up a fist, but she couldn't hit him because his arms were too tight. "Let *go!*" she managed to whisper, but he didn't.

"What are you going to do? And be *quiet*. Mithrus, if my mother finds me up here she'll tear my ears off."

"I have to . . ." Her pounding heart wouldn't let her breathe. "Avery . . . I have to . . . there's something I have to do."

"You should be in bed." He didn't move. "Are you, um, are you wearing a *sheet*?"

"Stop it." She tried to twist free, but he didn't let go. "Please. I *have* to go. Something's going to—"

"We can go to my dad and—whoa, okay, no, I get it. Calm down." He loosened up a little when she stopped struggling. "Okay. Come with me, all right? We'll do whatever you need."

Now she made herself heavy, resisting. "You're just going to take me to your parents," she accused. "You always tell. Let *go*."

"Look, I was worried about you, okay? You don't know what it was like, looking for you and not being able—"

"Why do you even *care*?"

"Shh, keep it down. This way." He could pick her up and carry her with not a lot of trouble, but he didn't, and her worn-out heart was full of something weird and warm.

Still, she had to get him to let go. "I don't have *time* for this."

"Just tell me what we need to do, Ell. Don't make me pick you up and carry you over my shoulder."

Irritation gave her fresh strength. "You wouldn't—"

"Try me. I just got read the Jack Act of '39 for taking on an *arachna*, even if it did save your life. I think I'm going to have nightmares about that thing, and what it was going to do to you. And you were *living* with it, right in its lair while it softened you up. I should never have left you there. If I'd just figured it out sooner—"

Ellie suppressed the urge to scream and punch him at the same time. At least the irritation kept her going. She didn't feel like collapsing now. "Listen to me."

"I'm listening. Come on." He loosened up even more on her and kept it slow, leading her the opposite direction down the hall. "Mithrus, what happened to your feet?"

"It's not important," she whispered. "I have to go to Perrault Street. Something's going to happen."

"We should *so* get my mom," he muttered darkly and hauled on her arm when she tried to jerk away. "Settle down. I'm just saying. Why do you need to go back there?"

"I don't *know!*" The heat in her throat felt like tears. "I just know something really fucking awful is going to happen, Avery, goddammit, can't you just *help* me?"

"I *am* helping you, shush up!" He sounded just as exasperated as she felt. It was a wonderfully comforting thought. "We'll get you something to wear, okay? And then we'll drive out to Perrault so you can see there's nothing you can do there. You have to promise to not get out of the car without me, okay? Seriously, you do realize my parents are going to kill us both if they find out?"

What, and they don't mind about you going down to Southking at night? "As long as I stop whatever's going to happen, I don't care."

"We."

She halted, blinking at him. "What?"

"We, Ell. You and me. *We're* going to stop whatever it is. If it even happens." He commenced with dragging her on, but gently, and she didn't resist.

"Avery?"

"Mithrus, what?" He sounded, she decided, downright *aggrieved*.

I don't blame him. Everything she wanted to say to him balled up inside her again, so she settled for the bare minimum that might, possibly, conceivably cover a fraction of it. "Thank you."

In the dimness, his smile was a balm. "Anytime, babe. Come on."

THIRTY-THREE

NOW *SHE* WAS THE SCARECROW, SHIVERING IN CLOTHES far too big for her. A pair of Avery's sweatpants, a T-shirt that hung comically loose and low, and the best they had been able to do for shoes was a pair of his mother's old slippers. They had diamanté flowers, and looking at the sparkles made Ellie a little queasy. So she didn't, just curled her toes inside the two pairs of socks Avery had insisted she put on as well. *You'd better not have any foot disease*, she'd said, and he had given her the sort of look usually reserved for people who pissed in your cereal bowl.

Which cheered her up *immensely*.

He cut the engine and the Del Toro coasted to a stop. He'd cut the lights too, and the stone wall rearing on Ellie's side of the car was more sensed than seen.

The sky would start lightening in the east very soon, but now it was the long dark time of early morning, when the last partygoers have staggered home and the streets are hushed and secretive. The core never birthed minotaurs during the darkest hours; even Twists would be wherever passed for home, in whatever passed for their beds. The streetlamps buzzed or flickered, weak against the darkness, and even the glow from the core was just orange-ish gauze stretched over a bleak hush.

"It's so quiet." She licked her dry lips, nervously. Her stomach cramped, and she realized she was hollow-hungry.

"Always is, this time of night." He glanced at her, set the parking brake. "Are you sure about this, Ell? I mean, we could just hit a drivethrough for a couple burgers and go home."

"I don't have a home." She studied the dull-red, venomous tinge to the Sigil on the gate. The high-heeled shoes were melting, their heels corkscrewed and Laurissa's trademark flourishes turned into jagged edges. The charmlight was *wrong* somehow, and she shuddered. "Why is it doing that?"

"If she's on poppy . . ." He didn't need to finish the sentence. "If I ask you how bad it was, are you going to get out of the car and vanish again?"

It was a valid question, given the circumstances. She looked down at her naked hands, and the bruises on her arms throbbed. "It was . . . pretty bad."

"My mother's furious, you know. She's going to bring charges. Laurissa'll get off lucky being sent to a kolkhoz. Black charming like that is a capital offense."

Good luck proving anything. "You're a lawyer now? I don't care what happens to her as long as she leaves me alone." It wasn't quite true. Testifying against Laurissa was an intriguing possibility, but not very plausible.

The Strep always got her way. She hadn't survived as a black charmer for so long by being easy to mess with.

Still, the hunched, thick-bellied shape Ellie had glimpsed ... how would it look in daylight, in a courtroom? And Rita, what would Rita do?

Maybe she'll tell the truth, if she doesn't have to be afraid of the Strep. Maybe. It was a long shot. But more importantly—

"So why are we here, again?"

I wish I knew. Somewhere inside, she probably did know, but the knowledge wouldn't surface. She was so *tired.* "Something's going to happen. I—*we* have to stop it."

"No clue what this something is?"

"None." Even as she said it, closing her eyes and knotting her aching hands into fists again, the image of the algae-coated swimming pool rose inside her head. It was a still, awful mirror, and a fat yellow moon above was reflected, a skull's grin on the choked surface. "It's in the back."

"What is?"

"The swimming pool." *Don't ask me how I know.*

"You're pretty weird, Sinder." He was already unclipping his seat belt. "Let's go."

"Wait." She grabbed at his arm. "It may not . . . look, it might not be safe."

"So we go together."

I have to know. "Avery . . . where did you get my hat?" *No, I don't want to know.*

I just want to hear him say it.

"I saw you on Southking, during the day. I was pretty sure it was you. I tried to get your attention, but you ran away." His eyes gleamed, and the tousled mass of his hair fell over them, a defiant wave she almost wanted to touch.

"Did you tell anyone I was charming unlicensed?" *Like you told about Laurissa?*

"Of course not. You know the kind of trouble you can get in, if anyone knew? Seriously, we can totally go find a drivethrough and go home. You're worried about being safe, well, that's safe. I'm a good driver. Not like your friend de Varre."

Yeah, Ruby's fast and reckless. But she got us away from a minotaur once. I never even thanked her. Now there was a squirm of guilt behind her breastbone.

They hadn't even considered letting go of her. *Not now, not ever,* Ruby had said. Cami didn't have to say it, it just *was*.

I've been really lucky. Shame woke up, hot and rank inside her ribs.

"Okay." She reached for the door handle, and he grabbed

her wrist. She was so thin now his fingers overlapped, and he didn't squeeze, but she flinched slightly as if he had.

"Look, you're . . . look, just stay with me, okay? My mother will kill me if anything happens to you. She's got her grandchildren's names all picked out and everything."

"What?"

He was already gone, and he shut the car door so softly she guessed he was pretty used to sneaking out at night. He came around to her side, and she had to press twice to get her own seat belt undone.

"Your mother *what?*" she whispered.

"Shh." He was actually grinning, but the tension in his broad shoulders warned her. "She really likes you, Sinder."

Great. I'd feel really good about that, but something terrible is going on, and we have to go. The sense of urgency mounted, pushing behind her sternum, thudding behind her heart, mixing uneasily with all the other feelings crowding through her. She had a sudden mental image of her own bleeding cardiac muscle, its walls thin as paper and the red fluid just a pale-pink, watered-down trickle. "Whatever. Come on."

The gate was open. Just a little, just enough to squeeze through. The throbbing bruise of the Sigil brightened perceptibly as Ellie drew near, and the metal hissed to itself. She brushed past, careful not to touch it, and Avery had to turn sideways and squeeze through, his breath hissing between his teeth a little as it crackled. The boundary charms still recognized Ellie, which was all to the good. But they were fading and sparking in weird ways, struggling against heavy invisible resistance.

The circular driveway was overgrown, and the gardens on either side were tangled and ragged. Had Laurissa let *all* the staff go? Poppy was an expensive habit, but still . . . she should have had plenty.

"Mithrus," she breathed, looking at the house.

"What do you see?" he whispered back.

"It's . . ." *It didn't look like this before. Did it?* She hadn't been looking, she'd been so focused on getting in to see Rita.

The massive stone pile slumped oddly, vibrating with distress. Two of the lower windows were broken and boarded, looking like pulled teeth. The paving was cracked, and the giant front door hung dispirited on its hinges, thin threads of smoke rising from heavy blackened wood. *Am I too late?*

She broke into a shambling run for the corner of the house; it seemed a million miles away. Weeds had forced themselves up through the gravel; her borrowed shoes slipped and scraped.

Then the screams began.

THIRTY-FOUR

AFTERWARD SHE WAS NEVER QUITE SURE HOW FAST she'd moved. Avery didn't know the grounds like she did, and it was dark. She was alone when she thrashed through the fringes of the overgrown rose garden, tearing long stripes in her borrowed scarecrow-suit, just as the kitchen door broke outward, shattering under the force of a black charmer's hateful curlew-cry.

An indistinct shape fell out, a smear of paleness striped with black fluid. *She* wasn't screaming, she was panting furiously, and her eyes were wide and white, rolling like a terrified horse's.

"*RITA!*" Ellie yelled.

Then things got very confused.

The girl didn't stop. The garden was full of graying predawn light, as if someone had flipped a switch, and now Ellie could see the blood striping that goddamn peach sweater, the rags of her skirt—it looked like one of Ell's school skirts, and for a moment weary anger filled her. Why couldn't the bitch wear her own clothes?

But then, did Ellie have anything that could be called her own? Did either of them?

"*Sweeeeeetheart*," a familiar, nasty voice crooned. "*Sweeeeet-heart come back here!*"

And there was Laurissa, shambling down the garden path. A bright gleam in one misshapen, trembling hand was sharp metal, and bile-fear crawled up in Ellie's throat again.

At least the monster that had been Auntie had been some-how *natural*, even its shadow full of writhing legs obeying the invisible laws of how the world should look.

This . . . Laurissa had . . .

The Strep's belly swelled, pendulous, but the rest of her was bony except for her shoulders, which had thickened as her head dropped forward. Her right foot dragged, the ankle corkscrewed and the instep clubbed, and her blonde mane had turned dark at the roots. Her forehead was thickening, heavy bone swelling under peeling skin.

A colorless smoke rose off her, blooming like ragged, silken petals, and Ellie could almost taste the rage and sick need. The Strep's anger wasn't burnt cedar now. Instead, it was rotten wood, not burning, just smoldering and sending up nasty toxic bitter smoke.

Soon the horns would grow and her shoulders would hulk,

and she would rage until she was spent. There wasn't any of the perfect, lacquered shell she'd fooled the outside world with anymore.

What had turned her into this? Did it matter?

Ellie had reached the garden path. The Strep crooned something else, seeing her, but Ellie bolted in Rita's wake. "*Stop!*" she yelled, her throat full of sludge-terror. "*Don't go down there!*"

Rita's sobs were harsh and clear between her hitching screams. She was getting tired. How long had she been evading Laurissa? That sharp metallic gleam in the Strep's hand, that was troubling, because—

The other girl skidded to a stop, pinwheeling her arms. She'd reached the slick concrete edge of the pool, grown over with moss—no more blue sky-reflecting eye and scrubbed-clean pavement. The garden was heavy with storm-rain, still dripping and fresh but with that rotten green undertone, a nasty smell lurking under the goodness of grass and trees. The reek reached down into Ellie's empty stomach, and bile whipped the back of her throat.

I am never going to eat again.

Ellie dug in her heels. The borrowed slippers squeaked through moss and dug against concrete, and she grabbed Rita's arm. Threw herself backward and they both fell, Rita's elbow whopping Ellie a good one between the eyes. A starburst of pain, but at least they fell on a soft squidgy carpet of moss.

Crashing in the bushes. Had the Strep blundered off the path? Where was Avery? If he got in her way ...

If he's part fey, will he Twist? Oh, God, don't let anything happen to him—

Rita swore at her, and Ellie swore back, both using filthy anatomically impossible terms that would have been hilarious if it had been Ruby or Cami.

I never told them I was sorry. The thought was gone in a flash. "Get *up*," she panted. "We can run. Come on."

"She's ..." Rita gulped, lunging to hands and knees like a primary-school kid playing horse. Her hair fell in her face, and it wasn't as thin and fine as it used to be. It was plastered down with the damp, and the mineral copper tang of blood filled Ellie's nose. Wet slickness coated Rita's upper lip. "She'll kill me. Kill us both." Hopeless, as if it was a done deal. "She's always ... she wants to, she always wanted to. *Always.*"

Don't I know it. Ellie thrashed, trying to rise. Every inch of her was worn through, rubbed bare. Avery's sweatshirt was covered in moss and guck, and a brief flare of regret went through her, as well as a burst of bright red relief.

They'd made it in time, right? Rita was still alive.

Amazingly, Rita hauled herself up and glanced at the path. "God," she muttered. *"God."* She leaned down, offering Ellie her hand. It was a quick, instinctive gesture, and Ellie grabbed before Rita could change her mind. "You've got to get out of here. If she—"

"I'm not leaving you," Ellie informed her. "You're a bitch, but I'm not leaving you."

"Why?" Rita cast another quick glance at the path. "Look, just get out of here."

Ellie clamped her fingers down, and the other girl flinched.

That's why. It passed through her in a scalding flood, every single reason.

Because the other girl *knew*. She knew what it was like to live with Laurissa, and she had it even worse than Ellie had. Because Ellie had Cami and Ruby, and even Avery, even though she hadn't known it. They were willing to come into a dangerous place for her, and even Rube hadn't said a single angry word. They just treated it like it was no big deal.

Like she was *worth* it.

Who did Rita have?

Nobody except Ellie. Laurissa had made damn sure of that. Where had Rita been stashed in New Avalon? Imagine just being left somewhere like a broken toy, by your own *mother*, the same mother who had stolen your Potential, scraped out the very core of what made you a charmer. The Strep had sent for her, probably when Dad died . . . why? What had she been planning?

Who cares? She tightened her fingers again, her entire arm cramping. "We will. The pool—"

"*There* you are." Heavy and misshapen, the words slurred,

and Laurissa blundered through a screen of overgrown azaleas. The metal in her fist was a butcher knife, one of Antonia's beautifully sharpened pieces of steel. "Naughty girls. Little *sluts*." Her eyes had become bulbous smears, and shimmering ribbons of thick reddish ectoplasm were beginning to rise on a corkscrew-draft of Potential. The throbbing dual swelling on her forehead had sprouted into tiny cancer-black spikes, and they twitched, thickening with scary speed.

Rita's mouth was loose and wet with terror. She yanked back, and her fingers slipped through Ellie's.

No—

Ellie faced Laurissa squarely. "Back off!" she yelled. *Where's Avery, Mithrus Christ, did she get him, what am I DOING?*

There was nowhere to go but into the swimming pool. Ellie's fingers flicked and relaxed, and Potential flashed. Her head ached, and she doubted her ability to even throw a pop-charm.

She wet her lips, or tried to. Her tongue was still dry, and her stomach was ragingly empty. "You wanted to steal my Potential too, didn't you." Her own voice surprised her, and the tone—soft but clear, almost adult—stopped the Strep in her tracks. "You couldn't figure out a way. Did you ever have any charm of your own? You must have, because you Sigiled. But then you thought of an easier way. You're a black charmer, and now everyone knows."

Rita sucked in a deep hopeless breath, panting. To hear someone else tell a secret you'd been holding like a spike in your chest, was it a relief for her too? Did it lift the awful burden to know someone else knew?

Laurissa lifted the knife. "Little rich girl." Her shoulders pulsed, swollen, and clear fluid dripped upward from her skin, riding the updraft of a minotaur's rage. "What do *you* know? Rich girl with her rich daddy."

You leave my dad out of this. "You're Twisted." The words stung her mouth. "You always were, but now everyone can see it." Another deep breath, and a massive wrecked scream filled her throat. *"You're ugly!"*

The Strep actually rocked back, on both her good foot and her clubbed one, and her mouth fell open, a grotesque caricature of surprise. Rita actually laughed, a high, shocked sound.

Gray dawn light strengthened. There was a *plink, plink* of water droplets falling, and later, Ellie could have sworn she heard a bird sing somewhere on Perrault Street.

The dark is broken, she thought, right before Laurissa, her distorted face suffusing with an angry brick-red, horns widening from her dropping, bone-thickening head, spat a curse that arrowed for them both.

THIRTY-FIVE

IT WAS A STREAK OF BLACKNESS, BOILING WITH RED AT the edges. This wasn't just a nastiness to bring some bad luck or a prank-curse to sting your target. No, this was pure black charming, meant to do more than hurt.

Meant to *kill*. It corkscrew-hissed through the wet air. Rita let out a little cry and stumbled back. Ellie stepped *forward*, directly into its path, and she lifted her hands.

This is going to hurt. She didn't care. Her head was full of sunlight and the buzzing of bees, and she heard Auntie's voice. Not the hungry howling of the thing on the stairs, but the patient teacher.

A mirror does not Twist. Impossible.

The space inside her head opened, only now it wasn't empty. Instead, it was brimful of liquid light, a humming, and her hands were loose and open. She caught the channeled Potential, her fingers tingle-stinging with pins and needles. It fought, heavy and slippery like an armored eel, and there was a horrific thick splash behind her.

Rita!

She couldn't look back.

The moment stretched, impossibly long. Two thoughts, lengthening like taffy between a candy-charmer's slipgreased hands, filling her, pulling her in opposite directions.

First: *I could throw this back at her. I could loop it there, just a touch here, and it would kill her. She wouldn't hurt me ever again.*

Second: *There's no time.*

If she spent even the scant moments to throw the charm back at Laurissa, striking in anger, Rita would hit the bottom of the pool. The other girl's lungs would fill, the thing that used to be Laurissa would howl and stumble back, bleeding just like she'd made *them* bleed, and when the Strep died Rita would too.

The choice trembled inside her. Hot rage and cold knowledge, exact opposites, and Ellie was the rope between them. A thin, fraying, tired rope who had already been drained past her capacity to stretch.

If I throw this back at her, I'll be just like her.

The curse spun, driving down into the ground before her, throwing up chunks of blackening moss and chipped paving stones, shrieking in rage as it burrowed.

Ellie, her arms opening wide, fell backward, borrowed slippers sliding again, for a long endless moment.

● ● ●

Smashing through the water, arrowing down, clothes full of viscous green. Tired, so tired, lungs burning, hand groping through the blackness. Eyes squeezed shut and fingers turned to claws, combing the jelly that passed for water here below the surface.

She sank forever, and finally, the thought came swimming up to meet her, a realization like dawn breaking.

I don't want to die.

Her questing hand touched something. Living warmth, her grasp curling in sodden floating hair, and she hauled up. Dead weight, tired muscles straining, and suddenly she was full of a terrible lightness. It was the last scrap of oxygen being forced into her bloodstream, her aching arms giving up, the smothering black around them bearing down on two guttering sparks.

When a candle is snuffed, does it feel relieved at the end of burning?

No. *A familiar voice, familiar warmth, and a cascade of blue sparks, crackling against inimical algae-laden water.* My brave, strong girl. No.

But the ring was gone, wasn't it?

It was never the ring, my darling. *Her mother's touch, light and warm and soft.*

One of her hands was tangled in the other girl's hair, the other reached up blindly, hopelessly searching for the surface. For light, for hope, for everything she found out she would miss if the dark succeeded in smashing them both.

It was never the ring, *her mother repeated, and warm fingers—*

too impossibly big, as if her hand was a child's and her mother's so much larger, tapering fingers capable of soothing any ill, righting any wrong—threaded through hers. It was always you. My brave, bright girl.

Pulling, then. Lifted, her arms stretched and a jolt of pain cracking in her back, and they rose on an escalator of bubbles. The blue glow became a brilliant point of white, and her mouth opened, an explosion of silver bubbles, and she—

—broke the green mirror's surface in a thrashing geyser, tasting mud and slime and rot, dragging at the hair in her fingers. Rita came up too, shooting out of the water like a dolphin, coughing and choking. They both struck out blindly, and there were hands and voices, lights and harsh sounds, and the choking screams as a Twisted creature rampaged away through blackening, curling azaleas, its body striped with slashes from dying roses.

THIRTY-SIX

LATER SHE FOUND OUT THAT AVERY HAD CLEARED THE
side of the house in time to see the Strep, her shoulders thickening and her belly swelling obscenely as she dragged one clubbed
foot behind her, scuttling off the kitchen step. He'd immediately recognized what was happening, decided that a minotaur
was too much for three teenagers to handle, and darted in the
kitchen to find the phone. Which was thankfully still active.

He'd punched 733 into the phone, and by the time the
Strep had found them near the swimming pool the night was
alive with sirens. At least Perrault Street was high enough on the
list of priorities that when someone called, there was an answer.

Then he had called his parents. It was the adult thing to do,
and she supposed she could be grateful. Especially once Mrs.
Fletcher—Livvie—found Ellie huddled, wet and covered with
green gunk, in the back of a high-crowned white ambulance
and swept her up in a hug, after scolding Avery and kissing his

cheeks and shaking him. *Don't you ever again*, she had said, over and over again. *What were you thinking? Don't ever, ever, ever again . . .*

It was a mother's song, and Ellie recognized it. Every string in her tired body relaxed, and she had finally, finally burst into relieved tears. The sobs shook her, but she didn't have to do anything about it. Someone else finally had the reins, was finally worrying about how to get things done, and the weight of responsibility had slipped from Ellie's aching, too-thin shoulders.

There were bright lights and a long juddering ride in the screeching ambulance, Mrs. Fletcher crammed in the back with a sobbing Ellie and a dry-eyed, green-streaked, catatonic Rita, who was whisked away as soon as the bright glare of Trueheart Memorial Hospital swallowed them both.

The weeping wouldn't stop, even while she was poked and prodded and had to answer all sorts of questions until Livvie Fletcher took over, her eyes gleaming under the fluorescents, and told them to *leave the girl alone, yes, she's part of my charm-clan, call Giles Holyrood—he's a charmstitcher with the clan—and let's not have any more nonsense.*

Avery was there too, in a chair with his elbows resting on his knees, just watching. She tried to gulp back the sobs whenever she glanced at him, since he was ashen and his cheek had a smear of green algae, flaking and cracking as it dried.

The charmstitcher, a tall stoop-shouldered man with dark

circles under his eyes and an amazing beak of a nose, eyed Ellie for a long time, standing next to the hospital bed. She *felt* his scrutiny and flinched under it, tiny diamond feet running over her skin.

An arachna, Livvie Fletcher murmured, her hands clasped like a little girl's. *And Laurissa Choquefort was forcing her to charm above her capacity.*

I doubt she knew this girl's true capacity, he'd replied solemnly, in a surprisingly reedy voice. *She'll Sigil, if she hasn't already. Now, Ellen—it's Ellen, right?* Her own nod, the tears trickling down her chapped cheeks. Would she ever stop crying? Rita had been taken away in a wheelchair, her large dark eyes fearful and help-less, still silent—

Ellen, I'm going to charmstitch you, and you'll sleep until you're healed . . .

She had fallen into darkness, relieved that she didn't have to run or fight or stay so constantly, painfully alert anymore. As far as she was concerned, she could sleep forever, though she knew she wouldn't.

Yet in the dark, she heard two things. A distant seashell murmur—*my brave girl, my brave darling, sleep until it's time to wake up.*

The other was a young man's voice, low and hoarse. "Just be okay, Ell. Please, just be okay."

THIRTY-SEVEN

"I AM NOT QUITE SURE I UNDERSTAND." MOTHER Heloise's broad pale face looked, as usual, slightly damp. Her habit was just as starched-penguin as ever, her small avid eyes just as bright. The charmlight around her, if Ellen concentrated hard enough to glimpse it, was eye-wateringly bright.

No wonder Mother Hel hadn't been afraid of the Strep.

"The clan will pay for her schooling," Livvie Fletcher repeated, quietly. "She's missed a great deal, but is willing to attend make-up classes."

Ellie sank down further in the chair, her hands laced over her midriff. It felt weird to be sitting in here without a Juno blazer on, but the leather seat was reassuringly sticky against the backs of her knees. At least she had a skirt, Livvie had seen to that. Wearing a pair of jeans to St. Juno's was just not done.

"Her stepmother . . ." Mother Heloise's gaze bored into Ellie's.

"Is responsible for that absence. She was forcing Ellen to charm and selling the resulting—"

"Yes, yes. Hm. Well. This is a very *irregular* situation." Mother Heloise folded her hands under where her breasts should be, and the light overhead in its cage of suppressive charms ticked slightly as its heat expanded.

Idly, Ellie wondered if she should shatter the light bulb. It wouldn't be any great trick. It might even add something to the festivities. Just a little pressure here, a little pressure there, slipping through the suppressors, and pow. Big fun.

Livvie continued, doggedly. "We're willing to—"

"Little Ellen." Mother Heloise still stared at her, as if she could see Mithrus Himself printed on Ellie's face.

Maybe she could just see guilt. Plenty of that to rumble around inside Ellie Sinder, that was for sure.

"I'm sorry." How many times had Ellie said that lately? If she was going to be a charity case, well, that was just the way things were. *It will get better*, Livvie told her, over and over. *I promise it will get better.*

Well, maybe Avery's mom could be trusted. Avery himself had been raked up one side and down the other for driving Ellie out to Perrault Street, but he'd taken it all with a rueful grin, and they hadn't hit him, either with charm or with fist. Mr. Fletcher had sounded like her own father, stern but fair, and Livvie, well, she was Livvie.

Right now she leaned forward a little, pale but composed, almost vibrating with tension in the chair where Laurissa had once sat. Ellie had that morning tentatively broached the idea of working to pay for her room and board, since the trust was tied up until she was eighteen. There was enough of it left to get her through college, though the Strep had burned a lot on poppy and God only knew what else.

Avery's mother had looked horrified, and now here they were, sitting in Mother Hel's office while Juno drowsed under a late-summer sky, its halls empty except for the sisters going about whatever they did when the girls had mid-July through mid-September off. It was too late in the day for even the summer school classes to be in session.

"Hmmm." Mother Heloise nodded, her chin dipping. "Ruby de Varre and Camille Vultusino. Your friends."

It was ridiculous, that she should feel caught out. Why would Mother Heloise know about that? "Yes ma'am. They're my friends."

Not an angry word from either of them. Cami simply hugged her and teared up a little, then brought out presents. Little things like hair ribbons—the thin headbands were out and ribbons were in now—and fresh luckcharm dangles, these ones not silvery as last year's had been but bugle-shaped, like bells or beads, and their tinkling had made a cold finger trace down Ellie's spine. Ruby brought a fresh paperback copy of

Sigmundson's Charms to replace Ellie's lost one, and a couple gossip magazines, their covers garish-colored.

One of them had a grainy painting of a half-minotaur Twist criminal caged behind true-iron in an inquest dock, a swollen misshapen thing sentenced to a kolkhoz for the rest of its life. Laurissa's pregnancy hadn't been real, just the first symptom of a black charmer's Twisting.

Now when Ellie heard a train coming in from the Waste she would think of the Strep, bone-shrouded head too heavy for her neck because the minotaur process had been halted midway by charmer cops throwing draincharms. She would think of the thing's bleak furious gaze scraping the sides of a dark, sealed car, speeding through the poison-black forest. Maybe she'd Twist back fully into a minotaur out there and run through the sinkstone and wire out into the Waste, where she could savage and howl all she wanted.

Yes, Ellie would think about it. And each time, she would feel scalding, shameful relief.

I didn't kill her. Instead, she had saved Rita. Who had disappeared from the hospital. Just like a cloud vanishing.

The police weren't happy about that, but there was enough evidence to take the Strep away—as if more evidence than her Twisting half-minotaur was needed. Poppy, black charming— Ellie's halting answers to their questions were accepted without question, even though she'd been terrified the Strep would appear at any moment and accuse her of lying.

Maybe she could have stopped all this earlier if she hadn't been so afraid?

The Mithrus Mother Superior made a small *hmmm* noise. "Miss Vultusino missed school during the winter and is attending classes through summer holiday. So is Miss de Varre, who I gather was not skipping to go shopping, as is her wont, but to search for her missing friend." Mother Heloise nodded. "Very irregular situation, indeed."

"I'm sor—" Ellie began again.

"Miss Sinder, this unfortunate series of incidents is *not* your fault. Mithrus, in His wisdom, knows that. I, though my wisdom is much less, do as well. And . . . Fletcher? Mrs. Fletcher, is it?"

"Yes ma'am." Livvie looked almost as uncomfortable as Ellie felt.

"Olivia. *Née* Starling, I seem to recall." Mother Hel's gaze grew a little sharper. "Top of your class, indeed. A mischievous little thing. Used to quite torment Sister All-Abiding Mercy."

"I grew up, ma'am." Slight hint of asperity, but Livvie's cheeks were pink.

A bright, watchful spark had kindled in Mother Heloise's tiny eyes. "You agree that little Ellen bears no fault for this . . . situation, do you not?"

"Completely, Mother Heloise." And Livvie Fletcher did a strange thing.

She reached over and took Ellie's hand, scooping it up from

Ellie's plaid-clad lap. She even squeezed, very gently, while staring Mother Heloise down.

Ellie's jaw threatened to drop.

"Very well. Sister Amalia will give you her schedule, she starts classes on Wednesday. I believe Miss de Varre is her transport on file; otherwise, you will make arrangements?"

"Certainly. She needs a new—"

"Uniform, yes, Sister Amalia has a package for her."

"I'll pay for—" Ellie began, because the trust had provisions for her schooling, and she'd offered to pay the Fletchers even though they wouldn't hear *any* of it. Was it just more charity?

Somehow, she didn't mind so much. Not at the moment.

"You will *not*," Livvie interrupted, firmly.

Mother Heloise went on, smooth as a ship sailing into harbor. "Miss Vultusino, I believe, signed the receipt. I am sure a thank-you note is in order. Manners are just one of the things a Juno girl must acquire."

Cami. Thinking ahead. And Mother Hel knew I'd be back. The weight in Ellie's chest lifted, and Livvie squeezed her hand again, gently, comfortingly.

"Your grades, Miss Sinder. Keep them up. Be a credit to us." Mother Heloise nodded. "Yes, indeed. Mithrus bless and keep us all, in this world of struggle and striving."

"Amen," Livvie murmured, and Ellie too. The ritual response

was comforting, as if they were sitting together in Morning Chapel, bored and warm and finally, blessedly . . . safe.

"Drive carefully," Livvie said, giving Avery a glare. "Do you hear me, Ave?"

He rolled his eyes. "Yes, darling mother. I'm taking Ell for cheeseburgers."

"Good." Livvie kissed Ellie's cheek, her soft perfume a cloak. "You didn't know I was a Juno girl?"

"No ma'—I mean, no. I didn't." For a moment she felt cold, even in the sunshine, and heard a rustling. She restrained the urge to look over her shoulder—there would be nothing there but Juno's empty visitor's lot. Empty except for Avery's primer-coated hulk and the Fletchers' heavy SUV imported from overWaste, its windows tinted and its radio sleek and charm-buffered, its ride as smooth as a white limousine's.

Avery was watching her, carefully. "Ell?"

"I'm all right. Just wondering about Rita. Marguerite."

"No word yet. We're looking. New Avalon's making inquiries too." Livvie tried a smile, but the worry underneath it made it crumble. "Who knows, she might be going to Juno too, if we can find her."

Livvie's dark eyes were troubled, and Ellie knew why. A teenage girl could go missing in New Haven and never be found.

For all *sorts* of reasons.

Ellie had nothing of Rita's to practice a locator-charm on, and Livvie would probably give her a scolding if she tried. There were a few weeks left before the charmstitcher would clear Ellie for even regular classwork again.

Why on earth would she leave? Livvie had asked, and Ellie had shrugged. It was no use explaining how even help could be a trap to someone whose own mother didn't want her. *She's not responsible for Laurissa*, Livvie had said . . .

. . . but Ellie knew, deep down, that it didn't matter. Rita would *feel* responsible. Just like Ellie did. Sisters in unwilling guilt, both of them, and Ellie couldn't even begin explaining.

There weren't words for it.

The big stone house on Perrault was being reclaimed and sold, the proceeds going into the trust for Ellie's eighteenth. Still, it would sit on the market for a while, because nobody wanted to buy a place that had held a black charmer Twist until they were sure the echoes had died down.

Livvie grinned, and you could see the Juno girl she used to be, probably popping vanilla beechgum and full of fire, just like Ruby. "All right. Have a good time, you two, and be home before dark. Dinner is at seven."

"Mrs. . . . I mean, Livvie?" Ellie reached out, tentatively. She touched the woman's arm, fleetingly, just above the elbow. "Thanks. I mean . . . thank you."

"You are very welcome, Ellie. You're safe now."

And the clan adoption paperwork on the kitchen counter. She could see it, black and white legalese, waiting for her signature so that the charm-clan could fold around her like a warm blanket. She'd looked at it for a long endless moment this morning, her heart in her throat.

You don't have to sign it, Livvie had said, softly. *Any clan would be glad to have you. You'll finish school, we'll see to it, and you can work anywhere you please. Even over Waste, if you . . .*

No, Ellie had said, with more firmness than she felt. *I belong here.*

Such funny little words. Such a funny feeling, to belong anywhere. Was she ever going to get the hang of it again?

The SUV's engine roused as Avery closed the passenger-side door of his own car. Ellie took a deep breath, and when he dropped down into the seat she scooted over and did the next awkward thing. Her lips met his cheek. As kisses went, it was just a shy peck, and she retreated to her side of the car with fire-hot cheeks and her heart beating thinly against her ribs.

She'd gained a little weight, but she still felt . . . well, oddly clear. As if sometimes the light would shine right through her. She couldn't decide if it was comforting, or . . . not.

Avery sat very still for a moment, before jamming the key in the ignition. "Wow." A goofy grin split his face, and his hair was a furnace of gold streaks. "What was that for?"

"For everything." She settled back, and the flush died down. He wasn't angry. It was a start.

"Any chance I can get a real kiss?" He darted her a shy glance, and Ellie ducked her head, her hair sweeping forward. It was still pale as Auntie's had been, but the waves in it were new. It was growing out nicely, and Livvie often sighed and ruffled it, just as she easily ruffled Avery's dark-gold head.

At least Ellie knew what to say to *him*. "Pushing your luck, Fletcher."

"Wouldn't be the first time. Ell?"

"Hmm?"

He twisted the key, and the Del Toro purred. The Marconi crackled into life, one of Hellward's slower songs lifting gently from the speakers he'd installed by hand. *That* was why the car was a hulk, because he wanted to fix it himself. He would even teach Ellie how to do some of it—she had helped with the wiring, snatching her fingers back when suppressors sparked against her Potential.

"So, are we . . . you know, dating?"

Oh, Mithrus. How am I going to answer that? She decided to take another small risk, since it seemed to be a day for it. "Kind of." Weighed it, found it wanting, so she added a little bit more. "I mean, if you want to."

"Finally." He rolled his eyes, dropped the Del Toro into reverse, and backed them carefully out of the parking space. It

was agonizing to go so slowly, sometimes, and he was irritating as all hell.

But he was steady. He'd grown up.

Have I?

"I thought you'd never ask," Avery continued, craning back over his shoulder as they reversed. He turned back to the front, and his hand not-quite-casually brushed her shoulder. "So I can call you my girl now?"

"I guess." A warmth began inside her, the last of the cold leaching away.

"Hot damn. Well, where do you want to go?"

Ellie leaned back in the seat and shut her eyes. *My baby has a witchy eye*, Hellward sang, scratchy and rough, but with a lilt behind the words. *She's my baby, all right.*

"Anywhere," she said, quietly. "Anywhere, with you."

EPILOGUE

IT WAS A RUINED LITTLE PLACE, AND SHE FOUND IT almost by accident, wandering aimlessly under black-barked elms. She'd had some vague idea of finding the train station again, but this town turned her around, and the terror inside her head had robbed her of much conscious thought. The sedatives they'd given her at the hospital wore off only slowly, and when she surfaced, weaving unsteadily in another girl's old, too-small, scuffed maryjanes, silver tinkles breaking free of their straps, she found herself staring at a blasted trellis.

Behind it was a scattered path of bony chips, gleaming in the dark. She plodded up the path, her mouth working slowly, her hair hanging in her face.

There was a dilapidated brownstone shack, more like a two-story shed, queerly melted and sagging as if acid had poured over the bricks. It smelled faintly of sugar and feathers, and she gave it a wide berth. Something in her recognized the danger—some aching space where once there had been a wellspring of color and light.

The well was dry now, drained by—

—Mommy?—

The thought mercifully fled as soon as it arrived, and she found herself crouching on the back step of the shed. This door was blasted off its hinges too, and the rustling inside pulled her forward. There was something not quite . . . right, here, something she might have remembered, if she could remember anything at all with her head a mass of whirling noise and hurt.

Inside the cavernous ruin, a carved bench and leather straps. There was something trapped there, a vaguely human shape rippling and bulging. For a long while the girl stared, her mouth slightly open and some faint color coming back into her cheeks.

It wore a blue velvet coat. She took a step forward.

Another.

The leather split along old chewed seams, and the thing thumped forward. It hit the sagging, rotten, runneled floor with a thud that echoed all through her, and she found herself on her knees beside it as the blue velvet roiled, its tanned breeches twisting and jerking.

She seized its velvet-clad arms and gained her feet in an unsteady rush. Dragging, the heaviness bumping and thudding, somehow trying to push itself along, they spilled through the back door and fell, and as they did the wellspring inside her roared to life. The hot flood hurt as it tore free, and the air was full of high crystal singing for a fleeting instant.

Stalk and sand became flesh. The scarecrow sagged, and his mouth finished its endless yawning scream. Blue eyes flashed, and the girl in his arms struggled. Her cry was swallowed as his own rose, and her thrashing grew more frantic.

"Stop! Stop!" He sucked in a huge breath, living lungs full of air now, and his grip on her tightened. "I am not—I am not her!"

It was the one thing that could have pierced her frantic thrashing. She went limp, boneless, and the damp hot pressure on her forehead was lips, printed over and over again on her sweating skin.

"My life," he kept repeating. "My life, you have found me."

The shack behind them folded down with a rumbling splintering sound. Three locked chambers upstairs full of diamond-twinkling dry-drained cocoons crumbled into sand, for the thing that had fed upon them and kept them wrapped in gossamer cerements had lost its last hold upon the physical world.

Sticks melted, and its entire sagging shape released a hot breath, a long, rank, foul exhalation as a black cloud rose from its pit. Tented together like drunks, they reeled to the bottom of the garden between ancient empty beehives, and there her strength failed. She folded down into the grass and he fell beside her. They slept tangled together like children under a tree next to a heap of simmering refuse, where another boy had called over a fence to the girl he loved so desperately. The morning dew coated them, but they did not care, and when they woke on a bright summer morning it was as if they had always been thus, adrift in a world with only each other.

The next morning, he found the ring in the ruins, and held it up. A glittering circle of silver, a sapphire that flashed blue in the sunshine.

"At least tell me your name." He poked at the debris with his foot. "Do you know that? Your name?"

His rescuer, hugging her knees as she crouched on the bottom step, shook her head. "I don't . . . no. Nothing."

"The spider here no doubt stole it, as she stole mine." Long and lanky, his blue eyes squinted against the sun he had not seen in a lifetime, his straw-yellow hair disarranged, the boy knelt. "It matters little. You are not alone."

A disbelieving smile broke over her thin, pinched face, and the ring flashed once more in benediction. He slid it onto her finger, and when she tipped forward into his arms, the scarecrow boy closed his eyes and held her close.

Rita-no-more, who no longer remembered the mother who had not wanted her or the orphanage's terror, finally began to weep.

finis